IN THE FAR COUNTRY

A Portrait of Three Generations

by

Warren E. Schwartz

American Historical Society of Germans from Russia
Lincoln, Nebraska

International Standard
Book Number:
ISBN 0-914222-14-7

Library of Congress
Catalog Card Number: 84-072555

Printed by
Augstums Printing Service, Inc.
Lincoln, Nebraska

Dedicated

with love and gratitude

to my father,

Edwin Schwartz

PREFACE

The episodes in this book are based on oral tradition. The characters, most of them now deceased, were real men and women known to my grandfather and to my father, whose reminiscences provided most of the material for this work and through whose eyes most of these stories are told. Both serve as major characters in the narrative. The book begins in a Mennonite settlement in Russia when my grandfather, John, was a very small child. It follows his people's migration to America in 1874 and relates their early experiences in what was then Dakota Territory. The narrative continues with my father's boyhood in Freeman, South Dakota, and — later — in Montana, where John homesteaded in 1910.

Although these events are historically accurate, the recording of history has not been my primary objective. Rather, I have attempted to recreate a people and their way of life — in this case a group of displaced Swiss Mennonites, who, due to the nature of their faith, remained a cohesive social and cultural unit for more than four hundred years. I have taken the liberty in some cases to fictionalize or embellish events in the interest of literary composition and to change a few names as I deemed appropriate.

Detailed histories and studies have been done on these people by a number of Mennonite authors. While I have relied on their work for reference, duplication of these writers has not been my intent. Customarily, when Mennonites write about themselves, they appear to have a tendency to become somewhat sanctimonious. Few Mennonite authors have endeavored to deal with their people from a humanistic point of view. *In the Far Country* views the lives of the "Schweitzers" from such a perspective and presents them to the reader as real people — neither paragons of virtue nor provincial oddities — but as people with normal human longings, strengths and failings. In this book these Mennonites reveal themselves as they once were and — to a certain extent — still are. The book is intended as a sympathetic tribute. Its humor and pathos should be felt and enjoyed by all — particularly by the Mennonites themselves.

For the fact that my labor of love has reached publication at this time, I owe special gratitude to Reuben Goertz of Freeman, South Dakota, whose help and interest in this work have been a constant encouragement to me. He brought my manuscript to the attention of his friend Adam Giesinger of Winnipeg, Manitoba, editor of the *Journal* of the *American Historical Society of Germans from Russia,* who became interested in it and promoted its publication by the society.

Warren E. Schwartz

PRINCIPAL CHARACTERS
AND FAMILIES

Jacob Schwartz (Schwartzeck) — a blacksmith

Marie — his wife

Jacob and Marie's children:
   Jake (Jäk Vetter)[1]
   Marie (Marhinja Bas)
   Johann (John)
   Anna (Hanju Bas)
   Joe (Joe Vetter)
   Bernhart (Bernhart Vetter)
   Freni (Tante Freni or "Fluss" Freni Bas)
   Jonathan (Jonath Vetter)
   Carrie (Tante Carrie or Caroline Bas)

Uncle Jacob — the blacksmith's uncle (a widower)

Uncle Jacob's children:
   Maria
   Francisca
   Andre

Andre (Schwartz-Andre) — another uncle, much younger

The blacksmith's brothers:
Joseph (Sep Vetter)
Johann (Blinde Hannes Vetter),
   a blind man

John — the blacksmith's second oldest son

Caroline — his wife (nee Kirschenman)

John and Caroline's children:
   Heinrich (Henry)
   Ida
   Lydia
   Edwin (Eddy)
   Hardwig (English version — Hardwick)
   Othelia (Tilly)
   Bertha (Bärbilie)

Anne
Carrie (died in infancy)
Mary and Jonathan (died in infancy)

John's brothers-in-law:

Uncle Soft (Zafft) — Marhinja's husband
Uncle Christ — Hanju's husband
Uncle Julius — Freni's husband
Uncle Rodolphe — Carrie's husband (does not appear in narrative)

John's sisters-in-laws:

Marja Bas — Jäk's wife
Julia Bas — Joe's wife
Anna Bas — Bernhart's wife
Freni Bas — Jonath's wife

Eddy — John's second oldest son

Some of Eddy's cousins:

Freddy
Tilda
Paul
John
Albert
Laura (pseudonym)
Bernhard
Herbert (pseudonym)
Johnny
Elena (pseudonym)

* * *

Christian Kirschenman — a farmer from south Russia (a non-Mennonite)

Christina — his wife

The Kirschenman children:

Jackob — a cossack
Christina (Reich)
Rudolf (pseudonym)
Sophia (Dirks)
Caroline (Schwartz)
Johann

* * *

Poltauwitz — a hunter and foreman on a Russian estate

Joseph Wipf — a Hutterite physician

Kreisch — a Mennonite mystic from Kotosufka

Mennonite preachers:
   Schrag-Andre (Andreas Schrag) — leader of the first immigrant
      group from Russia
   Mueller-Christ (Christian Mueller) — the blacksmith's childhood
      companion
   Dicke Kaufman (Christian Kaufman)
   Kaufman-Sep (Joseph Kaufman)
   H. A. Bachman — helped to organize first Montana con-
      gregation
   J. J. Balzer — an itinerant
   J. M. Franz

Roger-Jäk — a homesteader, John's companion

Katie — his wife

Jäk and Katie's children[2]:
   Emma
   Gust
   Erhart
   Henry
   Alfred
   Willy
   Clara
   Elsie
   Anna
   Raymond

Poltauwitz-Joe — the hunters son, also a homesteader; John and
Roger-Jäk's companion

Netha — his wife

Joe and Netha's children[3]:
Paul
Clara
Bertha
Eva
Olga

Anna
Freddy

Schenker-Pete — another companion and homesteader

C. J. Schmidt   Mennonite pioneers in
Andrew Buller   Dawson County, Montana

Peter — C. J. Schmidt's son (drowned)

Klaus — a carpenter

[1] Among the Swiss Mennonites the term *Vetter* which translates as "cousin" in modern High German, designates an *uncle*. Similarly, the term *Bas* designates an *aunt*.

[2-3] Not all of the names appear in the actual narrative.

CONTENTS

Part I

IN RUSSIA

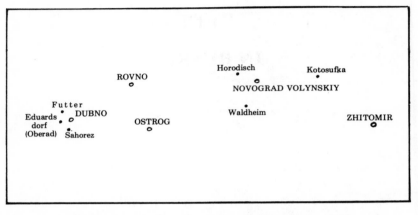

Swiss Mennonite villages in Volhynia in 1870.

The Mad Dog

John was not old enough to remember the time his father killed the dog. Yet he had heard the story so often from his brother Jake — Jäk Vetter — their father's namesake, that it seemed almost as though he could recall it himself. He remembered the muddy ruts in the lane where the pigs and chickens foraged and the row of small, rough-hewn houses in the village of Oderad, Volhynia province, where he and Jake had been born and where their father's blacksmith shop stood. He remembered, too, the gardens that were lush with beans — *Herrebohne,* "the Lord's beans" — the glow of the cornflowers and the extravagant beauty of the hollyhocks that grew beside each window and doorway.

Behind the houses lay the *Kurgan,* a large earthen mound where the children played and dug pits, unearthing bones of men killed, so they were told, in a long-ago war between Poland and Russia. Beyond lay the forest, sinister and mysterious, and beyond that was the steppe where lurked the dreaded *Kalmuke** — fearsome barbarians — each of whom had a single eye in the middle of his forehead. John had been warned by his parents not to stray from the village, for the *Kalmuke* loved to devour small children. At night he thought of them and trembled as he lay in his tiny bed.

But it was no imagined terror that caused people to flee in those days at the cry *"Wiediger Hund!"* Even the most intrepid knew the alarming portent of that call. A rabid dog was loose, running through the village, tearing demonically at anything in its path. Women snatched their children from doorways. Men, reacting with primeval instinct, broke from their work to seize the nearest object that could be used as a weapon. This was no lesson in pacifism — no evil for which one could return good. It was rapacious, unreasoning, animal rage, which no idealism could refute or vindicate.

Such things, however, were far from anyone's thoughts, Jäk Vetter said, on that day when their father took him to the shop to pump the bellows for the forge. John watched them go until they were a good distance down the lane. Then, after some short moments of child's deliberation, he determined to follow, picking his way among the ruts, his eyes inspecting everything as he went.

The hollyhocks seemed to return his gaze, beckoning him as they stood in a profusion of color along the fence. A pair of white butterflies danced among the blossoms as if holding a silent conversation with the ceaseless motion of their wings. John ran

*The Kalmucks were Mongol tribesmen that once roamed the Russian steppelands.

toward them, his tiny palms extended. But they remained beyond his reach; so, turning reluctantly away, he continued in the direction that his father and brother had taken.

* * *

By this time Jacob had reached the blacksmith shop where he set about kindling a fire in the forge and put little Jake to work pumping the bellows that hung from a large hook that Jacob had made. A *zabuk* he called it. The day was already hot and languid, and the shop became a furnace as the flame rose from the center of the forge where little Jake pumped up and down on the leather bellows. The boy soon began to grow tired of their monotonous heave and groan as they made the sparks gush upward, and his ears rang with the gonging sound of the hammer against red steel. Smoke stung his young eyes. Although his arms ached from their task, he knew he dared not stop; and to slacken even a little brought a sharp reprimand. He envied little John, who was not yet old enough to help at the forge.

Then he heard something from a distance — a shout followed by a loud commotion. At first it sounded almost like laughter. But, as the noise grew louder, there was an unmistakable note of terror in the voices. Little Jake saw his father's eyebrows rise. The sparks stopped, and the bellows rested. Now the cries seemed to come from the other side of the door.

"Bleib ruhig!" Jacob cautioned him and, still clutching the bulky steel hammer, moved toward the door.

As he stepped into the sunlight, a flying shadow leaped upon the blacksmith. Jake heard the hideous snarl, saw the flash of teeth and fur. Then the thud and crunch of something heavy jarred his ears. There was a shriek — then silence. He ran outside to see. His father was standing above the twitching carcass. Blood came from its nostrils. Jake trembled as he approached the dog. He would remember it all his life — the contorted face of the dead animal.

But there was something else . . . the bewildered figure of small John standing there, frightened and uncomprehending, now clasped tightly in Jacob's arms.

So Jake told the story to his brother and, in the years that followed, to his nephews — for he had no sons — of that day in the old village, far away in the Old Country.

An Evening Meeting

Jacob Schwartz, the man who killed the dog, was strong for his small stature. He was neither important nor rich — to have hoped to be either in the Mennonite community would have been considered a vanity, so at least the old people said. Yet there were some attainments of which he could be proud. He was, after all, better off than the illiterate Russians whose language he could speak as well as his own Swiss German — *Schweitzer Deutsch*. Also, he had some land and a trade. So he could remove his cap with a degree of urbanity when the Russian nobility — the *Herrschaften* — rode through the village.

His father, Christian, whom he could remember only vaguely, had come to Russia in 1831 from Galicia in Poland, settling in Oderad, Volhynskia Gubernia, where Jacob was born on October 20, 1839, and where Christian died of the smallpox.

Jacob remembered the difficulty of those times, caring for the two younger brothers, Joseph and Johann. He learned early to use the forge that strengthened his young arms and gave him his status in the village, although its lethal smoke even then had begun to weaken his lungs. He remembered, too, caring for his mother Barbara when she became an invalid and how he had to carry her in his arms until she died. He was always amazed at how light she seemed.

Then there was young Mueller-Christ, the boy with whom Jacob had grown up and who knew the benefits of both parents and some wealth. The Muellers had taken Jacob's family to live with them when old Christian died, and together the boys had learned to cut fence rails and to drive oxen over the threshing floor at harvest. Young Mueller relied upon Jacob as he would upon an older brother, calling him affectionately *"Schwartzeck"*. Jacob smiled as he thought about it now. It was hard to think of little Mueller — always so full of fun and advice — as a preacher.

It was 1873. He and Mueller-Christ were both married, and Jacob already had four children. Johann and Joseph had gone to Horodisch when the estates and common lands were divided by the government, leaving Jacob and the uncle whose name he inherited in the old village. Only a few families remained in Oderad and the two other tiny villages nearby called Sahorez and Futter. It seemed that things were going well for them until 1870 when an imperial edict — a *ukase* — terminated Mennonite privileges with a ten-year grace period. Since the time of Catherine the Great, the people had enjoyed considerable liberty, including local self-government and freedom from military service. Now all of this was to change. Once again they were to be uprooted. It was the story of their existence.

Jacob knew well the stories that the old people told about the time they were driven from Switzerland, from the beautiful Emmenthal Valley in Bern Canton; how they had dispersed — his own family fleeing to Bavaria while others went to Austria, the Rhine Palatinate, and even to America — that far-off wilderness which seemed more myth than reality. His wife's people, the Grabers, found a place in Montbeliard, France; and it was not until three generations had died that they were to come together again in Galicia.

But all of this now seemed so long ago. Here the Russians had given them the best land, had let them have their own schools, their own mayor and council. Here they could sing the old hymns and talk the old language unmolested. Any thought of persecution was all but forgotten. Suddenly now it returned. "We were too proud," Jacob thought, repeating to himself the old maxim: *"Stellet euch nicht dieser Welt gleich* — Be not like unto this world."

These words came to him again with their familiar reproach as he walked with little Jake and John, followed by his wife Marie and their daughter Marhinja, toward the oblong church building at the end of the lane. The evening sun had already begun to set, touching the log buildings with yellow light. The dry autumn air was filled with the smell of cut straw and chimney smoke.

"Ai, Schwartzeck!" Mueller-Christ called to him, approaching on his short legs, accompanied by his young wife, a quizzical smile drawn above his newly-grown beard.

"Dobryi vecher!" Jacob greeted them in Russian, slackening his pace until his friend caught up to him.

"Dobryi!" Mueller-Christ repeated and glanced benignly at the two small boys. "So this is the little one who was saved from the dog," he declared as though making a public announcement, placing his work-toughened hand gently upon John's head. To the Mennonites work was the norm of existence and, next to God, the only solution to life's problems. Even the clergy was not exempt from it.

Jacob drew his eyebrows together. "It was only the grace of God that saved him. Perhaps it will teach him not to wander about again."

The two men, talking in intermittent German and Russian, continued to walk together toward the church, followed by the others. This was no ordinary *Abendmal* to which they were going. Even little Jake was old enough to comprehend that. Old Schrag-Andre had returned from America where he had talked to President Grant about land for the Mennonites. The American railroad companies had offered favorable terms, and, above all, there was to be no military conscription for the young men.

6

Yet there was much confusion and uncertainty in the minds of the prospective emigrants. Were there not wild beasts and savages in America? Perhaps this promised land would prove to be an inexorably hostile place where no one could live. Then, too, passports were costly. These and other considerations were debated often at such evening communion meetings and were the subject of many private conversations.

"Die Sahorezer sind schon dort," Mueller-Christ observed as they approached the church and saw the people from Sahorez waiting there. These people and those from Futter belonged to the Oderad congregation and came each week in carts and on foot, even in the malicious winter when frost clung to the ends of the men's beards. Some still walked with the traditional staff, a remnant of the old days when the Swiss Anabaptists refused to carry swords and thus set themselves apart from worldly custom. Others wore tall boots known as *Rohrstiefel,* according to the injunction which commanded that one's feet must be elevated.

When they entered the long building, Marie, along with her daughter, took her place with Anna Mueller on the women's side. All of them were dressed in black, except for the tiny white caps which they always wore for church. At the end of the building the elders conferred at the *Ohmstübchen* — the place of honor. Their power was almost absolute in matters that concerned daily life or family disputes. Today, however, they were talking with particular concern among themselves as the wooden benches began to fill. For a decision such as this, that involved moving to another country, required the consensus of all the adult parishioners. At last there came the prayer, and the service began.

The familiar voice of the *Vorsänger* chanted the words of an ancient hymn, raised then with one voice by the congregation in a slow, monotonous cadence . . . the words *"O Jesu, meine Freude."* So they sang in the langorous evening stillness in a dispassionate and solemn way, as they had for three hundred years, a people until then separate from the vicissitudes of the world. To the east lay the great city of Kiev and the Dnieper River. The the north and east was Petersburg, the home of the tsar, and Moscow, where Napoleon stopped. In the west the German states were being united under Bismarck, while across the Atlantic Ocean ex-soldier Ulysses S. Grant, President of the United States, opened Dakota Territory to homesteaders and a man named Crazy Horse was preparing for a last great war to save his people . . .

In the church now the communion cup was passed with great solemnity as the service ended. More debate followed.

"But if we are to leave, it means we lose our homes and our livestock," protested one of the elders, while others nodded agreement with their greasy whiskers.

A Mennonite House in Oderad.

"Perhaps if we again petition the tsar . . ."

"It is no use; he will not listen to us. We are still *Ausländer* — foreigners!"

Jacob the blacksmith listened to all of this with profound interest. Then he rose to speak. "I, too, am afraid of this journey. . . . Yet I am willing to make it, trusting in our Lord for what is best. If there is one among us who will go, then I shall be the second."

There was a subdued murmur. At last old Schrag-Andre spoke: "*Geliebte Versammlung* — dear brethren! I know your misgivings, for they are my own as well. But we must not forget what the holy apostle tells us in the Book of Hebrews. We are ever strangers and pilgrims — committed to the promise of our faith. Nothing is permanent in the world. Only our souls can endure. Land, money, even family may be taken from us if it is our dear God's will. And it is upon His will that we must rely. Brother Jacob has said that if one of us pledges to be the first to go, he will be the second. I proclaim now before you all that I shall be that first pilgrim. Let us go to America."

Another Winter

The harvest was finished. Flails and scythes were put away, and the threshing floor lay bare. The last of the rye, barley and wheat was stored in attic granaries above the houses. Small children played among strawpiles that would be used for thatching and for fuel in the brick heating ovens, while the older boys and girls dug the last potatoes and stored them in cellars. Autumn sunlight lingered along the rows of houses facing a wide street, their peaked gables painted red and yellow — home, shop and stable under one roof. Inside the houses deft hands worked at weaving and cooking, while the scent of yeast-pregnant loaves and of curing cheese bags — *Faulerkäs* — filled every corner. Bean pods lay spread and drying, and wild plums boiled in huge vats upon the stoves. Along the tiny, wooden fences *Stangerose* and *Stolzeheinrich* dropped their petals. The once splendid yellow sunflowers stood like rows of stiff corpses in every garden. For the people life was work, and the work never ceased.

Snow had already fallen in the Carpathians, covering the marshes and filling the forests like some wondrous, incomprehensible mystery. The wolves anticipated the coming cold, sensing it with their own indigenous wisdom, knowing the mystery which they could not articulate — the mystery of which they were a part. They howled throughout the forests of Volhynia, their songs trailing ominously among the trees. *Sussel,* the gopher, heard them and quivered deep within his burrow. In the villages the pigs and sheep moved restlessly in their pens. "See, Papa," small John exclaimed. "The pigs carry straw for winter!" So he cited an old adage that seemed always to prove itself true — pigs carrying straw in their mouths meant cold weather. That winter he would watch the butchering of the pigs and listen to their terrified screams with a childish delight.

During such days, when his work was finished, Uncle Jacob, old Christian's brother and Jacob the blacksmith's uncle, who still wore hooks instead of buttons on his coat and who would not allow so vain a thing as a mirror in his house, paged reflectively through the parchment leaves of the *Praxis Arndiana,* the old devotional book that was brought from Germany. He had turned fifty-five.

At school small Jake sat with the other boys on long wooden benches and listened while Schrag-Andre showed them a book with pictures in it of the place called America. Jake's eyes gazed at the portrait of a fierce-looking being wearing feathers and carrying a club. He dreamed about the picture afterward and wondered what he would do should he ever meet an Indian, for he was only seven years old.

At home his mother was sealing the window panes with ground chalk and oil while the men cut logs in the woods with large hand-saws. The snow came into the village the following week, and still the woodcutting continued. Large sleds, filled with logs that would provide warmth, groaned over the snow drifts like boats on a white sea. The men worked in their woolen *shapkas* and *marinatkas,* resembling two-legged beasts as they moved through the trees and down the frozen lane. Uncle Jacob told his nephew about the time when the Dnieper was said to have frozen to the bottom. How vulnerable they were, thought the nephew, as they approached the settlement with its tiny window lights faintly telling of warmth in the awful cold. A sudden twinge of fear and helplessness touched him as he listened to the steady crunch of their feet in the snow and heard their voices in the morbid winter silence.

Inside, Marie and the girls had prepared the meal of soup and ryebread to be eaten with milk and *kutia,* which they made from wheat, poppy seed and honey. All now awaited the evening prayer, Uncle Jacob's daughters, Maria and Francisca, ate with their cousin's wife. Their brother Andre sat with little Jake, who was the same age, the two of them sharing the same wooden soup bowl. They waited until the men were served.

When at last the prayer was said, Jacob sampled his soup. "*Kalt!*" he muttered loudly for all to hear. "All day we work in the woods and come home to cold soup."

The girls looked at one another. "It is not cold," Marie protested, unable to discern the faint grin beneath her husband's full beard.

Uncle Jacob shrugged indifferently and, raising his own spoon, swallowed a large mouthful of vegetable-laden broth. The others did the same. Suddenly the uncle's usually half-closed eyes widened. Spoons dropped with a clatter; hands flew to stifle cries of pain. For a moment they looked at each other — then at Jacob, who continued to eat with a droll smile upon his lips. Someone started to giggle softly. Soon others began to laugh. And, like the fire, their laughter drove out the cold.

"It is true, as I heard it," Uncle Jacob insisted later that evening as they sat together by the huge brick furnace. Little Jake and Andre lay on their stomachs by the hearth listening. . . . "The girl died." In the corner Marie worked at the large spinning wheel while the firelight made lurid patterns upon the walls and ceilings.

"Because she did not believe in ghosts?" the nephew queried.

The older Jacob nodded soberly. "It was this way," he began. "The young people were talking about ghosts, and the girl — I have forgotten what her name was — she laughed at them. She said she did not believe in such things. So one day the boys thought they would play a trick on her."

The anxious listeners waited. The rhythmic whirl of the spinning wheel sounded faintly in their ears and threw grotesque, moving shadows across their faces. "They covered themselves with sacks," the uncle continued after a pause to dip snuff, "and hid in the loft above the barn, waiting for her. Finally she came to milk the cow. When she turned her back, they jumped out at her. She screamed and fell over — dead." There was another long pause. Jacob the blacksmith shook his head. "It is true," his uncle repeated philosophically. Outside a wolf's lament sounded incisively upon the winter air, while the snow's silent music played among the dark trees . . .

So it was during their last winter in Russia. So an old story, whose actors' names no one could remember, would be told again by the two boys who listened to it that night — little Jäk Vetter and cousin Andre — in another country in another generation. They would tell, too, how the men killed wolves by dragging a live, squealing pig behind a sled until the ravenous pack of animals was lured into range. Poltauwitz, the hunter, was always in the lead during such exploits.

"Let's go, boys!" he called to the men in the sleds, flailing at the horses with a large whip and holding his rifle ready. The wolves came like a swarm of black flies, snapping at the hoofs of the frightened horses and lunging at the terrified pig, only to fall under the piercing gunfire from the men in the sleds. An old gray wolf lay as though wounded until at last the sled passed over her, upon which she leaped against the belly of one of the horses, tearing out its vitals.

The dying horse was cut from the traces while guns continued to flash in the cold air until the bravest wolf fled back into the darkness of the trees, leaving a trail of blood and wounded carcasses, gray and grotesque, upon the snow.

* * *

At his estate in Zhitomir, Prince Lubinarsky, governor of Volhynia, waited to see what the Mennonites would do. He was a Ukrainian — not a Russian — and, like his people, despised the arrogance and stupidity of the Petersburg aristocracy. The nationalization policy of the tsar was foolish, he knew. If the Mennonites left, so would the prosperity that they had brought. The peasants envied them, but what of it? These German-speaking pacifists minded their own business. So what if they were a bit eccentric? At least they had made the land good for something. But politics was, after all, politics. Of one thing he was certain: if the Mennonites left the country, he would see to it that some of their money would remain behind.

Journey to Kotosufka

It was a day's trip from Oderad to Horodisch, perhaps the largest Mennonite village in Volhynia, where young Schwartz-Andre lived. This was not the boy who listened to the ghost story with small Jake. It was, rather, his uncle — whose name the boy had been given. Schwartz-Andre was also Jacob the blacksmith's uncle, although Jacob, who was thirty-five, was six years older and would sometimes tease the young man by addressing him with the old formal *Ihr*. But it was Andre who volunteered for a mission that would make him remembered long after his people had come to America.

For a long time he listened to the elders argue until the decision was at last made to leave the country. He was glad they were going to a new place. It was youth that stirred within him, saying, "Go! There is something different — something wonderful over there." In Russia there was only the monotony of the old life that made men weary in their habits before they reached thirty.

So when the question of passports came, Andre knew there would be a task for him. They were not Russian citizens, and it was already clear that the government was determined to make their emigration costly — fifty rubles per person. "The prince and his bureaucrats must have their money," Andre heard his father telling another in a tone that was more than a little vindictive.

But that was not all. The passes had to be purchased in Petersburg, a distance few dared to travel alone. A lawyer named Foss had been hired — or bribed — for five hundred rubles; and he lived in Kotosufka — a trip that would take a good traveler nearly two days on foot.

"And what of thieves?" someone argued. "Even a poor man is not always safe on the road. But a traveler with money . . ." They shook their heads and debated some more. Evidently no one wanted the job.

Andre listened contemptuously to their arguing. "Such frightened old women!" he brooded. "They all want to go to America now. But when it comes to a little risk . . ." Suddenly he was on his feet, his hands quivering slightly. He felt a tightening in his throat and swallowed hard. *"Ich nehm's uf!"* he heard himself say. The bearded faces turned toward him. There was a sudden silence during which he almost expected them to laugh.

They did not laugh, however; and it was not long after that he found himself on the road to Kotosufka, the money secured beneath a poor, tattered jacket. It was a lonely road through woods where one met few travelers, even in the day time. In spite of his earlier boldness, the stories told him by the old people returned now and made him uneasy. He walked faster, not daring to stop, even though his feet hurt him. The woods, dark even at midday, seemed to mock him with ghoulish noises.

"You are not a little girl. . . . You're a man," he tried to reassure himself. But the uneasiness persisted.

He spoke enough Russian to get by, so when he saw night overtaking him he knew he would be able to ask for a place to stay. But this brought a new question. The inn would cost money, and it would look suspicious for a poor man to pay for even the cheapest lodging.

Counting out a few small coins, he determined to stop at an inn, pretending that he could pay no more. The Jewish innkeeper looked at Andre's clothes with parsimonious scrutinizing eyes. "A bowl of *kasha*," he conceded at last, "no more!" He gathered up the coins and brought the mush to the table where Andre sat. He began to eat.

There were others in the place — rough-looking men with angry eyes — playing cards and drinking, seeming to watch his every move. Andre continued to eat, pretending not to notice.

"You — boy!" a harsh voice jabbed him. "You are not a Ukrainian with that accent. Are you from Poland?"

Andre stared helplessly into the face of a red-complexioned woodsman. "No — I'm Swiss," he replied in a voice that seemed to shudder.

"So what are you doing alone?"

"I'm going to Kotosufka — to my relatives — to find work."

"Bah! Damned foreigners!" the red-complexioned man muttered to his two friends and returned to his card game.

"Don't talk so rough to him, Vanka!" one of the others said. "Here, lad, have a drink on me."

"No —" Andre hesitated. "That is — I don't drink!" He felt himself cringe with shame and fear.

"Never refuse a Ukrainian, boy!" the second speaker snarled. "Here — Christ-killer!" he called to the Jew. "Some vodka for the foreign boy!"

The stuff stung the inside of his mouth and caused him to wince. In a moment he felt light-headed. "The devil's brew!" he thought. "I must not let it get the best of me."

But the long walk and the effect of the drink upon his still all but empty stomach were overwhelming. He could hear the card players talking together in low voices. "I must not let them search me," he told himself before falling asleep.

When Andre awoke, he was alone, still at the table. The fire had diminished to a red glow. A rat leered at him from a corner, then scuttled insidiously across the floor. Suddenly Andre thought of the money and grasped wildly inside his coat. It was still there. Moving the table closer to the fire, the young traveler pulled himself on top and tried to sleep again.

* * *

The sun had not quite reached the hilltops when he resumed his journey. Once he reached Kotosufka, it did not take him long to find the lawyer's house and turn over the money. It was dark again when he arrived at the same inn on the road homeward.

The Jew sneered at him disdainfully. "So, maybe now you will ask me to feed you for nothing?"

Andrew drew out his purse, watching the innkeeper's eyes grow large with astonishment. "Tonite," he smiled, "a bed!"

14

Into a Far Country

John was nearly four years old on April 10, 1874, when he sat upon the cart in front of his house and watched his mother load the last of the household items. It was a nice spring day, he would recall — a good day to play on the *Kurgan* or to chase gophers in the pasture. The hills were a verdant green under the clear Russian sky. But he knew that this day was different from others, because they were going away. Surely they would come home again, he thought, kneading his cap nervously with his small hands. But why, he wondered, must they take everything?

Throughout the preceding day and, now, since early morning, his father and mother, brother Jake and sister Marhinja were taking things from the house and barn and piling them into the cart. The same thing was happening at other houses down the street. It was a day the like of which he had never known. Normally there were men in the fields; John's mother would be working in the garden, and his father's forge would be hot. But the blacksmith shop was cold and forsaken now. It seemed almost like a Sunday. Yet there had never been a Sunday that saw so much excitement in the village. Small Jake and cousin Andre tugged upon the huge leather oxen reins. John pitied the large, dolorous-looking animals as they followed the boys submissively. He remembered the time his uncle had let him ride upon their backs when they pulled the plow.

"Let me hold the reins," he pleaded, longing to be useful.

"When you're a little older," was all Jacob said. So John remained sitting upon the cart and watched the drama with uncertain vigilance.

His father and Uncle Jacob stood at a short distance, talking with the other men. Surely, the boy thought, they must know what was to happen. Everything, he told himself, would be all right.

"John, put your cap back on. You'll drop it," brother Jake commanded him. Dutifully — but with habitual resentment at being told what to do — he obeyed.

At last everything seemed to be ready. The doors were closed, leaving the houses looking deserted and sad. Everyone had found a place to sit upon the overloaded carts and listened now as Schrag-Andre spoke. The men removed their caps, and John felt his own little *shapka* snatched from his head by his sister. There was a long prayer asking God to protect them on the journey. When the prayer was over they began singing as they did in church — a new song that someone had made, telling of a happy journey — *"Eine glückliche Reise."* It must be a good place where they were going, John thought.

"Is it far to America?" he ventured to ask his sister. He had heard the name often already. But the dimensions of his tiny world could not accomodate anything beyond the village.

"*Ach!*" Marhinja scoffed. "Such a question! It's on the other side of the world. So you must behave or we'll leave you with some Gypsies along the way."

"But when will we come home again?"

"America will be our new home. Now be still!"

Jacob gave a peremptory shout to the oxen, and the cart began to move. Little John felt the jolting of the wheels from where he sat securely on top of a big trunk's arched lid. It was happening. . . . They were on their way, moving past the houses of other people who watched them from doorways. Everyone was waving, crying and laughing at once.

"Often I have gone this way before," he heard Uncle Jacob mutter sadly to himself. "Now it will be for the last time — my house — the place where I raised my daughters — their mother . . ." The uncle's words were lost among the confused clamor of voices and the sound of the groaning wheels. No one seemed to be listening to anyone else. Only John saw the tears that shone upon the old man's face.

"*Ja huddie!*" someone called out in Russian. "Come here!"

A man was running alongside one of the carts. "We shall meet again!"

"What does he want?"

"He's from Kotosufka. He came all this way to say goodbye to his sister."

"In this world or the next." The man stopped running. A tortured cry burst from his lips. "*Zwecklos!*"

"*Adye!* Goodbye! Goodbye!" The man who had been running stood now and waved at them. John returned the wave and continued to look back at the lonely figure until the carts turned out of the village gate and proceeded up the road . . .

So they left forever the village where they were born, traveling over each Russian mile — or *verscht,* as Uncle Jacob called it — with what seemed to be infinity.

It was a two-day trip through country that most of them had never seen before to the train that would take them to Hamburg. They felt a bewildered fascination upon seeing the steam engine, hearing the shriek of its whistle, sensing the terrifying speed at which they moved. But the days of travel quickly dulled their sense of excitement, replacing it with weariness. The small children cried incessantly; and John, although feeling too old to cry, became sick from the constant swaying of the narrow coaches. It seemed as though they were always stopping at another town and waiting there forever. They had brought water along in jars, but that had soon grown warm and tasteless. Then there was the unending blizzard of soot and cinders that stuck to the sweat upon their skin, mingling with the stench of their bodies.

They crossed more borders than they could count, and each time there was an inspection by dour-faced officers who seemed to feel nothing but contempt for them.

"When will we come to America?" John continued to ask Marhinja until it became clear even to him that she herself did not know.

"Sit still, or these soldiers will take you away," was the only reply she made.

They came at last to Hamburg — the great German industrial city with its noise, filth and wonder. This was the world they were always told they must avoid. Suddenly it was there — roaring, grinding, screaming at them. And they were in its midst, thrust across centuries of isolation into the current of its life. The streets rang with noise. John stared at the confusion, thinking that there could not possibly be so many people in the world. There were hundreds of carts, carriages and horse-drawn omnibuses — soldiers, sailors, tradesmen and vendors. Everyone seems to be angry and in a hurry. He clung tightly to his sister's hand until they were settled in dingy quarters where only a gray light filtered through greasy, soot-darkened windowpanes.

"We will have a long wait," was all that Jacob said. And that night John could hear his mother weeping softly to herself.

During the days that followed, the adults talked again of the years of wandering, of their parents' reunion in Michelsdorf and of the sojourn in Russia. Now again in Germany they found themselves strangers among their own race, speaking a language that was all but incomprehensible to the people whose name it bore. The citizens of Hamburg shook their heads and looked curiously at these lost wanderers from another time.

* * *

It was a small group that left that spring — eleven families if one counted the married children — many of them with the same names: Jacob, John and Christian Mueller; Elder Andreas Schrag and his two sons; Joseph, Jacob, and Andrew Waldner (later changed to Waltner) and their mother, who had married into the Hutterites and returned to her own people after her husband's death; Jacob Schwartz, his wife, and his uncle of the same name whose wife was dead. It would not be until late summer when the remaining people from the villages of Waldheim, Horodisch, and Kotosufka were to follow. Once again they were strangers and pilgrims, uprooted and wandering through a lonely and indifferent world, led by the demands of conscience as well as expedience and held together by ancient family solidarity. Each left an empty house, a field that someone else would plow, a grave of someone loved — all to be forgotten in another generation's time.

They spent days waiting for the boat to Liverpool, during which they talked constantly of America and its promises of help from the Pennsylvania Brethren — descendants of those who had left Switzerland for America two centuries earlier — and from a man named Daniel Unruh — a Low German Mennonite already in America. Some lamented the livestock that had been sold at a loss: "We should have waited. . . . We were too anxious."

"It is in God's hands now," Schrag-Andre reassured them. "We are like the Israelites with the Red Sea before us."

Jacob the blacksmith cautiously explored the noisy foreign streets, asking questions of the Germans, bargaining with the Jews in Yiddish, a little of which he had learned. When they heard his name, they became affable toward him, thinking him to be one of them. He felt himself in the midst of a great tide of faces, his senses jarred by shrill cries and empty laughter — fat, lean, rich, shabby, great and mean. . . . All of humanity was there, smelling of smoke and grease, of oil and manure. And upon all of them was a look of bitter hopelessness — a look that spoke of bewilderment and mortality. "They, too, are God's children," he thought. "We are all from the same stem — the same humanity — from Adam, from Noah, from Jacob — whose name I bear, as did my grandfather and his father, as well."

Jacob knew little of his great grandfather, who had come from *Württemberg* — German, *Schweitzer*, perhaps even Jewish — a man, gone. "And we, too, will be gone," he reminded himself, "all of us tossed away like old ashes, forgotten."

He came upon a shop with a sign that read, August Buchwald — *Buchhandlung,* and went in. A small man with wire-rimmed glasses sat like a miniature king at a desk before a citadel of tall bookshelves and gave Jacob a pinched smile.

"Good afternoon, sir! What can I do for you?"

"I would like a Bible — a large one — for my sons."

"Ah, every day almost there is someone who wants a bible. It is still "the book." You would prefer Luther's translation?

"Yes, that would be fine."

Leading him to a nearby shelf, the salesman handed Jacob a heavy volume with a plain, dark cover and large lettering. "This one is an excellent purchase. It still contains the Apocryphal books."

Jacob studied the pages and inspected the binding. "Yes, this will do," he agreed.

"Now our sons will have the holy book in America," he told

Marie when he showed it to her. "They will give it to their grand-children someday."

It was May when they finally left for England.

* * *

Fearfully, John clutched sister Marhinja's hand that morning as she led him up the gangway. *"Siehst das Wasser drunde?"* she cried excitedly, indicating the water that undulated in the darkness between the planks. They were taken into large, acrid berths deep within the hold where they waited until the ship's whistle announced departure. On board, the small boys began to explore, running about in the hold and into the galley where peas and other vegetables rolled from end to end in large tureens as the ship swayed.

"There is a storm coming," someone said later that evening when the ship's motion became violent. Anxious faces gazed upward. There were groans of dismay and seasickness.

A big German sailor with red whiskers entered the hold and began fastening the portholes. "Tonight the ship will go under," he chanted, trying to conceal his mirth at the terror he aroused among the helpless passengers. But morning came, and the ship was still afloat, reaching Liverpool the same day.

* * *

Samuel Brooks, captain of S. S. THE CITY OF RICHMOND, studied the passenger list for steerage to America. Aboard was a group of German-Russian families belonging to some religious sect. An exact count was always difficult in such cases where there were children and grandchildren with similar names.

"Can't they think of anything besides Jacob, John or Andrew?" he complained to the first mate. "A wonder they can figure out who's related to whom!" His finger went down the list "Mueller, Waldner, Schwartz, Mueller, Schwartz, Mueller again, Waldner, Schrag, Waldner — women with an army of young ones — widow, too! Jacob Schwartz — two of 'em — farmer, age fifty-five; laborer, age thirty-five . . ."

So their names were placed into the infinity of emigration statistics, single daughters listed as spinsters, in-laws listed as children, ages and occupations arbitrarily recorded. Nowhere was shown the wonder, the anguish or the hope that constituted the life of this small migration. They were the first of their people to cross — fifty-five in all, drawn by faith, by necessity, by an inexorable human impulse that even their sequestered mode of life could not resist. There were to be many after them.

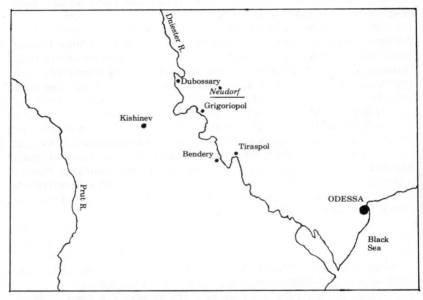

Map showing location of *Neudorf,* northwest of Odessa.

On the Black Sea

It was haying time in South Russia. The stone house where Christian Kirschenman lived in the German Lutheran village of Neudorf was cool and comfortable in contrast to the warm outdoors where men's weary arms strained in rhythmic momentum against the weight of cumbersome scythes. All morning they had worked until their muscles became numb and their hands were marked with blisters.

"The first day is hard, but after a while it will go faster," Kirschenman told his sons, Rudolf and Johann, as they rested from the noonday heat. Like their father they were small but muscular — good workers everyone agreed. "All night you will be cutting hay in your sleep," Kirschenman teased, his lips broadening into a grin as he filled his clay pipe. "And by morning you will be so stiff you won't feel anything at all."

Leaning back now in the shade of the acacia tree that grew in front of the house, he inhaled the essence of the tobacco and looked beyond the stone fence toward the orchards. The soft smell of fresh blossoms was mixed with a faint aroma of the distant sea. It was a good place, he thought. Although only a tenant, he still nurtured the hope of someday owning land that would be his and no one else's.

He thought, too, of the coming harvest when corn stalks would rustle in the wind. There would be potatoes, melons, pumpkins and squash to fill the cellar for winter. The grapevines that grew over the doorway would be heavy once more with fruit. A farmer lived the entire year in anticipation of such things.

"Papa," Johann called to him, "the storks are back." They looked above the tiled roof to the chimney where the large birds were arranging their nest.

Kirschenman nodded his head. "That means good luck — a good year for us."

Meanwhile the women were busily setting out the noonday meal of peasant bread, cheese and butter to be served with milk and tea. Thirteen-year-old Caroline was filling the *chainik* with hot water and tea leaves when she heard the sound of a galloping horse entering the gateway. Looking hastily through the open window, she saw the erect figure of her brother wearing his cavalry uniform and sitting astride a milk-white horse. "Mama," she cried. "It is brother Jackob!"

They ran from the house to where the young man had already dismounted. "*Ai, du Kasak!*" their father called out, breaking into a full grin at the sight of his son.

Eagerly they embraced, everyone talking at once. Jackob stroked his military mustache with an air of satisfaction.

"Caroline," he greeted his sister, kissing her. "I promised you I would come on your birthday, and here I am."

"That was all she talked about today," muttered Rudolf, who was always sullen.

"She is a good little worker," Kirschenman defended his daughter. "She and her mama were raking hay with us all morning."

As they continued their talk, Caroline ran quickly to the cellar, her bare feet striking noiselessly upon the trampled clay. She returned with a jug of *kvass* which she handed to her brother.

"Mama's good schnaps!" he exclaimed with delight. "Little sister doesn't forget." Pulling out the stopper he drank copiously of the home-made intoxicant. "And now," he said, licking his lips, "I have something for you." Reaching into his saddlebag, he produced a small blue tea canister and handed it to her. "It is from China. That is Chinese writing on it." There were exclamations of awe. Speechless, Caroline examined the gift.

"Tell us," Kirschenman asked his son after they had eaten and once again filled their pipes, "how have they treated you?"

The young soldier shook his head. "It is hard. We must keep our horses perfectly clean. They inspect us every morning. The officers wipe each horse with a cloth, and if they find the cloth soiled, they will strike you to your knees."

The others looked at him in astonishment. Kirschenman shook his head.

"Is there a chance of war?" their mother asked then.

"There is always such talk," Jackob replied with a shrug of his shoulders. "But you never know. Now they are afraid of the Germans because of what Bismarck is doing."

"It is good what he is doing," Kirschenman interposed indignantly. "The rest of Europe will see what our people can do with a man like that at the head."

"Only think, Papa," his wife cautioned. "We have sons. If we stay here, it may be their own people they will have to fight."

Kirschenman became thoughtful, the day's happiness interrupted by this misgivings.

Then Jackob spoke. His voice, too, had become sober. "There is something else I have to tell you. The tsar is going to call for more conscripts. Rudolf will have to go."

Kirschenman, his temper aroused, slammed his fist upon the table. "No! Not another son! Next they will want Johann. . . . We must not allow it. We are not Russians. Why must they take our children?"

"Because, if war comes, they are afraid to have so many German people in the country," Jackob replied. "They want to make sure of our loyalty. There is nothing we can do, unless . . ."

"The best thing may be for us to leave," Mother Kirschenman broke into her son's sentence.

The family had talked before of leaving the country, of going to America where so many others had found sanctuary. But such a move was not made lightly.

Kirschenman frowned. "They will not let us go."

"There are some Jews who can help us," Jackob assured him. "We will have to pay them, of course. But they can take us across the river Prut after dark."

Again their conversation became stilled, and a moroseness settled upon the small reunion. A decision had to be made. The risks were considerable. Caroline, not daring to speak, listened to all of this with concern.

Their thoughts were interrupted by the jingling of harnesses as a Gypsy wagon came through the gateway. Since the time her ears were pierced by an old *Zigeunerin*, Caroline had been fascinated by these dark-skinned wanderers. Although she told no one, she felt somehow that she belonged to them. Especially in the night, when the wind blew from the sea and the trees knocked against the roof, she would dream of running away to live their life in distant places, sleeping by their campfires and listening to their songs.

Now she watched them dismount in the yard and listened to their arguing with her father in broken Russian. She saw the dark-eyed children with their unsmiling faces staring back at her and longed to talk to them. One of the men was examining her brother's horse. Jackob laughed and offered the man a cup of *kvass*.

"That is like Jackob —" Rudolf snarled under his breath, "to waste good *kvass* on beggars."

As Caroline continued to watch, an ancient-looking woman wearing a brightly-colored shawl and large hoop earrings approached the house. Her face was like rough tree bark. She seemed to fill the room with her essence — old and mysterious. From a small leather purse she withdrew some coins, offering them to Caroline's mother for some bread and cheese. The deep-set eyes surveyed the household and fastened quickly upon the milk pitcher that stood in the middle of the table. She pointed to it. But Mother Kirschenman shook her head firmly. The Gypsy looked at her with intent eyes. "Tonight there will be a frog beneath your pillow," she decreed and left the house.

"A *baika!*" Mother Kirschenman scoffed contemptuously when the Gypsies had gone . . .

There was no more field work that afternoon. Jackob remained with them playing the favorite card game — *durak* — until it was evening.

"The fool wanted to buy my horse for just ten rubles," he laughed. "Only think — an animal like that!"

There was more talk about leaving. "The Gypsies cross the border all the time," Jackob reassured them. "It can be done."

Later, when the game was over, Caroline drew some water for Jackob's horse at the well. Her brother leaned against the stone curbing. "I must leave for Odessa tomorrow," he told her. "I will be back when it's time for us to go."

Uncle Jackob, the "Cossack".

She gazed into the distance in the direction of the great city. "What is it like?" she asked him.

"It is big — bigger than anything you could imagine. And there are more people there than you have ever seen in your life."

"I would like to go there someday," she said as she pulled on the winch. The water splashed into the trough.

"There are many cities," he told her. "Some even bigger. You will see them someday. But you must tell no one what we have talked about this afternoon. It will do us harm if anyone finds out."

She watched him as he walked back to the house. Then she turned toward the barn. It was growing dark — milking time. Tomorrow she would have to rake hay again.

Later that evening, as she entered the house with the milk buckets, there came a cry from her mother's bedroom. Caroline ran into the room and called to her mother, who was standing above the bed, holding the lamp in her hand and staring in terror at an enormous bullfrog upon the blanket.

To the Border

"We will take only what we can carry," Kirschenman cautioned them before sun-up on the day they were to depart. "It must not look as though we are leaving for good." His thick, work-moulded hands put clothing, cheese, bread, tobacco and some salted fish into a bundle. A few necessary things went along — some dishes, cloth, needles, buttons, and thread. Caroline was careful to pack the tea canister that Jackob had given her. It was the most precious thing she owned. She had been sure to leave plenty of grain for the chickens and some extra hay for the cow. "Someone else will have to milk you," she whispered as she stroked the familiar beast for the last time.

"And we are really leaving home," she thought sadly, stung by the sudden realization that they would never return. "We might even be caught and sent home. And Jackob — if they find out that he has run away . . ." No, she could not allow herself to think that. For a moment she longed to beg her parents to remain — to abandon the trip, at least for a while. Instead, she tied her kerchief about her head and said nothing.

"We can sell the team and wagon to the Jews; and I have put a little money away, in case they ask for more," she heard her father say to Jackob, now dressed in civilian clothes, as they discussed the route they were to take. Then the door was closed, and Jackob called to her to join the others in the wagon. They moved through the gateway for the last time, past the stone wall, the clay pit and the lime kiln. They passed farms and villages where bells quavered upon the Sunday stillness, and rich-looking houses ornamented with carved horses' heads.

"If we are stopped," Jackob instructed them, "we must say that we are only going to one of the border estates to help with grape picking."

The cart continued to wobble along the rutted lanes until nightfall. Then they slept. Days of traveling followed — a dream of faces forgotten, towns whose names they did not know. Behind them was the lost protection of familiar places that had been home. Beyond lay new country over which they were yet to travel — an entire ocean, and then America. Caroline lost count of the days and the places through which they passed.

Finally, one evening, they arrived at the Jewish settlement on the Prut, where Jackob led them to a stone house and knocked upon the door. Two men with full beards and locks of hair hanging by their ears came out to talk with Jackob. They looked at the horses and the wagons and, after some deliberation, agreed to take the family across after dark.

They spent hours sequestered in the strange house. The Jewish women spoke kindly and brought them a supper of bread and lentil soup. Then, when the moon had risen, Jackob and the two men with the earlocks came to tell them it was time to go to the boat.

"We dare not carry a lantern," Jackob said. "The moon will give us enough light."

Clutching their few belongings, they followed the Jews across fields and among bushes until they came to a small skiff.

"*Schnell! Schnell!*" Kirschenman urged them on. "It will soon be daylight."

In the east the sky was already beginning to brighten. Stars faded into pale light. Caroline trembled as she got into the boat. In a few moments they were free of the shore, the dark water tugging hungrily at the skiff. . . . Suddenly Caroline's father began to laugh, embracing and kissing her. They were out of Russia, safe and free to go to America as the Mennonites, whom they would soon join, had done nine years earlier. The ordeal and the agony were behind.

* * *

Who is there seer enough to say how a life's wandering shall result? A boy and a girl — a man and a woman — born in the same land, growing up apart, yet somehow brought together by incomprehensible circumstance into one life. There comes a time when each will sense an ancient kinship, saying, "I never knew you then; yet somehow I have always known you." And the one life fails to be complete without the other.

Another country, another place — strange and foreign — becomes home; and the places that were once familiar — the little pathways, hills, colors and smells never to be known again — become dim and lost. They are obliterated like smoke on distant hills in autumn, consumed and blown away, remembered only in minute, desultory fragments — a place to which no one can ever return, because its life, too, has changed forever.

Part II

DAKOTA — THE FIRST YEARS

The First Indian Visitor.

The Arrival

It was five o'clock on the morning of Tuesday, May 19, 1874, when Schrag-Andre's little congregation of eleven families arrived in New York Harbor. Weary of their monotonous voyage and still fearful of what lay ahead, they were herded through a place that Schrag-Andre called *Kästelgarten*, a noisy arena where clerks and officers took inventory of the shouting, importunate throng of voyagers that pressed through each gateway. Here annually came thousands of immigrants — Poles, Greeks, Irish, Italians, Germans, Jews, Scandinavians — most of them destined to populate the slums of New York, Chicago and the other great cities of the United States. The Mennonites were among the fortunate few who would find the dream they had been promised in the newly-opened territories of the Great Plains.

It was to the plains country that the railroad companies sought to lure prospective farmers by offering generous conditions that included lodging for immigrant families until land could be procured and farmsteads constructed. Schrag-Andre's correspondence with these companies and with President Grant greatly expedited the Mennonites' transit through customs. By four o'clock that same afternoon they were boarding a train on the Santa Fe Railroad, paying $17.65 for each adult passenger; and on Saturday of that week, May 23, the Mennonites became a part of Dakota Territory.

The small town of Yankton, begun as a trading post, was not even fifteen years old when it first saw these strangely-clad people. Their provincial dress and manner aroused as much wonder among the town's pioneer citizens as the Mennonites, themselves, felt upon debarking. They gazed about in astonishment at the diverse collection of worldly citizenry. There were well-dressed businessmen, soldiers with blue uniforms, tobacco-chewing cowhands and traders dressed in buckskin. The Mennonites, with their flat-brimmed hats and dark coats, drew curious stares — as well as a few sneers.

"Whatd'yaknow — Pilgrims!" remarked one onlooker.

"Yeah!" laughed his companion. "And it ain't even Thanksgiving yet."

These words were meaningless to the Mennonites, who knew no English. But the tone of the laughter was unmistakable to Jacob the blacksmith, who threw a vituperative glare at the two Americans.

"Such are the people of this world," Schrag-Andre cautioned his parishoners. "We shall have to do business with them from time to time. But we must avoid their ways as much as possible."

They were soon approached by a stocky, bullish-looking man with a stern expression. With him were two evidently important men in expensive suits. At once, upon seeing them, Schrag-Andre cried out and embraced the first man, who spoke to him in German:

"It is good to see you again, brother Schrag. God be with you and your congregation."

The elder's voice shuddered with emotion. "Once again He has shown His grace toward us by bringing us here safely . . ." Wiping his eyes with his sleeve, he spoke to his people: "This is our kind brother Unruh, whom I met on my first visit and who has been so helpful in finding a place for us here."

There were exclamations of approval. Unruh smiled with satisfaction. "I have brought with me two gentlemen from the railroad," he said. "They have arranged for you to stay here in a common house until you can take homesteads."

The officials spoke next, giving a brief welcome, which Unruh translated; and in a short while the newcomers were settled in a long, barracks-like "immigrant house."

On the following Monday the men went with Unruh to his ranch, which lay a two-day distance from town. Unruh was also a Mennonite, although of a different order, and had attained a degree of prosperity as a sheep rancher. "*Der Reiche Unruh*," they would call him — "the Rich Unruh." He gave them jobs shearing sheep and told them of land to the north, only a short distance from his own. They would not have to go to the Red River as first planned. Jacob had no difficulty finding work that summer as a blacksmith in Yankton. Soon he would have land and a home for his family. "We are very close now," he told Marie, "to the things we have hoped for."

In August of 1874, Peter Graber and Jacob Gering brought their families from Kotosufka. Later that month the mass migration, led by Elder Peter Kaufman, followed from Waldheim and Horodisch. Among them was young Schwartz-Andre, who had made the trip to Kotosufka with the passport money. He joined a group bound for Kansas. Jacob's blind brother Johann — "*Der Blinde Hannes Vetter*" — remained with those who went on to join the original settlers in Dakota.

So they came from Russia, from a land of hills and forest, to a country that was new and that would change their way of life forever. They moved out onto the prairie after the first winter, their wagons drawn by oxen for two days past small lakes and over grass-covered plains that were as unbroken as the sky. There they began to farm as they had in the old country, earning money to repay the Pennsylvania Brethren for the precious supplies donated during the cold months. Even after generations of separation, the American Mennonites willingly claimed their Russian counterparts. All were of one kindred.

It was a land of few hills and no trees — except along the rivers — its uniformity interrupted only by an occasional lake or creek bank and by the ubiquitous granite boulders that lay scattered upon its face. A few remaining buffalo lingered in places upon the great expanse — pathetic anachronisms awaiting their own belated extinction — reminders of a dead world. The new world that was being born was not yet understood. But what had been for years a fixed and firm pattern of life would not return, even for the Mennonites. The earth, itself, was changing, and they with it. Helpless against it, with their austere faces and childlike trust, they were drawn into the awesome flux of its life.

The Woman in the Buffalo Robe

John looked across the flat expanse of treeless prairie, so fresh and new in the light of that first spring, and listened to the calls of the meadowlarks. The sky was clear. A breeze was blowing, singing to him in a language known only to children. Among the stalks of new grass appeared bright faces, — daisies and purple turnip blossoms — *Wieseblume*. The house where he now lived was far different from the one he had known so long ago in Russia. It was merely a peaked roof set upon the ground and resembled a stiff, wooden tent. Outside, upon the trampled black soil, was a stack of dried buffalo dung, *kerpitsch*, that his mother used in the stove. That was all. There was neither village nor barn nor blacksmith shop. No hills met his gaze no matter how far he looked.

Beyond the house his lucid eyes followed a distant image — his father driving a plow with oxen against the horizon. Behind the plow the soil lay dark and naked — like an African's skin, Jacob had said. (John remembered seeing men with skin such as that at the railroad station in New York.) At the end of the freshly-broken furrow was a pile of round, granite boulders that had been cleared for the plowing. Only a few days before, they had been a circle — a ring of stones where, Jacob said, the people called Indians had lived. But the ring was soon dismantled, the plow slicing through the sod to expose stale bones and ashes. No one had yet seen an Indian.

John listened now as his father called impatiently to the sluggish oxen. For a moment the small boy pitied the animals. He saw brother Jake watering the stock down by the creek and began to walk in his direction when he caught sight of someting else moving in the distance. He remained, looking at it with wonder as it grew, coming slowly toward him, its image not yet clearly defined against the sky. An ancient song came to his ears, blown across the prairie grass — a song barely audible, strange — yet familiar in its plaintive, aboriginal longing — like the wolves' howling in the winter. He listened, awed and hypnotized by it. It was a woman's voice.

He was able to discern now a person dressed in something heavy and brown — a being like no one he had seen before — someone alien to him, yet somehow belonging to the prairie, lost and wandering upon it. He was tempted to flee. Yet he felt drawn by a strange fascination that would not let him move. Then he saw Jake running toward the house. "Someone is coming," Jake cried.

In a moment Marie and the girls were outside. All of them stood together and watched the approaching figure.

"It's a woman," Marie said softly. "An *Indianerin!*"

"See, she is waving!" Jake exclaimed.

Their mother continued to watch. Her eyes narrowed. "No, she is pointing with her finger."

With slow, fixed motion the twisted hand pointed forward, pecking at the air in the direction the woman walked. Still she approached, unmindful of the onlookers, until she was close enough for them to call to her. She stopped then and gazed at them but made no reply to their greeting. The white buckskin shoes remained still upon the ground beneath the cumbersome, brown cloak of animal hair.

"Bring some bread and milk," Marie ordered her daughters. "She may be hungry."

They returned quickly. The woman continued to stand, staring vacantly beyond them as though made of stone. Cautiously Marie approached her.

A sudden cry burst from the stolid figure, who fled with short, frightened steps. Marie halted, placing the food upon a rock and returning to the house.

"We must go inside. Perhaps she will come when she sees we don't wish to harm her."

Through the single windowpane they continued to observe the woman as she came toward the food. She examined it warily, then ate with a ravenous appetite until it was consumed. Throughout the rest of the day she remained nearby, wandering without purpose by the lake and among the piles of rock, searching with lost eyes, until it was evening. They brought her soup, which she drank from the wooden bowl. Then she returned to the rocks and, wrapping the large buffalo robe about her, settled upon the ground to sleep.

"Poor creature!" Marie sympathized. "She has no home."

"Her people must have sent her away," Jacob said. "They think she has a demon."

That night John lay awake thinking about the lonely, dark woman. Rising early the following morning, he left his bed and went outside, moving warily toward the rocks until he could see the brown coat. As he looked, the coat began to stir. The woman rose then and shook the dew from the great mass of animal hide, not noticing the small boy who watched her. She was not an old woman. Her hair was long and darker than a horse's mane. John waited.

Suddenly she was looking at him. Her eyes seemed wild — haunted. *"Hokshina!"* The strange word sang to his ears. *"Taku eniciyapi?"**

A thrill of fear ran through him, and he fled to the safety of the house.

Throughout the day she remained. Again they fed her; and still she fled at their approach, until one morning when she was gone, never to return to them. Still they could not forget her, and in many years John would again see that forlorn look of inscrutable dismay and loneliness which is known only to those who have lost their way upon this treacherous earth.

*"Boy! What is your name?" (Yankton Sioux)

Plagues, Fears and Sorrows

The first grave in that place was for the Mueller baby. John learned early the rituals of death — the dolorous hymns and wails of sorrow, which were so much a part of ancient custom that no argument of faith could lessen their intensity. In the old country it was a commonplace to see the death of children, their tiny corpses buried one upon the other in the wake of disease. Now the first had died in the new land to be put beneath soil never before broken for a grave — a maiden life in maiden earth.

Schrag-Andre preached the customary sermon, brief because there was so little to be said, about a life returned to God before it could be tainted by worldliness. The old people wept indulging their self-pity; but John watched, his child's eyes full of wonder, feeling, himself, the mystery and pierced suddenly by its touch. He remembered and was afraid. But the fear was one that could not be expressed; so he listened to the wailing and to the soft voice of the wind that blew upon their tears.

Sister Marhinja, too, was crying as she held his hands in hers. John knew better than to ask questions of her at such a time. Yet to himself: "Why should a baby die? Why did God allow it to be born to live only a little while? Will it always be small — even in heaven?"

These questions bore upon his young mind as he followed the older people. Singing, they walked across the prairie, Schrag-Andre carrying the small box beneath his arm to the place where the grave was. The sun was just setting.

* * *

Fire came, too, one day like a hungry animal across the dry summer grass. It appeared first as a fringed cloud upon the level horizon of an otherwise clear morning. Soon its acrid smoke darkened the entire sky, and those who knew its terror felt their hearts grow weak. Each house was protected by a circle of plowed ground. But, for anyone caught on the open prairie, there was only flight. . . . Smoke stung their eyes and nostrils as the flames came nearer. The noise was like thunder, and it seemed as though the very earth shuddered at their approach.

Jacob and Marie, with their children, watched the fire's advance, the narrow band of black earth surrounding them and the little A-frame house. There they waited helplessly until, like the angel of death, the fire passed them. The wife of Karl Preheim, their neighbor, was not so fortunate. Her burned body filled another grave.

* * *

In the spring of 1876 there was talk of Indians. Jacob returned from Sioux Falls one day and told of seeing soldiers there. Then in June it was reported that a man named Custer had been killed by someone called "Sitting Bull" in Montana Territory. "What if he should come to Dakota?" the people wondered, not realizing that they, themselves, were the intruders.

"We shall show love toward him. We shall not resist," Schrag-Andre declared. "This man Custer was a soldier. He lived by the sword and so he died. If our Father so wills that we must meet the barbarians, we shall do so with His love."

* * *

In the dry summer that followed there came locusts and fleas that covered the ground, making the whole earth seem to move like water. The old people looked at the up-turned points of the crescent moon and shook their heads. "It is a bad sign," they said to one another. "The moon makes a cup to hold back the rain." Deeper wells had to be drilled, bringing to the surface soft fibers of ancient wood that could be burned after it was dried.

* * *

34

In July of 1878 the rain returned, abrupt and unrelenting. The cracked earth became soft and liquid; and the lower places filled and overflowed to meet the rising water from the rivers. Jacob Gering — *"Der Blinde Jäk"* — lived eight miles north, near the Vermillion River. All but one of his children — the eldest daughter — had inherited their father's blindness.

Gering heard the thunder and felt the dampness in his blood — sensing danger as only a blind man can — knowing. "You must hitch the team," he ordered his wife. The yard was already a shallow lake, and the trail was covered. Quickly they threw a few things into their wagon and set out for higher ground. The team plowed through the mud-filled tide. Suddenly there was no more footing for the horses. The wagon veered. Gering felt it lift beneath him. He heard his children's screams. Then the cold mass clutched his body, pulling him downward. The roar of the water surrounded him. He felt something — a feather bed cover. He grasped it. It floated. He called to his son.

Together, with blind instinct, the two struggled, groping in the moving mass, until they touched a tree limb. They were safe. From there they could hear the pleas of terror from the others. There was nothing either could do. "They cannot swim," Gering's son wept. "Their skirts are too heavy."

"Can it be?" Gering cried. "Is it a punishment?" Tears flowed from his sightless eyes as he continued to listen to the screams growing fainter until there was only the sound of water, the shapeless darkness and the horror of certainty.

* * *

"And why should God, who had already inflicted such misfortune upon a family by making them blind — why, tell me, should He bring upon them added punishment?" Jacob often asked such questions of Mueller-Christ, sometimes merely in an effort to baffle the young minister.

Mueller twiddled his thumbs. "It is not for us to know. It is a matter of faith. 'Whom He loves He chastens.'"

"And still I must ask — because God has given me a mind to think, to reason — why was it so? Could it have been otherwise? Was it predestined — for what?

"No one can answer. Yet each of us must suffer in some way; and, when we do, we know that it must be right. We can only wait upon the promise of our God."

"So it has been since the beginning," Jacob concluded. "So it is we turn our faces to that mystery we call God. So it is that faith is born."

The Children

So quickly that no one could say exactly how it came about, the land was transformed, divided by roads and fences marking boundaries where newly-cultivated fields grew wheat, rye and corn. Treeless timber claims became groves of young saplings that would mature and remain after the hands of those who planted them were gone. The place was, as men said, becoming civilized. Yet, in spite of such transformations, the terrain would be forever flat and undistinguished — endless acres of plowed ground and pasture — the sort of place where a visitor might return a hundred years later and say, "Yes, I remember how it looked, but there is nothing left now — nothing familiar — only a cornfield where a house once stood." There would be nothing to reassure him that it was indeed the place he had once known. It was a monotonous and undifferentiated country.

But the lives of the children who played upon that earth remained perennially, spontaneously, happy. One of them was John, now almost twelve. Among his comrades — boys of his own age — were one called Roger-Jäk, whose parents came from Indiana to take a farm that once belonged to an Englishman named Rogers, and two others — a boy called Schenker-Pete, whose father had been an innkeeper in Russia, and Poltauwitz-Joe, the son of the Russian wolf hunter, who came at a later time than the rest. The four of them were thrust together with an intimacy that belongs to such a society where many generations have known one another as brothers and sisters of one family. Such an intimacy, therefore, could not really be called friendship, because it was not based upon a chosen acquaintance. The four boys had simply been born as parts of the same generic unit of humanity — leaves upon a single branch — and therefore accepted each other without thought or preference. So it would remain until they became old men.

Such matters did not concern them, however, in those early times. They knew only that they were boys and that the world was fascinating and new for them as they played together upon the meadow, listening with delight and wonder to the calls of the meadowlarks.

"Then what do you think the meadowlark is saying?" Schenker asked them one day. They thought for a moment. It was, assuredly, a most profound question.

John, who had already become analytical, replied, "He knows German. . . . He says, '*Wo bin ich do-hie geflohn?*'"

"And what does the other one answer?"

"She says, '*Hier bin ich geflohn.*'"

This was indeed a remarkable insight, the others concurred.

But it was Roger-Jäk who thought of something better. "No, he talks English. He's an American bird." So saying, he tilted his head backward and extended his elbows, crying, "Pin-less-liberty!"

They laughed then and resumed their play, jabbering in their emphatic Swiss dialect interspersed with a few Russian and newly-learned English words — words such as "liberty," which they recited now in school. When it grew late, John's father came to remind the other boys to go home.

"The sun is still high," Pete protested; "and there is only a little way to walk." So he remained with John until dusk came and their faces grew dim.

John at last made the awful pronouncement: "Now it's time for you to leave. You must hurry or be late for supper."

"All right," Pete hesitated. "But walk with me a little way."

John looked doubtfully at his companion. "Are you afraid?"

"No, no! But walk with me a little way. . . . When once I am by the Englishman's house, then I am soon home."

So John walked with him to the Englishman's place, which was over half the way. ("Englishman" did not denote the man's true ethnic origin, but simply meant that he spoke the English language.) "Now you can find your way alone," John said.

"But come with me a little farther — until I can see my house. Then I will be able to go alone," Schenker implored.

John relented and continued to humor his companion in the childish game that has been played by everyone — the fanciful flight from imagined and unknown terror to a point of imaginary safety — a tree, a rock, a post, an invisible line beyond which no harm can pursue. At last they saw the light from Schenker's house, and John was left to return alone in the darkness.

He knew he would be late for supper and was afraid of his father's wrath. The night wind spoke to him of unknown mysteries while the stars glistened — so close that he felt he could touch them. Through the shadows he hastened toward his own lighted window — that familiar place that meant security. It was his own house, different from the others because it was his. He knew the other houses and the people who lived in them. Yet he would not go to them to live. There was only one place . . . one door . . . one table and bed that he knew as a part of his existence.

Then, without warning, in that strange, night-altered world came the thought with cold and piercing acuity: "But these are strangers, too — these people who are called my brothers and sisters — even Mama and Papa — strangers whom I never knew before, calling me by a name which they have given me that is not my own. I do not know my real name." The fear came very close to his heart as he neared the house and touched the door latch. Then, seeing the familiarity of the lamplight upon those fleshy faces and the flicker of a smile drawn upon his father's lips, he was once more reassured. He looked around the table at his brothers and sisters, who, with himself, now numbered eight.

Brother Jake had grown tall — almost a man, patient, always good-humored. "You are the oldest," they would say to him. "You will be the one to show the others the way they must follow." So Jake became, in truth, the older brother of whom everything was expected. There was no malice in him — even when his father once beat him for not bringing a horse that was left hobbled in the pasture. . . . The knot was swollen with dew and would not loosen no matter how hard the boy tried to undo it. He had tried to obey. . . . Now he only laughed about it — told it as though it were a joke. John, however, would not have laughed. Even then he was easily bitter.

After John came Joe, gentle and unhurried, then Bernhart — the prankster — and now baby Jonath. There were the three sisters as well — Marhinja, Hanju, Freni. The youngest daughter, who would be called Carrie, was not yet born. Together they lived in the new frame house which Jacob — the blacksmith turned farmer — had built for them.

* * *

There were, besides the family home, two other spheres in which the children learned of life. These were the school and, of course, the church.

The school which they now attended was no longer taught by church elders. It was an English school. Still it was their own — a place where they learned to read the new language, sitting upon wooden recitation benches with others whom they knew by such names as Jockilie, Janju, Danelka, Stoddler, Zonzel. These names were not recorded in the church register, but they were far better known than those given formally at birth. These children would continue to be replaced by their younger brothers and sisters, who would repeat the cycle of learning and growing up, until the last one had reached adulthood. Lessons were learned to be forgotten and relearned. But the small, peculiar things, the trifles that bore no significance except for them — these they would always remember. "*Schüler, lern* — school-boy study!"

"*Was hast du do?*" John's little brother Jonath once asked the boy they called Dundel on their way to school.

"*Kutter!*" the small scholar declared, munching contentedly from a sack of sugar.

"Let me have a piece," Jonath pleaded.

"There are no pietheth," lisped the other. "*Eth thin feiner.*"

They could not know that little Dundel would, himself, become a teacher someday.

* * *

But it was the church that retained the task of initiating every young person into the mysteries of life and the other world. And it was, more than anything else in Mennonite theology, the rite of baptism that conferred upon an individual the status of adulthood and membership in the *Gemeinde* — the communion of believers.

"This is the sacrament for which our fathers were put to death in Switzerland when our people were still called Anabaptists or Re-baptizers," Mueller-Christ expounded to John and the other adolescent candidates in the catechism class. . .

"It is a profession of your faith in Almighty God, in which you present your bodies, as He so instructs us, 'a living sacrifice.' For as you so profess your faith, you have dealt a death blow to the Fiend who seeks to devour you . . ."

Yes, the Fiend! John seemed to remember it from somewhere long ago — the beast that sought to devour him — the terrible fear that leaped upon him in his dreams . . .

"This is the beginning of a new life for you," Mueller-Christ was saying from behind his beard, his voice sounding suddenly strange and frightening, "a new life as a child of God."

"But what is God?" John wanted to ask, suddenly doubting. "And what is all this talk of water and blood — or original sin — inherited guilt?" Suddenly it was shattered like glass upon stone — the illusion of security. And again the beast leaped at him. And when he knelt that day before the elders, trembling, and felt the water poured upon his head, it seemed as though he had been struck unconscious by a great, invisible hammer.

January, 1888

Since leaving school, John, who had turned seventeen during the previous summer, remained at home to work for Jacob. In the harvest season he had hired out to the Rich Unruh to earn money picking corn and threshing rye. It was hard work, but it was good to have spending money. Moreover, it was a rare opportunity to associate with different people — men who smoked cigarettes and told vulgar jokes. Then there was the Lutheran girl, a year younger than John. Her name, the men told him, was Caroline.

Now it was winter again. The small boys and girls were in school, and John was already growing weary of the snow and the tedious cold. He had purchased a clarinet with the money he had earned at Unruh's and spent the winter days teaching himself to play it. But still he thought of Caroline. His first conversation with her had been only casual. Now he would have to wait until spring before there would be another opportunity.

"This is devilish weather," he complained aloud to Marie.

"Be still," his mother reproved him gently. "There is no good that comes of calling upon the evil one."

Although January was always a cold month, there came a day which was surprisingly warm. "It's a good chance for us to haul the rest of the hay from the field," brother Joe suggested to John. So the two of them left with the horses and the rack. They were not gone long when Jacob, who had been chopping fire wood, felt an abrupt change in the wind and looked out to see an approaching sea of clouds.

"I must warn the boys!" he called to Marie and hurried into the field.

But when he reached the haystack there was no sign of either John or Joe. He called out, but his words were torn away by the momentum of the wind. He felt his face stung now by tiny, frozen crystals. Snow whirled through the sky until he could barely find his way back. He spotted some loose hay upon the ground as he went. Perhaps he had passed the boys in the snow, he thought. If not . . . he would not allow himself to think further.

Trembling, he reached the barn, felt for the latch and opened the door. "Thank God you're safe!" he cried when he saw them.

But it was not to be so for the man called Hannes Kreisch — a distant neighbor. . . . It was a long walk from the John Cotton School, where Kreisch's son had gone that morning. Now it was time for the boy to return. Yet already it was impossible to see from the window as the rush of the blizzard tore at the house. Darkness came and with it a sickening fear.

"Perhaps their teacher kept them," Kreisch tried to console his wife, who began to moan. "No doubt he saw the storm coming." It was a small hope.

Neither of them slept that night. Kreisch prayed incessantly with his bizarre, tremulous voice. "Dear God, deliver our child from death. Restore him to us."

The following morning, when it became light, Kreisch wrapped himself in a heavy *poldoni* — an overcoat he had brought from Russia — and walked across the silent, white fields toward the schoolhouse. The early morning smoke that rose from the chimney was the only evidence of life in the still, cold air. His own body felt lifeless like the dead cattle that lay in frozen humps on the prairie.

Anxiously he rapped upon the door, hoping with every shallow breath that inside he would find his son. The door opened. Cotton, bewildered, looked at him above his spectacles.

"My boy!" Kreisch almost whispered.

Cotton's brow furrowed. "Isn't he with you?"

"He did not come home."

"But they left yesterday before the storm. Your son, the Graber boy and the three Kaufman brothers together. . . . They said they would make it in time."

A silent terror was written now upon the faces of both scholar and farmer, each knowing without speaking the words. "I will go with you," Cotton offered quietly.

Together they went across the snow, examining the drifts and the frozen cattle . . . still nothing. It was not until some days afterward that the five corpses were found huddled together, their youthful faces looking like chiseled stone upon the white snow. "O God!" Kreisch's voice broke in despair. "Is it my blame or Yours that I find my child here, frozen among the beasts?" His agonized words resounded upon the deaf, cold air.

Then he knelt beside the dead child that had been his son and began to mutter and expostulate over the corpse, imploring the soul to return to its body. The men who had come with him watched the mad scene with a kind of morbid fascination.

"*Absprechen!*" one of them whispered, referring to Kreisch's supposed powers as an exorcist, often called upon to speak incantations over the sick. But now it was death, itself, he had to expel. Beside himself, the desperate man began to shake the stiff form of his son and to blow upon its face, at last collapsing upon it, weeping frantically until the others led him away.

The children's bodies, which were bent together like twisted nails, had to be taken indoors to thaw. There was much wailing among both men and women. Again the old question returned: Why this punishment? And again they shook their heads and murmured, "It is not for us to know."

At the Rich Unruh's

On Turkey Creek below Turkey Ridge was the estate of the Rich Unruh. He was, as everyone knew, the first Mennonite to settle in Dakota Territory, and through his help the *Schweitzers* had found a place there. He employed a number of domestic as well as farm workers, not only Swiss and Dutch Mennonites, but

German Lutherans as well, all having come to him from the Old Country knowing no English, speaking a variety of German dialects and all in need of work. He housed them in living quarters which he erected on his farm and gave them a diversity of tasks that included haying and sheep shearing for the men, and house work and gardening for the women.

Here — after their flight from Russia — the Kirschenmans came, part of a Lutheran minority in an expansive Mennonite settlement. Here Caroline grew to womanhood with hard work her only schooling; and there was always work for her — even on Sunday when the others rested. "It is good to be busy," her mother had often told her. "A good worker is, after all, what men value in a young woman; and that is what you must strive to be if you are to get a decent husband."

And such considerations were on Caroline's mind on this particular day in 1890. It was a warm June Sunday, and the family had just finished dinner. Caroline had put on her pretty blue dress (the men often complimented her on it) and walked down to the creek, a short distance from the main house. Although it was indeed a nice dress, something was lacking. If only she had a new pair of shoes, she wished.

At the creek there were large boulders where her father sat with her two brothers, along with the other hired men and young Dan Unruh, the master's half-grown grandson. Together they smoked cigarettes and laughed, cooling their bare feet in the stream. Brother Jackob, the cossack, was now married and gone.

"*Ai*, Caroline!" they greeted her as she approached.

"How she dresses for us!" someone teased.

"No — not for us! She expects her suitor — that little Mennonite!" They laughed and made her blush.

"*Dummheit!*" she retorted with mock indignation, noticing the resentful glint in the eyes of Carl, the man whose attentions she had always ignored. He said nothing now, however, sitting sullenly by himself.

"What do you say, Carl?" brother Johann said, turning to him. "A fine girl, *nyet?*" At this the young man rose to his feet and stalked away. There was more laughter. (Caroline felt a special closeness with Johann for she had nursed him through smallpox.)

"No, she wants the young Mennonite," Kirschenman corrected, his dark eyes twinkling whimsically above his cropped beard.

She could not be angry at her father because of his teasing. He never failed to be gentle toward her. She found a place on the boulders a little distance from the men and, carefully removing her old shoes, eased her feet into the cool water.

Her father rolled another cigarette and handed it to small Dan, who sat beside him. "It is time the young one learns to be a man," he said, as the delighted youth accepted the honored token. "Be careful not to burn yourself," Kirschenman added, smiling, and lit the boy's awkwardly-held cigarette.

They smoked a while then in silence. Suddenly Kirschenman's voice erupted in a short, painful cry. Someone had dropped a hot ash upon his bare foot. The others laughed as the impulsive Kirschenman leaped up with a shout and hurled a blast of invective at the culprit. Only Caroline was not amused. She was well-acquainted with his volatile temper that often caused her embarrassment. Her mother, too, was easily angered. (Caroline remembered the time Mother Kirschenman had gotten into a fight with one of the other women, striking blows and pulling hair until Frau Unruh sent them both from the house. That, too, had provided entertainment for everyone.)

Now it was her father at whom they laughed. "He jumps as well as he runs!" someone taunted.

Kirschenman's anger subsided as quickly as it had arisen. He, too, began to laugh, remembering the often-repeated story of how Unruh had offered a dollar to the fastest runner and how Kirschenman had won the race upon his strong legs. Unruh gave him the dollar and said, "Now I have found the man to herd sheep for me." Had he known, he would not have run as fast, Kirschenman said. Again now they settled themselves and resumed their good-natured talk.

Something flashed in the water at Caroline's feet. She saw it shine and knew at once what it was. She watched its gradual, almost imperceptible movements as it rested for an instant, suspended in the water, magnificent and silent. Quickly she thrust upon it with both hands. There was a loud splashing. It fought. Yet she clung to it determinedly. "A *Hecht!* A *Hecht!*" her father cried. They all came running at once.

"One does not often see a pike here," said brother Johann. "He must have come up from the river."

Kirschenman, who seized the large fish from Caroline, drew out his knife and, with deft incisions, soon had the pike opened and cleaned. He returned it to her then. "It is your fish. Take it to the house." So she carried it to the kitchen. Little Dan ran after her.

"You will cook it for us tonight?" he asked.

She nodded, a thought starting to take shape. She had a dress . . . but shoes! Yes, she would prepare the fish for the master.

* * *

John came later that afternoon, riding horseback. He was indeed a small man at twenty, standing shorter than Caroline. Yet he was well-proportioned with a full face and sharp, blue eyes. She smiled when she noticed that he was attempting to grow a mustache.

"You want to be a *Kasak* now?" she teased him, thinking about her brother's full growth. "Mennonites do not wear such things."

"It is not forbidden," he snapped with indignation.

"*Ach,* what does it matter?" she reproached him. "Always you get angry." She took the horse from him and led it toward the barn. It was a rather pathetic-looking animal. "Some oats he could use," she thought aloud. John made no reply.

When the horse had been stabled, they walked back to the house, not crossing the veranda but going to the side of the building where there were some shaded benches.

"I caught a fish today," she informed him proudly after they were seated. "Tonight I am going to cook it for Unruh. Then maybe he will give me money for some shoes — if we are to be married."

John saw through the ploy at once and resented it. "So maybe you think I can't buy shoes for you even?"

"But you must save your money. We will need land and a house. Those things must be saved for. We will both have to work if there is to be bread."

He did not reply to that. These were considerations with which he did not like to grapple. The deeper things — yes! But the demands of marriage — money, a house! "It will still be a while," he said at last . . .

Already three of them had been married — Jake now living on his own place; Marhinja with Wilhelm Zafft, the corpulent Lutheran from Poland, whom they would come to call "Uncle Soft"; and Hanju with Christ Senner, one of their own people. Now it was John's turn. "You should find a good woman," Jake had instructed him earlier . . .

"But it has already been a year, and we should think about these things, if it is ever to be, Caroline insisted. "You must not be afraid to find work. Maybe the railroad would take you in Freeman."

He snorted contemptuously. "Now it's a railroad man you want me to be."

"Only think, John," she persuaded, "the money!"

Yes, the money! Also there was a chance to go to town. Even a place as small as Freeman, that lay on the new track, had its saloon. It would be a change from the monotony of the farm. "Very well," he conceded after some thought. "I will go there tomorrow." They continued to visit for the remainder of the afternoon.

"I will have to help with supper," Caroline said at last.

"Next Sunday I will come again," John said as he rose to go.

"I might have a job by then." As he spoke, he was not aware of someone leaning from the window above.

When he was about to step away from the bench, a sudden surge of cold liquid fell upon them both. They screamed, shuddered and choked at once. Before they had a chance to determine where the water had come from, the window banged shut above their heads. John's eyes darted upward.

"What stupid *Narr* . . . ?" he began to curse. But Caroline laughed, ignoring his rage. "*Ach*, John, it's that crazy Carl."

"He should have a good thrashing," the furious man fumed, aware that his own diminutive size made this prospect unlikely.

The others came in, drawn by the commotion, and began to laugh at the ridiculous sight of the two dowsed lovers. "Well, Caroline, you are now baptized like a Mennonite," brother Johann hooted with glee.

Caroline flushed, and John became even more beside himself with anger. Dripping wet, she led him quickly upstairs and found a dry change of her brother's clothing.

Still muttering invectives, John sulked out to the stable and was about to mount the poor horse when his hand felt something sticky. "Axle grease!" Someone had greased the horse's back. This was indeed the limit. He began to curse the whole lot of them. "No decency! They only want to make a fool of me," he cried.

Quickly Caroline found an old cloth and began to clean the horse. "John, you are such a baby," she reprimanded.

Without bothering to say good-bye, he mounted the horse and, giving the animal a fierce kick, rode away.

Shaking her head, Caroline returned to the house to prepare the fish for Unruh's supper. But little Dan was too sick to eat any of it. His first cigarette had proved too much for his small stomach.

A House and a Family

Had anyone asked her then why she married John, Caroline might have found it difficult to give a reason. Many factors, with which Caroline was already acquainted, stood against the marriage. She was a Lutheran, not a Mennonite. John's people would scorn her because of that and because she was a mere servant girl with no education (although she had taught herself to read the Bible). Then there were John's own shortcomings, which she knew perhaps as well as did his own mother. "Wait until you are older," her parents cautioned her, as parents have always done when the time came for the children to cease being children. But Caroline had made up her mind.

"Somehow," she told her mother, "I feel that I knew him before — long ago."

She valued John's intelligence and his friendship. He was neither a cruel nor an offensive man. What was more, she has succeeded in winning his favor because of her industriousness and good character. Since she could first remember, she had been taught that it was her duty to cultivate these attributes. Such things were highly valued by men, whom it was her task, as a woman, to please. Finally, John had offered to provide her with the two things she most desired — a house and a family.

* * *

The house he built for her was a small, two-storey, rectangular affair with two doors, both facing south. It stood by a small lake on a quarter section of land that old Jacob helped him to buy. Directly adjacent was brother Joe's farm, and across the road was a place belonging to Jockilie Schrag, whom John had known since childhood. John's was a modest place. Yet he was still, after all, a very young man.

On quiet days he would stand upon the porch and look out at the country. He could call across the pasture to Joe's and hear a reply in the early stillness — if the wind didn't blow; and, to the southeast, he could see Jockilie and his wife, Freni, working in their fields. Jockilie drove the plow . . .

"Freni, why are you seeding there?" he called out to her.

"But I am not seeding!" she cried from her seat upon the drill.

"Well, why not?"

They could not suspect that John was listening to them with great amusement. Such was Dakota life.

In June of their third year together, Caroline was pregnant with her first child. She and John went in the wagon to visit her parents, who by that time were living on a leased farm three miles northeast of John's near a schoolhouse that was thereafter always called the *Kirsch'man Schul.* Reaching their destination, Caroline leaped from the wagon seat to the ground to embrace her mother.

"The baby! You must be careful," the heavy-set woman reproached her.

"*Ach*, it will not be hurt," Caroline laughed.

But the child came too soon, born at seven months and weighing three pounds. "Only a little longer than a fork handle," she would recall in later years.

"*Er wird nicht sterben* — He will not die!" Doctor Wipf, the Hutterite physician, reassured her as he wrapped the tiny infant in cotton gauze. The baby lived. They named him Heinrich.

Caroline remained at home raising the baby and doing the work that had to be done if there was to be bread. Although there was never much money, John and his brothers always managed to get jobs in the threshing season, keeping record of their accounts in a small black notebook: Joe Schrag $11.84, Peter Stukey $20.00, Joseph Ries $51.58, D. Goertz $16.69. At the top of the first page John had written a quotation from the Bible: "Let not your left hand know what your right hand does."

On Sundays the brothers fished and hunted ducks at the place called Silver Lake; and when there were no ducks, there would perhaps be a stray farm goose or a chicken brought home in the game bag. John's shotgun was always loaded, waiting for any ducks that might fly over the house. Once it slipped to the floor and discharged, leaving two gaping holes in the staircase.

The family's furniture was an odd collection of pieces large and small — an enormous bookcase from the Hieb Store in Marion, which they converted into a kitchen cupboard and lined with flowered wall paper; a small, wooden bed covered with a heavy coat of brown varnish (the *Krechsel Bett* they called it because it always creaked); a wall clock with carved ornaments and a glass door that was bought the year the baby came; a large, hand-crank roller organ from the Zickrick Saloon in Freeman; a tall wardrobe and a hooded trunk with a false bottom, which had been brought from the Old Country and which brother Jake gave as a wedding present. (It was the same trunk upon which John had sat when they left the old village.) These things became a part of their lives and of their children's lives, each a tangible memory. But most precious of all to Caroline, was the small blue canister that brother Jackob had given her on her thirteenth birthday. It remained always in a special place in the big cupboard.

Yet the strongest memories were of things that could not be touched or put away — warm evenings when John sat with his brothers in front of the house, smoking hand-rolled cigarettes or drinking *Honigschnaps* and joking about their hunting trips. Someone would always tell the story of the time they had gone to fish at Silver Lake, where one of the so-called "Low-Dutch," threatened to sue them for trespassing. They gave him the name *Menschefresser* because, Joe said, he had the face of a cannibal.

Bernhart held up one of the fish, replying, "Your fish? I can find no name on it."

Or they would amuse themselves by telling of the eccentricities of their neighbors. One of these was the stingy Geitze, who rode past the house on his way to town.

"Geitze is already out of matches again," they would laugh among themselves, because it was said that he customarily asked the storekeeper for a mere handful of free matches to avoid buying the entire package.

There was another neighbor, a rich man called Spitzberger, of whom John once drew a caricature and labeled it "Mr. Pointhiller."

But their greatest joy was to play music together — John on his clarinet or autoharp, Bernhart on the fiddle and Jonath on the mandolin. It was for them an ideal life, free from concern and secure in its tranquility. There would always be something to eat, and the work would always be done.

The Church

John sat in his place by the church door and watched the austere pageant that he knew so well. Behind the great *Kanzel* sat the three elders — Mueller-Christ, short and rustic-looking, peering at the congregation over his wire-rimmed glasses — still a farmer wearing farmer's trousers; Kaufman-Sep, the jeweler, sitting in the middle, always well-dressed, his hair and goatee clean and trimmed; and Dicke Kaufman, an enormously fat man with a full beard and bullish voice. Schrag-Andre was dead, as was old Uncle Jacob. Gone were the fat-brimmed hats, the hooks and eyes and the women's little white caps.

But the *Gemeinde* — the essence of religious as well as cultural solidarity — continued as always to set the standards for the people's way of life. Everyone had a role to perform — some capacity to fill. John was now the *Kirchediener* — or custodian — for which he received a salary of one hundred dollars per year. The original *Kirchediener,* old Sep Vetter, declined the task when age made it difficult for him to fulfill it, upon which the office was given to Jockilie and to John.

When he first undertook the task, John set about repainting the tarnished chandelier that hung from the ceiling in the church sanctuary. Such ornamentation would have been unthinkable for the old people, but a new feeling of prosperity had come with the present generation, prosperity being, after all, a sign of God's favor. And it was this feeling more than anything else that caused the trouble which followed.

Now old Graber-Anders, the *Vorsänger,* rose to his feet and began to chant the words to the hymn *"Lobe den Herren"* with habitual monotony. A story was told many times of his once having remarked that his glasses were smeared; and the congregation, taking his words to be those of a hymn, began to sing, *"Was ist denn los mit meiner Brille?"* John often wondered whether or not it was so.

When at last the hymn droned to its conclusion, accompanied by another worldly innovation, an organ, old Mueller-Christ inhaled a whiff of dry snuff and then blew his nose deeply into a red handkerchief. Replacing the handkerchief, his eyes tightly shut, he began the prayer: *"Lieber Himmlischer Vater..."* His high-pitched voice, almost like a child's, implored God's mercy upon them all. He twiddled his fleshy thumbs in steady motion as he spoke.

When Mueller-Christ finished his long prayer, Kaufman-Sep rose to the fullness of his own tall stature. The youngest of the three, he was a paragon of the newer trends in form and habit, having come to Dakota with the Waldheimer people — those of the *Spitzige Kirche*, who joined the others when their church building was blown over by a cyclone. He began to weep as he exhorted them to absolve themselves: *"Ihr sollt euch absolvieren!"*

John heard the rasping sound of a cough from the bench along the wall where the oldest patriarchs sat, reflectively chewing tobacco or dipping snuff as they had done every day of their adult lives. He did not have to look. The sound told him it was Gräber-Hans. Now there would be more tobacco juice to clean from the floor, he thought. Each of these old ones had his place upon the bench, which he repeatedly took week after week, evidenced by dried, brown stains on the floor or by a polished spot on the wall where he rubbed the back of his head. John had seen a picture of an American poet named Whittier. He knew the man immediately. It was Gräber-Hans.

Finally now Dicke Kaufman began to preach. His was by far the longest sermon. His voice thundered at them like the wrath of God until, as some said, the windows could be heard to rattle. He had come to America with the Horodischers and was known and loved by all of the Schweitzers, including those in Kansas and Nebraska.

When the sermon ended, John felt Jockilie's hand on his shoulder. "We must get the basins," he reminded him. It was already time for communion — after which there would be footwashing. The small children were sent outdoors. Then the blessed bread and the cup with its fermented contents were passed along the benches. There was a youth among them who, they said, was feeble-minded. He waited until the cup came to him, drank from it, and moved to the next bench in time to sample the wine once more. It was also said that this same boy ran to a small rise beyond his father's house every evening to watch the sunset.

Now there was a clatter of tin basins. John and Jockilie brought water in pitchers. Each person selected a partner whose feet he washed in the manner of Christ at the Last Supper. It was intended as an act of humility. Yet each of them used particular discretion in choosing the person with whom he washed. As they performed this rite, they sang another hymn, concluding with the

Bruderkuss — the kiss of brotherhood.

When all of this ceremony was finished, a general meeting was called for which most of the parishioners remained. There was that day a matter before them that would cause intense debate. The South people wanted a new church closer to them.

"It is only because they have the money," whispered John's brother-in-law, Christ. "Showing off! That's all it is. All they have to go is an extra two miles."

"If they decide to separate, they are going to demand their share of the money, too," John replied. "They'll want every penny that's theirs."

The argument began at once. Outside, the children played among the waiting horses and listened to the rancor that came from within.

Old man Geitze, the wealthiest and most notoriously frugal of the South people, was demanding payment of his share in the treasury. His resentment toward the *Gemeinde* grew from a judgment made against him earlier by the elders when he purchased a cow at a local sale. Seeing it inferior to one bought by a poorer man, Geitze took the better cow for himself. The issue came before the elders, who warned him of God's judgment in the matter. *"Einmal wird Er richten,"* they cautioned him. "God will someday set this matter right."

"For sure he will!" Geitze retorted as he left the building, keeping the cow he had taken.

"Now he will see that he gets what is his — and a little more, too, if he can manage it," John told Christ as they continued to listen.

The older man smiled beneath his handlebar mustache, "Next he will want to saw off a corner of the church and take it home. Wait and see. . . . He will come walking down the road, saw in hand, one of these days."

They laughed quietly.

Meanwhile John's father and old Poltauwitz, the wolf hunter, sat with the other old men, conversing in Russian. *"Pravda!* That's true, indeed!" Poltauwitz was affirming, nodding his head to something Jacob had said.

"Someday they will be gone," John thought to himself. "We won't see them again with their beards — only a place where they once sat." He looked about the crowded sanctuary. "And this building, too, will be gone." It seemed to him suddenly so ludicrous to argue over something that, when it came down to it, meant nothing at all when one was dead.

The room was filled with faces, some old and austere, others fat and contented — almost bovine — and still others that were wasted and anxious. As John studied them, there rose again within him a fierce yarning to know the "why" of all of it. It was that same implacable longing that he had felt since childhood: "Why are we doing this? Does life seem so good to us that we fear its ending, or so bitter that we can only hope for something better afterward? That is the whole matter of religion — the unknown and unknowable."

It was then that John's second brother-in-law, Zafft, interrupted the proceedings. The elders and everyone else turned toward him as he pulled his huge bulk upward from his seat. Because he had broken his back in a fall from a scaffold, he always stood in a stooped position. Yet he made a commanding figure in spite of his ungainly stance. The others listened to him because he was one of those men whose strength commands a natural respect.

"I think it is enough for today," was all he said and turned to go, waddling out of the church toward his buggy. The rest looked at each other. Then, one by one, they left their places and followed him. The meeting was finished.

"*Lieber Himmlischer Vater*"
Mueller-Christ

Part III

THE SECOND SON

John's House.

Days at Home

His earliest memory was of the time he sat upon his father's lap in church on the men's side, eating peanuts that John had chewed for him because he still had no teeth. He was a year old when the new century arrived, although he was too young to know it. But as his consciousness grew more acute, he became aware of a house that was the realm of his small life's activities — and beyond the house a garden, warm and green, smelling of earth.

In the garden he saw his mother moving slowly among the potato vines with her hoe and singing to herself, "*Ich weiss dass mein Erlöser lebt* — I know that my Redeemer lives." He was more than familiar with the words. She had sung them to him countless times whenever she rocked him to sleep. They were good words. . . . He did not have to know what they meant. There was also in the garden another being, like himself, only somewhat larger. (He had as yet no concept of age.) This was Heinrich, now called by his English name, Henry. There were two others, who were like his mother, called Ida and Lydia — his sisters, whose task it was to care for the baby brother named Hardwig — a name that their father had read in a German novel . . .

In naming his children as he did, John had broken with a custom of generations. "Our little ones," he told Caroline, "will not be condemned to bear our own names or those of our brothers and sisters." So it resulted that the three small girls who were to follow Hardwig would be named Othelia, Berta and Anne . . .

"Eddy!" Henry called to his brother, dragging a large garden thing along the path. "See what I pulled out. . . . It's a rutabaga." Eddy looked at the huge root and at the dull green stalk that his brother held. That was how he learned about vegetables.

He wandered among the rows of growing plants until his eye caught sight of something across the lake. It was alive and moved. Perhaps he could have it for a pet, he thought. "*Was iss das?*" he asked, pointing it out to Henry.

"It's a badger," Henry said, his voice becoming excited.

"Can we keep it?" Eddy asked.

"No, it will eat the chickens. I will tell Mama. She will go and make it dead."

Eddy watched them go to kill the badger. He was sorry, partly for the badger's sake, partly for himself because it could not be his. So he became aware of the place that was his world.

It was a place where swallows came each spring to build nests of mud above the doorway where Eddy played. Fascinated by their industry, he never tired of watching them as they flew to and from the lake with tiny specks of mud and grass. "Who taught them?" he wondered. "How do they know what to do?" They continued their work, oblivious to him and to the snipes that darted above the glimmering lake, calling shrill taunts to each other.

When Hardwig was old enough, the boys played together along the lake with their mischievous cousin Freddy, Uncle Joe's son, almost their brother. In the evenings there would be the familiar sound of the groaning roller organ — the *Dreh-Orgel* — playing "Nearer my God to Thee." Henry liked playing the organ, and sometimes John would accompany the songs on his clarinet.

In the house there was the smell of wood smoke and of good things to eat, as Caroline and the girls prepared supper; and afterward John would go onto the porch to roll a cigarette. "Do you see the *Irrlichte?*" he would say to the boys when they followed him, looking at the strange, moving lights far to the south where the marshes were. "Some people say they are ghosts, but they are really something called swamp gas," he explained to them.

So the evening hours passed while the wall clock counted the minutes with the tireless motion of its small pendulum. Warm lamplight flickered upon the papered walls, making the printed design seem alive and illuminating the austere portrait of a man who, Henry said, was the German king. When at last he was put to bed, Eddy lay quietly listening to his parents' voices from below until the lamps were put out, leaving the house smelling of kerosene.

When morning came, he awoke and felt the warmth of the sun upon his small carved bed. He heard someone outside humming a tune and knew that it was Uncle Joe — Joe Vetter — who came almost every day, entering the house without knocking and drinking from the coffee pot that always stood upon the stove. Eddy hurried into his clothes and down the stairs, hearing the lively concourse of familiar voices that he would remember as long as he lived, not for what they said but because they were a part of his life.

"So, here comes the early riser," John would tease, winking to Joe, who laughed —

"*Ach,* my boy will be in bed yet for an hour. He gets tired out after all his pranks."

"These two of mine can think up their own share of devilment," John laughed.

Quickly finishing their breakfast, Eddy and Hardwig were soon on their way to Uncle Joe's place to find their cousin, crossing a field of daisies that grew nearly as tall as the boys. There they spent the entire day, watching Joe work at his forge as their grandfather had done.

"Run to the house and bring my good steel file," Joe ordered Freddy that afternoon. "But don't strike it against that big rock," he cautioned, indicating the large granite boulder that rested in the front yard.

Quickly the boys did as the uncle instructed. As they left the house, Freddy stopped beside the great rock. His eyes studied it curiously and examined the file in his hand. "Let's see what will happen," he suggested then. "I won't hit so hard." The file struck the rock and snapped in two.

"It just fell apart," he sobbed to Joe, as he returned with the broken tool.

* * *

Uncle Jake came almost as frequently as did Uncle Joe. They loved him. To them he was always "Jäk Vetter." He would tease them often in his own gentle way and was always telling stories or giving advice on something or other. His was a kindly face that looked at them with one eye. The other — made of glass — was put out by a piece of kindling wood when Jake was younger.

He came to the house one day when Anne was a baby and lifted her from her cradle. "I think I will take this small one home with me," he teased. At once little Othelia leaped upon him, clawing and screaming, until he was barely able to keep from dropping the tiny girl. . .

Anne was the last child. With her there were eight — nine if one counted another infant, who died earlier. They were all delivered by Doctor Wipf, the Hutterite. His was another face Eddy came to know. Wipf visited them when he was called upon, accepting what they could afford to pay him. Always he had time to talk, and at such times they would ask him again to tell the story of how he had been driven from the Hutterite colony.

"How did it look?" he would say, twitching his small, penciled mustache. "They sent us — my brother and me — to learn medicine because the colony needed a doctor. So we went to school where everyone wore good suits — and there we were with our black hats and lice in our beards. What would you have done? We decided to dress like everyone else, and so we did until we went home."

"And that's when they drove you out?" John would ask then, although he knew the story well.

"*Das wird schon!*" Wipf replied. "They said it was contrary to the rules of the *Bruderhof.* Well — so it was perhaps. They said if we wanted to be English, we should go live as Englishmen and be worldly. So we left." He paused then to wipe his tiny eyeglasses and placed them into his pocket. "Anyway — we would never go back, either of us. Once you have been on the outside, that is where you want to be."

Sometimes they asked him questions about medicine. "What about this disease called tetanus?" John inquired once. "They say it's caused by rust."

"Rust!" scoffed the little doctor. "I wouldn't be afraid to take rust and rub it right into my skin." They looked at him with amazement as he moved his hand vigorously across his forearm to stimulate the act.

Eddy listened to the conversations and marveled at the stories, never daring to interrupt or question. Each face, each voice, each event constituted a fragment in a configuration of impressions that would remain with him — days that came and went, blending into a single continuum of life — days, people, memories.

Each year in the summer the families gathered at the *Grossvaterplatz* where old Jacob still lived on the land he had homesteaded. It was a trip toward which Eddy looked with dread, fearing the wrath of that stern old patriarch. Only after many years would he be able to look back upon those times with a wistful sentiment, realizing that in fact his grandfather was the most gentle sort of man. . .

It was no great distance from John's house to Jacob's farm. Yet it seemed to take forever traveling by wagon along the fields and fences that lay between. Before they reached their destination, they could see from a distance the dark-wooded timber that had come to be called the *Schwartzwald*, which Jacob had planted years before. Many agreed that it was indeed the best grove in the township. Then, gradually, as they neared the house, they began to sense the stifling sweetness of clover blossoms that grew along the roadway where the old man kept his bees.

There were, on such days, many people beneath the trees outside the two-story farmhouse that stood so stiff and erect with its peaked gables. Eddy could discern Jäk Vetter, telling jokes to make everyone laugh, and Uncle Christ, the philosopher, expounding Swedenborg's metaphysics, together with Joe Vetter, Bernhart Vetter and Uncle Julius Ewert. Uncle Jonath was there as well, still a very young man; but Uncle Soft and Marhinja Bas had gone to live in Kansas. Eddy's other aunts were present, their long dresses and wrapped hair making them appear old before their middle years — Hanju Bas, Julia Bas, Anna Bas, Freni Bas and Tante Carrie — the youngest.

Jacob's brother — blind Hannes Vetter — and their cousin, called Russ-Jonath, were there, too, among an assortment of other blood kin and married relations, which included the Poltauwitz family — Joe, who was always exclaiming, "By George!"; Janju, whom they called Vanka; Stoddler, the stammerer; and, of course, the old wolf hunter himself.

They could see his carriage flying through the dust from a distance, drawn along the road by Judy and Spot, the two pinto horses he had gotten all the way from Montana. Close behind

58

followed the pair of hunting dogs that always accompanied him. "His lordship comes! Get ready to remove your caps," they cried in jest, remembering the Old Country. In truth, Poltauwitz, who had been a foreman on a Russian estate, had gained the highest status attainable by a Mennonite in that country — not by any means a nobleman, although they jokingly called him "lord" behind his back. Yet everyting in his manner bespoke a mimic aristocracy.

When the carriage clattered to a stop at the gate, it was greeted by a swarm of children, who took turns admiring the horses and awaiting the usual favors from the *Herrschaft's* wife. The heavy-set matron, debarking as gracefully as possible, smiled and called out to them. "How many good children do we have here?" She was greeted by a chorus of gleeful shouts. "For each good child I have something." So saying, she produced a small bag containing, as everyone knew, sweet, sugar-covered lemon drops. "I want only good children now," she chuckled. There were more shouts. Each child in turn then, no matter how obnoxious, in fact, was his reputation, received one precious piece of candy.

The *Herrschaft* himself meanwhile assumed a seat under the trees with Jacob and the other old, bearded men and began to joke with them in Russian. Eddy and his cousins listened from a safe distance.

"How can they understand each other?" the boys wondered. "They even laugh together."

"And Grandpa even! Look how his tongue moves!"

Eddy and his cousins could speak both German and English. Those were languages by which one could make oneself understood, although German was by far the better language for telling a joke. But this eerie-sounding gibberish was totally incomprehensible. "They must be crazy to talk like that," the boys concluded.

After a few moments, Poltauwitz's discerning eyes caught sight of Eddy. "Come here, boy!" The command was not harsh but was given in a way to indicate that obedience was expected. Eddy approached apprehensively.

"So this is your grandson," Poltauwitz remarked to Jacob, as though such a common acknowledgement coming from one of such status was the most coveted honor imaginable. "A fine boy! Go now to my carriage and find my coat. . . . It's right there on the seat. If you look in the pocket, you'll find my pipe and tobacco. Bring them to me, and I'll give you something."

The carriage had cushioned seats and smelled of leather. Eddy reached into the deep pockets of the large overcoat, which seemed almost sinister to him, and found the corncob pipe and the tobacco. Returning, he handed these to Poltauwitz, who offered him some small coins. "A good boy — yes!" the old man repeated, his eyes gleaming.

Eddy watched as the pipe was placed among the brown lip whiskers and auspiciously lighted. He could not then realize that in the spark that drew fire and made the pipe's contents burn he was seeing a last glimmer of another time. He continued to watch for a short while and then ran off to play. What would have given others a sense of self-importance had only caused him embarrassment. . .

Soon it came time to eat. The children clustered into the house where the table and sideboards were covered with dishes of hot *Käs Pyrohy* and *Kraut Knepp,* as well as the highly-relished Russian pancakes called *Nalysnyky.* First it was the men who ate at the great table. The dishes were heaped with generous helpings, constantly replenished by the quick hands of jovial Mennonite women. There was continual laughter and loud talk amid the clatter of forks and spoons against heavy china. In the kitchen Aunt Carrie, the only one of John's sisters still living at home, was busily buttering thick slices of bread for eager young hands.

"Now, Eddy, what do you want? There is honey, plum jelly or apple preserves."

Shyly he indicated the plum jelly.

"Here you go then," she said, handing the bread to him. "Oh, such a cute, freckled face — I could kiss it!" The older women laughed while his cousins taunted him mercilessly. He felt the blood rise in his cheeks and hurried away.

When he had finished eating, Poltauwitz took out his pipe and, winking at the other men, recited a proverb: *"Und nach dem Essen, nicht vergessen. . . . Und das steht in der Schrift."**

Everyone talked; no one listened. All were caught in some mad hilarity that would be forgotten the following day. Still the droves of cousins flooded through the doors and across the yard, reveling in the day's jubilation.

Presently they heard the shrill sound of their grandfather's voice; *"Ai, ai, ihr Kasaki!* Stay away from the bees!" he warned them when they approached too near to the beehives. At once they left their play, more afraid of his anger than of possible bee stings. But from a distance Freddy mimicked him, crying, "Starra — Starri! I am stung by a bee!"

* "And after the meal, do not forget (to smoke). . . . And *that* is in the Scripture." The expression's irony lies in the use of the word *das*.

"Poltauwitz is leaving," someone called them. They gathered quickly at the gate to see the *Herrschaft* off. "*Prididomene!*" he called to Jacob, as he slapped the horses' reins.

"He says, 'Come visit me sometime,'" Henry told Eddy, who stood beside his brother. Henry, Eddy thought, must know everything.

Schwartz-Grossvater and Poltauwitz.

A Wedding and a Fire

"We are going to Pete Schrag's house today," Eddy's sister Ida said as she shook him awake one morning. His eyes, still dazed from sleep, stared bewilderedly about the room. It was earlier than usual. Although it was winter, the upstairs bedrooms were not heated, and he could see his breath when he spoke.

"*Warum?*" he asked, half awake.

"There's going to be a wedding. Come! Mama says I must clean you up."

Wearily he pulled himself onto the cold floor while Ida shook Hardwig. Together she hurried them downstairs and into the warm kitchen where, one at a time, they were dunked into a tub of hot water that waited steaming before the stove. Ida's less than gentle hands, hastily scrubbing the small shoulders, tugged at arms and ears with merciless severity. Being bathed in the summer was not so bad. . . . In fact, it was even fun when they were allowed to wash in the lake. But in winter, even when the stove warmed the room, it was a chilly business.

Eddy recognized the voices that were coming from the front room — they belonged to Joe Vetter and Julia Bas.

"You will soon need a bigger house, John," Uncle Joe was saying, "with six children now and one more on the way."

"Little ones are such a blessing," Julia fussed. "Of course I am well-pleased with the two I have. Freddy wanted to come early so he could play with your boys. But I guess there won't be time."

"We won't be ready for a while," Caroline commented hastily as she laid out the children's clothing. "You go ahead of us."

"Oh, what nice little suits!" Eddy heard his aunt exclaim. "Yes — perhaps we will go then. You know there are always so many people, one never gets a chance to talk to everyone. Of course, the Schweitzers always like a good *Hochzeit* — it gives them a chance to visit."

Eddy heard them moving across the floor and listened as the front door was opened — that familiar sound peculiar to each house and known only to its own inhabitants. As they left, Eddy knew that his father would follow them to their sled and talk with them there, as he always did.

Caroline came into the kitchen now. "Ja, the Schweitzers like to visit," she remarked in a tone that was slightly vindictive. "Hurry, Ida! We will yet have to bathe the little one."

Eddy could not know then what it was that his mother felt. But in later years he would remember and understand the alienation that she endured — making him bitter to think of it. Often he was to observe her sitting alone at gatherings, ignored, while the other women chattered among themselves. She never berated them for their clannishness or their snobbery, no matter how deeply it cut her.

* * *

Following the ceremony, the wedding procession arrived at the Schrag place for the noon meal. There was the usual array of sleds and teams collected around the house, as well as the noise and confusion of people. Eddy ran off to play with his cousins in the snow until the call came for them to eat. Suddenly another cry was heard. "There is smoke in the house," someone hollered in alarm, as the guests fled outdoors.

People were gazing excitedly at the rooftop while several of the men ran in different directions shouting orders to one another. "Buckets!" "A ladder!" "*Schnell!*"

A ladder emerged from among a cluster of heads and was propped against the eaves. Pete Mistschook, the self-appointed fireman, pulled himself to the roof's peak. "Bring water — quickly!" he ordered.

Eddy poked his way through the crowd, managing to peer into the smoke-filled kitchen. "The stove must have overheated," he heard someone say.

When the water bucket came, it was hoisted up to Mistschook, who promptly poured the contents down the chimney flue. Soot-laden water flushed through the stovepipe and onto the floor with a loud hiss. There were dismayed groans.

"Why did you pour it down the chimney?" an irate voice demanded.

"Why, because that's where the smoke is coming from!" snapped the indignant fireman.

Eddy noticed Uncle Jake standing at the base of the ladder, gazing quietly upward with his one good eye. "Nu! Where else should the smoke go?" the uncle asked with disdain.

There was nervous laughter. Mistschook, flustered and angry, pretended not to hear it. "Bring an axe!" he cried.

The axe was brought and lifted up to him. Furiously Mistschook hacked an opening in the roof. "Aha! There is something red in there!" he exclaimed in triumph. More water was taken up. Again there was the hiss and sizzle of dowsed flame, and at last the fire was out.

Uncle Jake looked down at Eddy. The glass eye glinted in the sun. "Son we had a big fire today," he smiled.

Later the roof was repaired and a patch of tin fixed over the hole. For a long time it remained; and, whenever the sun reflected upon the tin, it could be seen for a great distance to remind them of the fire.

Wind

The wind comes often to Dakota. It is an angry wind, unrelenting and haughty, blowing for many days without respite or mercy, ignoring those whose lives are compelled to endure it. Over long periods it can spawn dreadful loneliness, and occasionally its force is even more destructive.

In 1905 Roger-Jäk, the boy who imitated the meadowlark, lived with his wife Katie in a small house south of John and Caroline's. The wind came that year with a vehemence such as they had never seen before. All day they listened to it and felt the tiny house shaking helplessly around them.

"Perhaps it will quit at sundown," Roger hoped, gazing through the windowpane. . . . But the gale only increased with the darkness and brought rain. The house trembled. An abrupt bang of thunder shook the ground just as Roger lit the lamp. He looked at his children in the dim light — Gust, Henry, Emma and Erhart. Their faces were sober, looking back at him, anxious and trusting.

"If we had a cellar," he thought aloud.

"Yet I said we should have made one, but you would not listen," Katie scolded him.

Roger, not listening, continued to study the darkening sky. There was heavy rain now against the window.

"We must move the table," he said finally. "If the window goes out, the lamp will fall over." Motioning to Katie to take the lamp, he began to lift.

There was a sudden noise like a giant hammer. The floor seemed to come up beneath them, as if raised by a huge hand. There was no more sense of up or down — furniture, broken boards and glass flew on top of their screams. . . .

When Roger became conscious once again, there was only damp darkness and the triumphant wailing of the wind. He looked about, dazed and uncertain. Then he began to remember. . . . He called out his children's names. There was no reply — only the wind. Picking himself up from among the shattered lumber that had been a house, he tried to stand; but the wind nearly bore him off his feet. "Dead!" The thought paralyzed him for an instant. "All dead!" He began to weep. Searching clumsily, he found a pillow to cover his face and began to walk.

He was still weeping when he reached his cousin Schpook's house. "My children are dead. All of them!"

The cousin listened helplessly to the distraught man. "Perhaps in the morning," he suggested. . . .

* * *

"You must take the team to John and Joe's places," old Jacob instructed his sons, Bernhart and Jonath, the following day. "See if they are safe. John has only a small house."

Obediently the young men hitched the horses and started north. The spring morning was warm and still, but everywhere there were signs of the wind's scourge — fallen trees, roofless barns, overturned wagons.

"There — the Roger place!" Jonath exclaimed, pointing to the the pile of broken wood where the house had been. As they approached, they discerned figures moving about, probing the wreckage — Roger, Schpook, Katie and the children.

Roger motioned to them. His full, Teutonic face beamed. "They are safe!" he cried. "She got them all into the barn. Safe!"

It would be some years afterward, when he was living in Montana, that Roger was to find a small shingle nail embedded in his scalp. "A souvenir of the wind," he laughed whenever he told about it.

The Burial of *Dicke Kaufman*

Christian Kaufman, the elder born in Russia, the obese preacher whose voice rattled the windowpanes, died on August 16, 1906, in the heat of late summer. He had been an itinerant, traveling from one Schweitzer congregation to another throughout Dakota, Kansas and even Minnesota. When he died, there was much mourning among the Mennonites.

From all over they came on that hot day to see him buried — so many that the old church (later to be called the "North Church") could not contain them all. Strings of buggies and wagons came down roads from every direction. Each contained a family: a mother and father, a wizened old patriarch who still wore his untrimmed beard, a kerchiefed grandmother and an assortment of children of various ages. Eddy and Hardwig sat together with Henry, jammed tightly in the seat of the spring wagon as it clipped along. Their vehicle was joined by others along the way until there was a long caravan of black carriages on the dusty roadway.

"They must need a preacher in heaven," Eddy said. "That is why he died."

"Everyone has to die," Henry replied. "He was an important man; so he will be important there, too."

The small boys' eyes expanded when they reached the church, which had now become an island surrounded by a prodigious collection of black carriages. The waiting horses seemed to sense, as well, that this was no ordinary church day. Inside, the boys sat next to their father and watched the proceedings. There was the noise of heavy shoes upon the floor, the intermittent sound of coughing from the men's side and of weeping and sighing among the women. Some of them had come great distances. The heavy, dark clothes of mourning and the closeness of so many living bodies made the hot afternoon even more uncomfortable. The room smelled of sweat and death.

Then it began — the long ordeal of eulogies and hymns, telling of the *schoenes Land* to which the elder had departed. Eddy, who comprehended little of what they said, remained in awe of their lamenting. It did the dead man no good, he reasoned, if he was already in heaven. Did they mourn because he had gone to a better place — or for themselves because they were left behind? Still, he concluded, it was better to be alive.

Then he heard a slight groaning — a lifeless, inhuman sound — from where the dark coffin stood. "It is a different kind of coffin," he heard Jockilie whisper to John. "They have a glass cover over him inside the box."

"But what is that noise?" John asked, also in a whisper.

"We packed him in ice. But if he bloats any more, the glass may break. That is what you hear. He's pushing up against it."

Eddy looked again in the direction of the coffin. Flies, the harbingers of decay, had begun to collect around it, holding their own service for the dead man. Still the funeral proceeded, and the glass lid continued to groan.

"Come, we will have to move the coffin to the door," Jockilie told John while they were singing the final hymn. When the hymn was concluded, the mourners rose and pushed toward the entrance where the coffin now stood. The quiet sobs became an intense wailing as the throng gave way to self-indulgent emotion. They leaned over the open box to gaze upon the old deceased man, from whose face Jockilie quickly managed to wipe the collection of putrid foam. "Move on! Make room!" he ordered them when they lingered too long over the casket. But already the entrance was blocked so that no one could pass.

"Outside. . . !" John motioned to Jockilie. "*Weg mache!*" he snapped at the lamenting women. With imaginable difficulty the coffin was placed on the porch outside the church. There it was met by an additional congregation of mourners who had not been able to enter the building. The weeping continued as they clustered into a heavy knot around the morbid object. Again the coffin was moved . . . this time completely into the open yard.

Still the pressure mounted against the glass. Again the lid had to be lifted and foam wiped away from the silent lips — lips that once proclaimed faith with powerful oratory. The bloating had swollen them now, drawing them apart so that it appeared almost as though the dead man were about to speak.

There was no chance in all of this for a small boy to approach the casket, surrounded by so many sobbing and curious people, so Eddy stood by himself at a distance and continued to watch. He saw Jockilie run to a nearby buggy and grab a horse whip. Returning, the *Kirchediener* began to prod at the crowd until at last it began to move. Eddy then saw his father coming toward him. In a moment he felt himself lifted up higher than the people and carried over toward the coffin. He could see the glass window with the bearded face pressed against it. And as John held him, the seven-year-old boy gazed down upon the countenance of the great man.

Hunting Season — 1906

When the autumn came, John and his four brothers placed their shotguns into the wagon and went hunting after wild hens and ducks. Since the time of their boyhood, large game had become a rarity, made increasingly scarce by the ubiquitous farms and settlements that left little sanctuary for deer or antelope. Only wild fowl remained in abundance. It was a pleasant, warm time when the aroma of distant smoke rested upon the air on still, autumn days, and threshing stacks stood like small hills in every direction. The horses proceeded with habitual acquiescence among drying corn shocks where crows hunted like huge black insects for stray kernels — "karnals" Jonath called them. Joe Vetter drove the team, allowing the horses their own pace, not forcing them.

Dutifully they ambled along trails they knew as part of their own patterned existence. Eddy felt sorry for the horses as they went, the gray dust rising beneath them. He sat quietly in the box listening to the groan of the wheels and to the rattle of the tie chain as the men talked.

"So we will all soon travel in automobiles," Jäk Vetter was saying. "How will it be, then, with no horses to hitch?"

John rolled a cigarette and lit it behind his cupped hands, letting the smoke escape in a cloud. It floated in a thin stream behind the moving wagon. "It will be no different to us then because of the way things happen. We get used to anything after a while."

Then Eddy saw what looked like an enormous sack drifting in the air some distance from them. "Look, Pa!" he cried, pointing to the object.

"It's a balloon!" John explained, pausing to contemplate the airborne device. "They fill it with hot air. That's what makes it float."

"They had one in Yankton a year ago," Jake added. "Some people even bought tickets to go for a ride in it."

"But now there is even a machine that can fly," said Joe Vetter. "What will come next, I wonder."

"Maybe the Last Judgment," Jake said, half whimsically. . . . Yet there was something ominous in his tone. . . . "If it is as it says in the Scriptures — when we expect it least."

They remained silent for a while. Eddy smelled the scent of the cigarette smoke and listened. John began to sing:

The Yankton boys are clever and the Yankton girls are kind.
I soon forgot my sweetheart, the girl I left behind.

Finally Joe said, "But how can it come to an end just like that? When you look around you and see it all, can you imagine that it will someday not be?"

Bernhart, who had said nothing before now, gazed thoughtfully toward the ground. "Sometimes I wonder if it is true at all what we are told — even what is written in the Scripture. Maybe, after all, there is nothing after we die. No God — nothing!"

Eddy, as he listened, thought, "How can he talk like that? If it is in the Bible, it must be so." It would be some years before the same doubts would return to plague him. He looked for the balloon again; but it was gone, vanished among the clouds.

"Like a thief in the night," Joe quoted.

"Someone is waving at us," John interrupted them. Another wagon stood at the edge of the field. A man was standing upon the box.

They returned the wave, but the man continued to gesture in a way that became frantic.

"He wants something," Joe said, pulling the team to a halt. The gesturing was followed by a faint cry, and the brothers turned the wagon in the direction of the appeal.

"There is someone else — someone on the ground!" Jake exclaimed as they neared the spot.

Eddy would always remember the sight of that body lying upon the field. It was the first time he saw so much human blood. It terrified and fascinated him at once. There was a gaping red aperture in the prone man's forehead that made the boy shudder. John leaped to the ground and walked toward the other man — a stranger.

"He says the gun discharged when they jumped off the wagon," John told them after he had spoken with the stranger.

"His own gun or the other's?" asked Jake.

"He doesn't quite explain that," John said. "He seems pretty confused."

"There will be an investigation, no doubt," Bernhart surmised. "We'll have to take him in and report it."

The surviving man, as it turned out, was a Hutterite from Freeman. The dead man was named Weigum and had been the other's hired man. This Eddy heard from the uncles as they returned to Joe's place with the wagon. The Hutter followed in his own wagon with the corpse.

They stopped first in front of John's house where Caroline and the children gazed uncertainly at the small cortege.

"Do you want to see him?" Jake asked her, after they had told her the story. Curiosity outweighing her apprehension, she followed him to the back of the second wagon where he lifted the canvas that had been put over the body. Eddy heard his mother scream and saw her turn away from the sight. They waited then until Joe had called the sheriff, and the wagon was finally taken away. No one talked to the Hutter, who remained by himself throughout the affair, unable or unwilling to look at them or to speak. Eddy pitied him.

Later, as Uncle Bernhart had speculated, there was an inquest during which some said that Weigum's death had not been an accident. The Hutter, however, was exonerated. And it was a while before the brothers went hunting again. Eddy, too, felt a quiet dismay at what had happened.

"It could have been one of us," he thought, beginning to comprehend the awfulness of death as never before. "Maybe Uncle Joe or Uncle Bernhart — even Pa! It could have been one of them." It was only chance that dictated how life was to end. A man had gone hunting and had died. No inquest could revoke that death. No one could be held accountable for circumstance. For on that day, unexpected, the Thief had come.

Das Christkind

"In Russia they say He wanders about the country knocking on people's doors, and those who let Him in are blessed." Uncle Jake leaned back comfortably in the great chair, his hands folded in front of him, and gazed upon memories. The others sat about the room and listened to his stories. Everyone felt a sense of childlike anticipation . . .

It had been a night of much festivity, beginning in church where everyone saw neighbors and exchanged wishes for a good Christmas. They sang the seasonal hymns, sharing the *Abendmal* and the *Bruderkuss* with a special affinity. Past enmities were forgotten — or at least suspended for the evening.

Afterward, a row of sleds left the church, following the road past Spargler's house toward Uncle Joe's. "Do not lose your way now," they called good-naturedly to one another amid laughter and the jangling of the large sleigh bells on Uncle Christ's team. Even the horses seemed to sense the festivity of the time. To the small children, lying beneath blankets in the bottom of the sled, it seemed as though the vehicle was moving backwards by some strange duplicity of motion. It was a time of excitement and mystery.

Reaching Uncle Joe's house, the children were lifted from transports and hurried across the snow. Lamplight appeared suddenly in the windows and fell upon an ice-covered path leading to the open doorway. Inside, Julia Bas busily stirred the fire until the room was warm and comfortable, while Uncle Joe lit the candles upon a decorated plum bush that served as a Christmas tree and went outside to stable the horses. Everyone was treated to wine, *Kneebrot*, and *Makuchen*. There was laughter and loud talk. When at last the hilarity subsided, a relaxed pleasantness pervaded the room.

"Sing us a Russian song," Caroline asked Uncle Jake.

Smiling, he rose to his feet. "Well, maybe I can remember a song," he said evasively, pretending to be hard-pressed to recall even one of the many he knew. "This one is about a man and a saw," he announced after some contemplation, the lamplight reflecting upon his glass eye. "The man is saying, 'How much wood can this lovely new saw of mine cut up!'" Clearing his throat, he sang:

"Jak dam ludna bilka berdzam, azhenov! Nabaroth!"

When he had finished, there was more laughter and wine followed by stories, at which Jake was also well-accomplished. Foremost among these was the tale of the *Christkind* — the child of Christmas, who visited homes on the holy Eve with sweets and presents for children . . .

"I remember some left dinner plates for Him to fill," Jake said.

"They even did that here for a while," John added, fingering his cigarette holder. "But the Americans talk only of Santa Claus. . . . They hang up stockings for him."

Jake nodded. "Yes, times change."

Outside, the night was still. A calmness settled again upon the room. The wood fire rattled noisily in the heater while lamplight glistened upon the empty glasses and made the designs on the wallpaper seem to dance. It was a good time — a time when sadness was forgotten, having no place on such a night.

Then came a sudden rapping at the door. It startled them all. Julia rose to her feet.

"Wer kann's sin?" she asked, curious about so late a visitor.

The door was thrown open, and a shower of small colored objects flew upon the parlor floor. With gleeful alacrity the children were on their knees, eagerly gathering the pieces of peppermint, chocolate and licorice.

"*Das Christkind! Das Christkind!*" they shouted.

The older people laughed, sharing the amusement, remembering. But Eddy caught a glimpse of someone in the doorway. It was only for an instant before the door banged shut. But it was sufficient for him to see that Uncle Joe was the *Christkind.*

Der Schlofprediger

"But have you not yet seen the Sleeping Preacher?" Auntie asked Caroline one afternoon that winter. "I did not believe it at first. But now I have seen him with my own eyes, and it is true. He preaches in his sleep."

"*Ach!* He's just pretending!" Caroline scoffed at the other woman's superstition. "How can he preach, then, while he is asleep?"

Eddy and Hardwig listened to the above conversation from the doorway. Eddy, too, was incredulous. "They look down on Ma because she can't read," he told his brother. "But she has more sense than to believe such a thing."

"But maybe it is true!" Hardwig protested.

If so, it would be a marvelous sight to see — a preacher who gave a sermon while asleep. Eddy and his brother continued to listen.

"You must see for yourself," the aunt insisted. "You will talk differently afterward."

For the remainder of the day Eddy thought of nothing but the *Schlofprediger.* "Perhaps it is the devil who talks through him," he heard the old people say. "But, then, how is it he can speak from God's word?" So they debated among themselves, and in the evening John and Caroline went with the children to hear this mysterious man.

To Eddy, the church always seemed different at night — almost as though it were a building he had never seen before. Even with lights and people, it seemed uncomfortable and disquieting — *unheimisch.* Particularly on that night it gave the boy an eerie sensation as he looked about at the people and at the scene in the front of the sanctuary. Behind the pulpit, where a small lamp burned, stood a bed upon which lay a strange man, fully clothed and, by all appearances, asleep. There were a few hushed conversations among the expectant congregation.

Eddy observed old Hannes Kreisch, the *Absprecher,* sitting among the others. The frail old man's narrow eyes gazed penetratingly at the sleeping preacher's prone body. Eddy had heard stories from the older people of how Kreisch, whose son had frozen to death, muttered incantations and breathed upon the sick and of how they became well the following day. The sight of the old man made Eddy even more uneasy.

Now everyone became completely still, as the man on the bed began to stir. He placed his feet upon the floor; his eyes, however, remained closed.

"Is he asleep?" someone whispered.

"So it seems. . . . Yet how does he know what he is doing?"

Someone guided the man to the pulpit where he began to chant, his voice rising and falling in eerie cadence: "It is the Holy Ghost — the Holy Ghost that calls, calls you to repentance. Make straight — make straight the way!" His hands gestured wildly, throwing flying shadows against the back of the church. The content of the sermon was of only minimal interest to most of the listeners, all of whom were far more intrigued by the strange phenomenon itself than by any message they might have heard.

Suddenly the speaker cried out: "Despair not, dear brother. Your son is with God."

There was a restive murmur among the congregation. Old Kreisch gasped and buried his face in his hands. The speaker fell silent and, after a moment, was guided to the bed, where he rested. The more curious among the congregation went to observe him closer, and some claimed to have spoken with him when he awoke.

"He says he does not remember anything," they reported.

"He does not even know what he said."

Eddy waited close to the door, having no desire at that time of night to go out alone. At last he saw his mother and Julia Bas leaving the church.

"No, he was not asleep," Julia was saying. "I watched him very closely as he waved his arms so, and yet never once did he hit the lamp in front of him."

The School

"When can I go to school?" Eddy asked with increasing frequency as he grew older and saw Henry, Ida and Lydia departing each morning for that mysterious place.

"When you are older," came the discouraging reply.

Then, one autumn, he was told that he could go with them. On that day Caroline dressed him in a pair of pressed trousers and a new shirt. It was almost like going to church, except he could not ride to school in the buggy. "You will have to walk," they told him.

It was not a long walk, however, to the Ben C. Graber school, where John's children were enrolled. Besides teaching, Ben "Poststarr," as they called him, had been a mail carrier for many years and lived in a large, white house that could be seen from Eddy's home. The Mennonite parents knew him and entrusted their children to him because he was one of their own people — not of the English. Like every other child, Eddy knew Ben Poststarr. Yet having to be in so strange a place — without his parents — was a dreadful prospect for the small boy.

Although more than a little afraid, he took consolation from being with Henry and his sisters, who, knowing the procedures, laughed and talked together as though it were an ordinary day. Eddy felt a tightening in his stomach as they neared the one-room schoolhouse that was painted a sterile, shining white. There was a clatter of shoes in the entrance where tin lard pails, "dinner buckets," were left upon a bench. Shouting and laughter from many young voices rose in a keen pitch of excitement. Lydia took Eddy's hand. It felt warm and comforting, guiding him to a small desk. There he sat, almost motionless, waiting. The room smelled of pencils and chalk.

"You must behave now," Lydia said in a way that was more an encouragement than it was a caution, "and do whatever Ben tells you." Lydia was always gentle with him.

Finally everyone was sitting in a seat. There were a few other small boys whom Eddy knew, each looking on as apprehensively as he. Ben's large form rose from the great desk at the front of the room. The others rose to their feet, and in a sonorous voice Ben began to pray in English. It was the first English prayer Eddy had heard. Could God understand English, he wondered. . . . This was followed by a prayer to the flag and a hymn, after which everyone was seated again. The flag prayer was also strange to Eddy. "The Pledge," he heard it called.

At the front of the room was a long, wooden bench. Ben referred to it as a "recitation bench." Now the older children moved there and began to read aloud from books. Eddy listened and heard names — George Washington and Thomas Jefferson. Still he waited, watching a pair of flies that hunted for an opening along the window panes. He felt sorry for the flies and wanted to let them out, but he knew that he dared not leave his seat.

Later, Ben came over to Eddy's desk. He leaned over the boy, almost covering him it seemed, and showed him a slate and a pencil. Every nerve in Eddy's small body seemed to quiver. "Now, Eddy, here is how we print your name." As he spoke, Ben formed letters on the empty face of the slate. The boy looked at them. "That is myself," he thought. "That is who I am."

"Now you try to print the same letters."

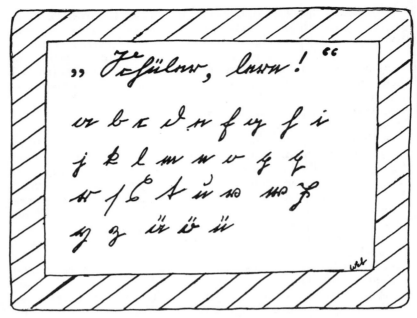

German Alphabet in Gothic Script.

Laboriously he worked with an unsteady hand until he had copied the letters almost perfectly.

"That's pretty good. Now practice it as many times as you can. I'll come again to see how you did." With that, the teacher left him and went on to another scholar.

So Eddy's education began. His slate would be with him always. Paper was expensive and, therefore, seldom used. In winter he watched the girls clean their slates with snow and set them in a row along the porch to dry, a ritual which to him seemed unduly fastidious.

* * *

As his school days progressed, Eddy began to observe people as never before. There were those whom he despised, others whom he admired and still others who evoked his pity. He felt young Pete Graber's embarrassment one day when Pete's slate pencil squeaked so loudly and continually that Ben finally said, "Pete, must you make so much noise?" Then there were those who seemed almost impervious to ridicule, such as the boy named Louis Wilde, who was an attraction because of his ability to stand on his head. But the Zinders — a collection of rather rag-tag children

— were often the object of cruel humor in a community that was contemptuous of any odd behavior. The Zinder boys, it was said, trapped skunks and came to school with the animals' scent upon their clothes until one day the smell became so unbearable that Ben sent them home. Their sister was nicknamed "Puppet" and was laughed at because of her large, bulging eyes and gaping mouth. Years later Eddy would see her again, — a grown, well-dressed and pleasant-spoken woman.

The Zinder children were not the only victims of social censure. Even such polite, neatly-dressed Germans as the Kettlers were not readily accepted when they moved into the Mennonite community. "They are not of our people," was the usual, condescending statement given with regard to such newcomers. Eddy watched the Kettler girl on her first day of school. At noon she sat, timid and alone, eating her lunch and carefully picking up every crumb that fell onto her lap. The small scene, observed by no one else, aroused a profound sympathy within his young heart.

From observing these children and others, Eddy began to formulate his own understanding of that enigmatic thing called human nature. Why was it that some people found satisfaction in showing off — in being better than the rest? Why did they delight in feeling superior, and why was it necessary for some to abuse others in order to achieve that status? Each wanted to know something of importance and was, in turn, envious of those who knew more than he. Each wanted to be recognized as someone of distinction. Yet those who sought such distinction most seemed invariably farthest from it. . .

"Eddy, what state do we live in?" Ben asked him one day.

He hesitated for a moment before venturing to say, "America." He cringed at the derisive laughter and felt his shame redoubled when the little girl named Sadie piped up with the answer, "South Dakota!" He would not forget. . .

Eddy was a shy boy — still something of a stranger to himself — and, perhaps for that reason, developed a feeling of compassion for the ostracized and the downtrodden. From early childhood, when he saw the loneliness in his mother's face, he learned to detest pride and ostentation. Yet he found it impossible to speak out against such injustices, an inability that made him all the more angry with himself.

Neither was he without his antagonists, although they were few. Chief among them was the Schrag boy — some years older than he — who hounded him continually until the day when Eddy's pent-up fury sent the larger boy sprawling among a clatter of dinner buckets. It was shortly afterward, as he walked past the barn, that a flying clod of earth just missed hitting the back of Eddy's skull. But the adversary never again confronted him.

* * *

"Fuchs, du hast die Gans gestolen — bring sie wieder her!" the girls and small boys cried in delight when winter came. The older youths, disdainful of such childish amusements as "Fox and Geese," spent their recreation time skating upon the frozen creek. Eddy, Hardwig and Freddy, who had no skates, watched Henry and his friend, Lewis Waltner, with envy.

"Don't go too far down the creek!" Ben cautioned them. "You will be late."

"Ring the bell early," Lewis said. "Then we will have time to come back."

"All right! Five minutes early! But if you are not back on time — no more skates," Ben decreed, smiling as he watched them go.

In a few minutes he returned and rang the bell that carried far in the still, winter air. Shortly the small figures approached from around the bend in the creek. They skated in a row, laughing and calling out, each striving to reach the building first. Later that afternoon it grew warm, and the surface of the ice began to soften, forming a level plane like shining window glass. "It will freeze tonight, and there will be good skating tomorrow," Henry told Lewis after school. The small boys listened.

"Let's go on the ice," Freddy urged his cousins with a sly smile that always indicated some mischief. Pretending to skate with their shoes on the slushy surface, they soon left the once smooth layer of ice as rough as a plowed field. So, in spite of the hard frost that came that night, there was no skating for anyone on the following day.

The *Hochzeit*

"It will be a big wedding," the girls said to each other. Eddy listened to his older sisters as they dressed him and Hardwig. "They say it is four couples. No one remembers when there were so many." Although the girls were greatly excited, Eddy and Hardwig exhibited only casual interest in the affair. After all, what was there to get excited about a wedding? Of course it meant good things to eat and games to play outdoors. But all this fuss the women and girls made was foolish, the boys concluded.

"Ouch!" Hardwig cried. "Not so hard!" Ida was always inclined to be rough when she combed their hair.

"Maybe that, too, will be my fault," Eddy said vindictively. "I'm always to blame whenever you cry."

"Be still now," Lydia reproached them both. "You want Jonath Vetter to be proud of you on his wedding day — especially if they take pictures." She began to hook the buttons on Eddy's shoes, repeating. "Only think — four couples!"

"But why would Jonath Vetter want to get married anyway?" Eddy asked.

"Such a question!" Lydia scoffed. "You think he should be a bachelor all his life?"

"But now he will never play with us anymore," Eddy said with regret, recalling the time when their young uncle discovered them playing at threshing and made a noise like a steamer's whistle to delight them.

Meanwhile, John was fastening his shirt collar. "So the Kadünners are going to be married into our family now. Well, Jonath could have done worse."

"Yes, your baby brother has found someone," Caroline laughed. "It's a good match. They even look alike."

This was indeed to be a wedding of which they would speak for years to come. It was common for more than one couple to share the expenses of a marriage celebration. But four bridal couples involved eight families, including almost everyone in the community upon their combined guest lists.

So it was a grand procession that led from the church to Spitzberger's farm south of Freeman on that June day in 1907. Carriages, trimmed with colorful tassels and bright flowers, stretched in a line for nearly a mile down the road in a gay caravan. The trees waved above them along the way as the four couples, accompanied by their families and the clergy, rode in elegance to the place where the celebration was to be — the *Hochzeit,* as they called it.

The Spitzberger house, imposing because of its size and design, was built of homemade brick with brightly-colored dormers. It stood amid a thick growth of trees on a small hillock above a pond. Here, with noise and laughter, the families left their carriages and proceeded toward the grove where they assembled for a picture: Spitzberger, himself, stood proudly with his wife behind their daughter Caroline, with Sep Vetter, Kadünner, Alte Senner — imposing with his full beard, Grandfather Jacob and the others with their wives. The bridal couples assumed the foreground position. The girls, conspicuous in white gowns, and the young men, looking somewhat uncomfortable in starched collars, their faces clean-shaven, made a marked contrast to the drab styles worn by the parents.

Then began a feast of pork, beef and potatoes with kraut — all the fat and starch that comprised traditional German diet. There were also small cookies with pink and white icing, which delighted the children. At the bridal table sat the four pairs of young peopie with their parents and the ministers — short, jovial Mueller-Christ and the younger Kaufman-Sep, each with a glass of good wine and a mug of beer.

The beer was drawn from kegs and vended among the tables by men who wore red ribbons about their arms and walked along the rows of raucous merry-makers. The noise and laughter intensified until at last someone noticed a boat along the shore of the pond. . .

"Ha! It's time for the newlyweds to go for a cruise."

"Yes! Yes!" insisted a chorus of eager voices.

"Come! There is no backing out!"

So the reluctant couples were all but pushed into the one small boat, which began to wobble beneath the weight of its eight passengers and caused the young ladies to cry out in a way that was more than a little affected. At last the vessel left the shore, escaping the clamorous partymakers — much to the relief of its occupants.

Eddy, Hardwig and Freddy, together with their young cousins, Paul and Albert — Uncle Bernhart's sons — watched as the boat moved away. "There is nothing for us here," Freddy remarked, casually jabbing into the soft mud with a stick.

"What should we do?" Eddy asked.

"It's not a far walk to Freeman," the cousin replied. "Maybe we could go there."

"Yes — let's go."

It was not that often that the boys went to town, and they had never been allowed to go alone. Now, however, no one seemed to notice or care what they did. So they began to walk along the road, past fields of young corn, toward the small town — the only municipality in their diminutive world.

"Freni Kadünner is our aunt now," Eddy said, contemplating this alteration in the family genealogy. "We will have to call her Freni Bas."

"And we must say *Ihr* to her."

They laughed, thinking how strange it seemed to have a new aunt. But it was thus that the pattern of domestic order was perpetuated. They would not have thought then of addressing their elders with the familiar *du*. It was one of the many small, unwritten rules of custom that constituted the pattern of their upbringing. . . . To violate such rules would have meant to defy the very order of things.

The boys were, as yet, too young to comprehend the central role of marriage and the relationship it bore to one's status both financially and socially in such a meticulously-ordered society. To marry into wealth was a virtue; to marry beneath one's family status brought censure; and to marry an outsider was all but disgrace. A story would be told for many years of a Schweitzer girl who became engaged to a Lutheran:

78

"Yes, but who will marry them?" asked the guardians of social propriety.

"Oh, perhaps one of the saloonkeepers — Koerner or Zickrick."

But these matters were for adults to debate. The cousins thought now only of the warm day and of the adventures that awaited them in town.

"If we wait by the railroad, maybe we can see a train engine," Albert said.

"Someday, I'd like to ride on one," Eddy responded.

Before long, however, they observed someone approaching from the opposite direction. As he came nearer, they could see the stout form of Sep Vetter, the old *Kirchediener,* who had apparently left the party and was now returning.

"Ai, where are these boys going?" he asked cheerily when he encountered them. "To Freeman? No — there is nothing for you there. Go on back to the party where you belong. Along with you now!" Reluctantly they obeyed him.

"But what was he doing there?" Freddy asked. It was one of the insignificant events from childhood that, for some unknown reason, is remembered. So it was on that day when Jonath Vetter and Freni Bas were married.

Part IV

HEARTACHE AND LAUGHTER

A Mother mourning for her child.

The Death of Cousin Tilda

The clock's patient momentum continued throughout that long day. As evening approached, the relatives began to arrive, nodding unspoken greetings to one another. John and Caroline, bringing only the older children with them, were among the first to come. Eddy, seated uncomfortably between his brothers, looked about the familiar room. Lamplight reflected in the mirror on the parlor organ — the chief attraction in Uncle Joe's house. The organ was silent.

Recently Eddy had learned to play the instrument, teaching himself to find melodies and simple chords. He wanted to play upon it now — to make some sound that could reach above the persistent silence in the house. But he knew that even to think such a thing was sacrilege. For on that night death demanded reverence.

He looked at poor Freddy, who was sitting alone beside the organ. Never had Eddy's cousin looked so bewildered or forlorn. The other cousins were there, too, together with Eddy's aunts and uncles. All were silent. There was no teasing or laughter. Except for an occasional nervous cough, no human sound was heard above a whisper.

"Listen, you can hear her."

"She weeps."

"It's Julia — not the girl. She knows Tilda is dying."

"Hush — be still!"

They did not go into the death room yet. Uncle Joe and Julia Bas were there with Doctor Wipf and Kaufman-Sep. Now all that any of them could do was wait.

Suddenly the door opened revealing a sickly light from the dreadful room as the irascible little doctor emerged. He brushed past those who stood outside and hastened to the telephone that hung upon the wall. The sharp ring of the bell startled everyone. Wipf listened a moment and turned the crank again impatiently. . . . "Will you women hang up those phones?" he snapped into the speaker. "Foolish old gossips!" he muttered. "Every time they hear a ring, they have to know who is talking."

At last the call went through. *"Ja, ja — da wert's!"* He hung up the receiver and hurried back to the room, closing the door behind him.

They looked at one another after he had gone. What could it mean? Diphtheria was a hard death. It had visited them before, and sometimes the afflicted had managed to recover. But, when medicine failed, there remained only God . . . and the tenacity of the human spirit.

After a while there came a soft knock upon the front door — another visitor. Jäk Vetter opened the door. The grandparents, Jacob and Marie, their faces reflecting a weary resignation to suffering, quietly entered the house. The others rose and offered them chairs. Grandfather gazed about the room at his family. *"Dobry vecher!"* he whispered to them in Russian, his voice weak from asthma from years of inhaling smoke at his forge. They knew that he was powerless to help the girl. Yet all felt some comfort at his presence.

Together they waited for the inevitable announcement — Jonath moving his feet nervously under his chair, John rolling a cigarette, Bernhart picking at his nose. . . . After a moment Jake cautiously opened the door and entered the girl's room. He emerged again with Joe, who approached his father and kissed him. The diminutive old man whispered into his son's ear and took his hand — remembering another, smaller hand and a crying child that he had consoled long ago. Again they sat and waited.

"They say the throat rattles when the spirit goes." Joe sighed. "It is a bad death."

"Do not talk so," Jake reproached his brother mildly. "Our dear God can still save her."

"It is not His will for it to be so," Joe shook his head. "It must be this way now."

Eddy listened, intrigued, knowing better than to speak. Yet, what was all this ritual of dying, he wondered. Was it indeed "God's will?" Doctor Wipf, the uncles, grandfather, even the preacher — all of them were helpless and afraid. If God was love and to go to Him was joy, why then were they so sad and fearful?

Julia Bas entered the room now, her eyes red from weeping. "Joe, the children should come now and say goodbye to her," she said.

Eddy did not want to see the room. Yet they would all be forced to look upon her — as though at that point such things were of any consequence to the dying girl — the cousin with whom only recently they had played and laughed. Now with an inexplicable, morbid fascination they followed each other into the room — first Ida and sister Lydia with their cousins Frances, Lydia, and Elsie, then Henry, followed by Eddy, Hardwig, Freddy, Paul and Albert. Theirs was an upbringing that made them ever conscious of death — even in childhood.

Each in turn they approached the bedside, not knowing if the girl was at all aware of their presence. Her drugged, half-closed eyes expressed only a profound agony. Every breath was taken with a groan as though she were being strangled by unseen hands. The children looked at her in silence. Eddy's turn came. Lightly, furtively, he touched the already chilly hand and drew away in terror. Beside the bed, his small, somber face reflecting the soft glow from the lamp, sat Doctor Wipf. Occasionally he felt for a pulse in the slender wrist and wiped the child's moist brow. In the corner sat Kaufman Sep with an open Bible on his lap, his head bowed. Both seemed quite oblivious to the children's presence. The moaning continued. Julia Bas, her eyes intent on every slight movement or nuance in expression, began to weep again.

At last Joe and the grandparents entered the room. The others followed. They stood a short distance from the bed and remained motionless, no one speaking. Now the breathing diminished, the groans becoming fainter.

"Did she try to speak?" Anna Bas whispered.

Julia did not seem to hear, but Jake shook his head.

"She will soon be with God."

Joe began to sob. "It will be over then. *Arme Tilda!* Poor girl!"

Doctor Wipf felt again the limp arm and, looking toward Julia, shook his head.

"She is gone now," Jake announced.

The waiting was over at last. Julia gave way to the full intensity of her despair.

Joe leaned over her, helping her to her feet as the others left the room.

* * *

They buried her with many tears, and Julia's weeping seemed to have no end. "My poor little girl! What was it all for? What sin did she or I commit?" She asked these questions repeatedly, knowing all the while that no one could answer them. But there came a day some weeks later when she came running excitedly to John and Caroline's house.

"Tilda spoke to me this morning," she announced ecstatically.

"I was sitting in the bedroom. So hard I was crying that for a while I did not know even where I was or what I was doing. It all seemed to be so hopeless."

"Then it was as though someone was calling me, and I knew her voice as only I could know it. Like in a dream it was. Yet I know it was real — because for a little moment I thought she was still with me here." She suppressed a slight, excited sob and wiped her eyes.

"'*Mutter — Mutter!*' she said. '*Warum weinst du so viel?*' I looked about me. No one was there. And again — 'Why do you weep so much? Your tears are staining my nightgown.' That is what she said — my little daughter. I did not dream it."

Many times thereafter they were to hear her repeat her story. No one could express anything but wonder at it. Perhaps a voice from heaven, said some — or, as others insisted, merely a bereaved woman's hallucination. All of them shook their heads when some years later a daughter was born to Julia's own brother, Janju. For as the child grew, Julia declared to them, "Yes, that is Tilda — reborn."

The Children and the Old People

"How do you suppose it feels to die?" Eddy asked his cousin one day shortly after Tilda's funeral. "Does it hurt, or does God take away the pain?"

"For some it hurts," Freddy affirmed, repeating what he had heard from the old people. "But that is because they are going to hell. Those who are ready for heaven do not suffer at all." Freddy had been unusually serious since his sister's death.

"But how can that be?" Eddy asked after a moment's reflection. "You remember how Tilda suffered. Did that mean she couldn't go to heaven?"

Freddy became indignant. "No! Didn't you see? She died just this way:" Dropping his head backward, he closed his eyes to illustrate the peacefulness of the girl's passing. "She knew she was going to be with God."

They resumed their play then, allowing the old belief its precedence. . . . A calm face in death saw heaven; an agonized countenance anticipated hell. So it was repeated in the hereditary, unwritten doctrine of many generations.

But these were matters for the old to deliberate. For the children such sage conjectures seemed remote and unreal, because life for them was still bright and wonderful — a lighthearted game, played according to flexible rules.

* * *

When spring came, the meadow was again filled with daisies and with the laughter of the little girls who played among them. Othelia, who had nearly caused Jäk Vetter to drop baby Anne, and tiny Bertha, whom John called "Bärbilie," ran among the brilliant flowers.

"Come, Bertha! See if you can catch me," Othelia cried. "I bet I can beat you to the big rock."

She bounded away, confident of victory, when suddenly she found herself upon the ground, dazed and breathless. Not until she touched her hand to her forehead and felt the bruise upon it, was she conscious of any pain. Then she saw the half-buried stone upon which she had stumbled. But she would not allow herself to cry or to show any weakness in front of her little sister.

Quickly she rose to her feet, saying nothing to Bertha, and ran toward the house to find her father.

In the house, John sat upon a chair, bouncing little Anne upon his knee and chanting: *"Huppa, huppa, reide,"* while the gleeful baby laughed. His clear blue eyes grew suddenly large when he saw Othelia. . .

"Ai, ai, Katzedreck! Morgefrüh ist alles weg," he soothed her, as she buried her face in his arms. The touch of his hand made her forget her pain.

But it was Bertha who was the most independent and resourceful of the small girls. Wishing for an excuse to visit Julia Bas one day that summer, she determined to appoint herself an errand. Finding no one in the kitchen, she took the sugar bowl from the table and, emptying its contents into a canister — for how could she borrow sugar with a full bowl? — started across the meadow to Uncle Joe's tall, white house. Tingling with excitement, she approached the kitchen door. She ran across the planks that had been placed there for a walk and entered the house. Now she could impress her aunt with the importance of her mission.

"Mama needs some sugar," she declared to Julia, who replied:

"Well, some sugar she will have," and filled the bowl.

So Bertha returned and quietly replaced it with her small hands, telling no one.

* * *

On Sundays when the weather was warm and church was finished, grandfather Jacob came to visit John and Joe. He sat with his sons on the porch and talked of the Old Country. On such days, if Jonath and Bernhart happened to be present, the brothers played on their instruments, the notes carrying far upon the sultry summer air. "Play us yet another song," Jacob would say then, his eyes gleaming with delight and pride — upon which, after some deliberation, fiddle, clarinet and mandolin together evoked the hymn "Joyful We Adore Thee."

The old blacksmith listened to the melody with reflective silence and watched the grandchildren, who swam and played nearby in the cool lake water — to the distress of the shrill-calling snipes. He smiled to himself as he watched them and looked down at the rumpled paper bag he held upon his lap. Jäk Vetter — the eldest son — sat beside his father.

"For all of mankind life remains an ordeal that must be borne by each in his own way," Jacob told his sons when the music was finished. "Perhaps it begins with that first reach beyond the womb, or at a much later time when the youth leaves his father's house and knows he cannot return. Yet between the moment of birth and the departure from the house, that, even when he is gone from it forever, will always be his home, there is a joyful time that stands still for a short while and then leaves forever. . . . That is childhood."

His voice broke with a sudden cough. The asthma had become worse during the past year, so that daily now he drank the old remedy of whiskey and black pepper, mixed with hot water. He resumed his discourse . . .

"Youth is a time when all life seems made for pleasure — when the company of other children reflects our own joy. There is for us, then, no other feeling but happiness. But soon — so soon — we grow old; and all our dreams and the plans of our youth are gone. Some — thanks to God's will — have borne fruit; others turn to ashes. But we accept it, because we know there is nothing else we can do. That is what old age teaches."

His sons, themselves no longer young, listened — for they knew he spoke wisdom.

"So many thoughts there came to me when you boys played your music," the old man continued. "Now that we are all of us together, I wish to say what I have had on my mind for a long time."

As he spoke, he reached into the sack. The brothers gazed reverently upon the familiar object their father withdrew from it.

"I know there are not many years left for me," he told them, clutching the book in his still firm hand. "This is our dear God's will — that we leave for our children a foundation upon which to build for the coming generation. And here is the only foundation — which belongs by right to the eldest of my sons." He nodded to Jake, who remained silent, understanding . . .

"And he has been a good son. He has obeyed his parents and been true to God. He has worked hard and raised his daughters in a good way. But he has now daughters only." He turned to John, his voice growing uneasy. "So it is now for you, the second son, to take custody of this holy book, which, as you know, I bought so long ago in the city of Hamburg. It is for your sons to own when they have their own families."

John hesitated before accepting the gift with which he was charged. He looked into his father's face — a face so familiar that he could not consider it other than beautiful — and was suddenly overcome with a feeling of unworthiness. Each year left him older, more weary and disheartened — lacking his father's faith and wisdom. His own soul seemed soiled and tattered. He regretted the frequent nights of drinking, the moments of anger he showed toward Caroline, his lack of material success.

"It is for brother Jake to say," he suggested then. "Perhaps he should keep it for a time until my boys are older."

Jake, however, shook his head. "No, John. Let us leave it as our father wishes. It makes no difference to me now."

At that moment Eddy, Hardwig and Freddy came running from the lake with Ida and Lydia angrily in pursuit. All of the children were dressed only in their soaked underwear.

"Come back with our garters!" Lydia screamed. "Daddy, stop them!"

"Be still now!" John responded. "Do you want Grandpa to think you are such bad children?" But as he spoke, he looked at his sons and felt at once a new sense of duty. Yes, he would accept the Bible as an obligation to his children. He would see to it that the trust was not misplaced.

* * *

Janju — Poltauwitz's son and Julia Bas's brother, whom the old people called Vanka, came walking into Jäk Vetter's yard one morning that summer. "What are you building here?" he queried after a moment, watching Jake pound nails into the studding rafters for a building. "A new shed?"

Jake continued to hammer. An ironical gleam reflected in his one good eye. "*Was denkst?* Should I build an old one?" he replied.

Janju chuckled good-naturedly beneath his mustache. After another moment, he noticed that Jake was clinching nails in the direction of the wood grain. This was not good because the clinching could come loose after some time. "The other way," he directed, indicating that the nail should lie across the grain.

Again the one good eye twinkled, and Jake lifted the nail point and bent it in the opposite direction, still with the grain. "*Nu, dann mein'twege,*" he shrugged.

"No, no! *Den ander Weg!*" Janju protested.

Again the nail point was lifted and the nail clinched in the original direction.

"*Ach!*" the short man grumbled. "Now I give it up."

Jake laughed. He always enjoyed a good prank.

* * *

Grandfather Jacob's brother Johann, who had also come to America, became blind in his last years and was given the name "Blinde Hannes Vetter." His children gone and his wife dead, he came to visit his brother and nephews. Assuming the usual cordiality demanded on such occasions, they asked him about his children.

"Which is older — Jake or Lizzie?"

"*Ach — Ich weiss es nyet,*" he laughed . . . "I cannot say for sure. It is already so long since I have seen them."

* * *

On his farm near Turkey Creek, a man named Jacob Preheim showed his grandsons a piece of sturdy canvas. "Here," he said, extending the material to one of them, "Pull on it with all your strength. It will not tear." The boy pulled and, with his young muscles, tore the cloth. Dismayed, he returned the ruined piece to the old man, who examined it. Looking up at the boys, he smiled. "*Mit Gewalt kann man Eisen breche. . . .* By force one can even break iron."

* * *

Along the road going toward Freeman, a wagon stopped to offer a ride to a small, ancient figure. "*Wo gehen Ihr hie, Grossmutter?*" asked the driver. The tiny face, marked like a plowed field and framed in a black kerchief, looked up at the speaker and declared, "*Ich will nach Kotosufka. . . .* I am going to Kotosufka."

Striking Out

Of his mother's parents, the Kirschenmans, Eddy knew little of consequence. Old Christian, the man who had won the race for Unruh, moved to North Dakota shortly after the beginning of the new century. Uncle Jackob, the Cossack, soon followed. Since their departure, there was little that came in the way of correspondence save a photo of Uncle Jackob's family and, later, a black-bordered letter that announced the death of Caroline's mother.

That letter, when it arrived and was read aloud to Caroline, caused Eddy to think of a day that clung faintly in his mind — a hazy picture taken from his infant consciousness. . . . He had awakened from sleep that day and was lying upon the small, wooden cot in the early evening. Perhaps his mother had left for a brief time; perhaps it was winter and thus had grown dark early. He could not say. But across the room from where he lay sat a heavy, old woman wearing a scarf and knitting. Soft lamplight shone against her plump face as she continued her handiwork, unaware that he was awake and watching her. His small eyes studied the old woman, knowing somehow that she, too, was his grandmother.

The scene returned to him often afterward, like the memory of some distant vision or long-ago dream. It was the only time he could remember having seen her; and thus it remained with him for the rest of his life — his only memory of the grandmother who had been frightened by a bullfrog in Russia before he was born.

Not until he grew older, however, could Eddy fully comprehend what it must have meant for his mother never to see her parents again. That, too, she accepted, enduring it as she had so much else. Yet the grief must have been there — inside her — and the longing that could never be satisfied.

The other members of her family Eddy knew far better. His Aunt Christina married Mathias Reich, a drayman from Marion, to whom they referred afterward as "Uncle Rich." Aunt Sophie married Peter Dirks, a large man who lived seven miles from John's place and whom they visited once or twice a year.

The two remaining uncles were Johann, whose face was badly scarred from smallpox, and Rudolf, whom Eddy's father cursed as a miser. Yet when Rudolf's oldest daughter died, Rudolf rented an expensive horse-drawn hearse to take her body to the church — the first use of such a vehicle in the community. "Worldly," the old people called it; yet what could be expected from the Lutherans?

"He tries to make up in death for what he denied her in life," was John's scornful interpretation of the affair. But his contempt for his wife's brother became even more acute on the day when cousin Elena came to the house.

Eddy was home with his mother that afternoon when a frantic knock was heard upon the door. Opening it, Caroline saw her niece standing on the porch with a suitcase. "Oh, Tante Caroline!" Elena sobbed, embracing her.

Surprised, Caroline glanced beyond the girl, looking for a wagon or buggy in the yard. Seeing none, she exclaimed, "Elena, you are alone! You have walked all the way?"

"Oh, Tante Caroline!" she repeated. "Please, I must come in."

Still clinging to her aunt, she allowed herself to be led to a chair, oblivious to Eddy's curious eyes.

"But where is my brother Rudolf — and your mother?" Caroline, too agitated to sit, looked again at the suitcase.

"I have come alone," the girl declared, regaining some composure. "I have run away."

Caroline stared at her. "But what does this mean? Rudolf will come to look for you, and think only how your mother will feel!"

"Mama will understand . . . I will not go back! It does not matter what Papa does. I will not go back!" She began to weep again. Calming her, Caroline led Elena into the kitchen and prepared tea.

"You see this old tea can?" she asked her niece in an effort to cheer her. "Your Uncle Jackob gave it to me on my birthday before we came to America." Elena did not reply.

"Now tell me what happened," Caroline demanded after the tea was poured.

"Papa is always punishing us," Elena began, "always beating one of us. Never can we go to town; never can we buy something that is new or nice." She restrained a sob and continued. "Yesterday he made Mama fix some soup from beans that we had canned long ago. It was sour. . . . We couldn't eat it. But when we told him so, he got his strap and stood over us until it was gone. We all got sick."

"Now I have decided that I can stay there no longer. I am old enough that I can leave home. Why, I am almost twenty. I can make my own money and buy my own things. That is what I am going to do. Only please let me stay with you — just tonight!"

Caroline listened quietly, wringing her apron in her hands, as she often did whenever she was disturbed. "I do not know what John will say — but you can stay for now."

It was not until sundown that John returned from the field and Caroline was able to tell him the story. As he sat at the table, his sharp eyes glanced uncertainly at the girl. "You cannot remain here," he said at last, speaking with finality — there was little commiseration in his voice. "If Rudolf comes for you, what could we tell him?"

"Only think, John," Caroline pleaded, knowing that it would be to no avail and that John was already on the verge of losing his temper. "She is my niece. We cannot send her away."

John's eyes flashed. "So when your brother comes," he snapped, "then I have to explain to him why I have his daughter in my house. Suppose he brings the sheriff — then what?"

Everyone became silent. John looked around the table and rose to his feet.

Elena left her chair and went to him. "Uncle John, I will not stay if you say no. Only please take me to Freeman. I can find a place there. I have some money."

He looked at her thoughtfully. "Perhaps I can do that," he said at last. "Get your things and I will hitch the team. It is a warm evening — good for a short trip."

At once Eddy was at John's side. "Let me go, too, Pa."

John threw a distracted glance at his son. "Oh — I guess you can come along for the ride," he agreed.

The seat jiggled upon the spring wagon as the team pulled them toward the small town. On the way Elena told them of the many outrages she and the other children had endured. "Poor sister," she lamented. "If she had lived, we would go together. But I know I am old enough."

John exhaled cigarette smoke from his thin lips. "Yes, you are a woman now," he reassured her. "Perhaps you can work for some of the rich Hutterites in Freeman."

Leaving her at the rooming house, they drove down the street, stopping at the Zickrick saloon on the corner. "Don't leave the wagon now," John instructed Eddy.

Eddy saw his father pass Alec Wipf, who had been in the Spanish-American War and bore a scar on the side of his face where a bullet had struck him. Wipf was a Hutterite and, therefore, partly friend yet partly alien to the Mennonites.

They acknowledged each other with a nod.

"Well, Schwartz, what brings you to town so late?" Eddy heard Wipf ask in a jovial tone.

John explained the reason for the trip.

"I tell you, Wipf, sometimes I get disgusted with life. . . . You know what I mean?" he said, rolling a cigarette. "It seems that a man can't get ahead these days."

Wipf laughed. "Well, you don't want to give up. . . . Say, you might have heard about that lottery they're having in Chamberlain?"

John shook his head.

"It's Indian land put up for homesteading," Wipf explained. "It won't hurt to put your name in. Quite a few of the boys are going from here on the train. You might have a chance to get yourself a nice farm."

"I'll have a drink and think it over," John laughed as they parted.

* * *

It was late when they started for home, passing the railroad where John had worked as a youth. A single kerosene lamp glowed in the window at the depot.

"Do you think Freeman will ever have electric lights like the big towns?" Eddy asked.

"Oh, someday, I guess," John replied affably.

They continued to drive in silence for a while. Then Eddy spoke again. "Pa, do you think Elena will be safe? What if Uncle comes for her?"

"Oh, I don't think she has to worry," John laughed. "The only reason he wants her is so she can work for him. But if she refuses, there isn't much he can do. . . . How would you like to live in Chamberlain, Eddy?" he asked.

Eddy was estatic. "You mean where there are Indians — with bows and arrows?"

John laughed. "Well, maybe they don't have bows and arrows any more. But I have a notion to put my name in that lottery. And — if nothing comes of it — well, there are other places. Here it will always be the same tiresome life year after year. . .

"We need to do just what your cousin has done — to strike out — find ourselves what the English call an 'opportunity.'"

"An opportunity!" It sounded like a good word to Eddy.

Laura, the Forgotten Sister

She watched them go to the field that day without her, and for a moment after they left her sight she felt almost at peace. "To them it is a normal day," she thought, remembering now a small girl who had been eager to follow and to pursue every childish caprice in a world that was all happiness. She could see that small girl now, running barefoot along the road, and wanted with all her being to follow. "But it is too late," she reminded herself. . . . "She is gone."

Turning away from the kitchen window, she crossed the room and stood for a moment in front of the stove. The morning fire had subsided to warm ashes. "Be sure to fix dinner for us," her mother had said before leaving to pick corn. "You can clean the house, too." Oh, yes, she could clean the house! The thought almost amused her. How ordinary a thing it was — yet how she wished it could be her only concern at that moment.

But what was done was irrevocable. At first she had tried to put it out of her mind. But it was with her even in sleep — a nightmare which became even more dreadful after she awoke. How could this thing be, after all? Was it really happening to her? She walked into the bedroom and stood by the window, being careful not to look at herself in the mirror. Her own eyes seemed to reproach her every time she saw them, until she no longer dared to see the reflection of her face.

As a small child she had heard the words of the Bible that said, "Vengeance is mine . . . I will repay;" and yet they had always seemed remote and enigmatic to her. But now she understood that, and the understanding caused her to shudder. The heartache was intense — too intense even for tears, which she never dared to shed until she was alone. Now, however, they came in an overwhelming surge of remorse and desperation. There was no one to console her — not even God.

Often she thought of the English boy, whom she could not blame for refusing to marry her, even after this. But how wrong it was — how fatally wrong to use another person like some dispensable thing that could be cast aside when its usefulness was gone. Human feelings could not be handled so capriciously. Yet, after all, what could she really expect from him? She realized that he was in many ways a spoiled child, used to having anything he wanted. He knew nothing of obligations. He could never be a husband. How foolish even to consider it! But for her the obligation would not go away. Soon it would be obvious to the others that she was with child. It would mean *Meidung* — avoidance. She would be shunned by everyone, even by her own family.

"What have I done?" she moaned, covering her face with the palms of her hands. For a long while she remained standing by the window, transfixed — unable to think.

Outside, the day had grown warm. The locusts made a clattering noise through the dry grass. A wagon moved down the road in the distance. Laura thought of her father and mother and of her sisters working gaily in the cornfield and almost begrudged them their happiness. Then, remembering what it would do to them to know her sorrow, she felt a sudden surge of terrible shame. They trusted her virtue. It would never occur to them that she . . . "I have disgraced them," she said aloud and wept again.

From the parlor came the absurd call of the cuckoo clock, mocking her, reminding her of the little time that remained. Slowly she went into the kitchen. She picked up the broom and stood with it for a long time. The little girl came to her again. "She, at least, was without sin," Laura smiled to herself.

"Why are you crying?" the small girl asked. "It is such a nice day outside. Come and play with me."

"Not today, but sometime soon."

"No," the child teased. "You must come with me now." Laughing, the girl disappeared, and Laura was alone again.

There was, after all, still a chance. If she miscarried, all would be well. If not . . . it would not matter, she reasoned. Either she would live without the baby or die with it. There was no other way.

At noon the family returned with the loaded wagon. It had been a good year — a good crop. They entered the house and called for Laura.

"Sister, what are you doing?" the other girls asked, cheerful and teasing. How silly she looked, bent over on the floor with the broom in her hand! Why didn't she move, they wondered. One of them poked her. . . . Then they saw the blood.

A Whip for Pete

Pete had gotten his father-in-law out of jail for the last time. "Why is it always up to me?" he lamented to his sister's husband. "He has other children. Let him stay with them. Then, the next time he steals something, they can pay for it."

To have a kleptomaniac in one's charge was sufficiently disgraceful. But the circumstances under which this occurred made the matter even more humiliating for Pete. The mill which he and his brother-in-law had planned to build seemed indeed to be a good investment. Who would have thought anything could possibly go wrong? All that was needed was a bit of extra money. So if the old man, after a little persuasion, was willing to mortgage his farm — what was so bad? True — the mill failed after all, as anything can. But even a safe investment has its risks. And for the entire family to turn to him, demanding that he care for his father-in-law, seemed unfair to Pete.

"Well, they have made a fool of me and they can have their laugh," he grumbled. "But if he would only at least stay put! You leave him alone, the next thing you know he's picked something up. Then I have to either return it or pay for it."

The brother-in-law listened to all this with a feigned sympathy that he employed every time he heard the story.

"He's an old man; he should know better," Pete continued. "But does he admit it? Oh no! I go and get him out of jail and what does he say to me . . . 'You know, our dear Apostle Paul was also in prison.' There's no reasoning with him."

Meanwhile the subject of these disclosures remained sitting on the wagon seat in front of the house. His small eyes scrutinized the farmyard with casual indifference, not seeming to notice the two men who stood along the fence discussing his misbehavior. His expression remained unchanged except for an occasional twitching of his lips beneath a white goatee as the spring sunlight reflected upon his partly-bald head. He looked remarkably like an ancient dwarf in a fairy tale, which may have been the reason for his nickname — *Kleinsige*, "the Smallest One."

Having at last concluded his argument, Pete rose up onto the seat next to the old man, slapped the reins and guided the team onto the road that led toward town.

"Fahren wir heute nach Kotosufka?" the old man inquired.

"No, we aren't going to Kotosufka," Pete replied wearily. "We aren't in Russia now . . . *Ach,* if I only had a whip to make these horses go faster!"

So they proceeded to town where Pete drew the team to a halt in front of the store and helped his father-in-law down. Noticing the buggy parked nearby, unattended, *Kleinsige* wandered over toward it. In the holder stood a fine buggy whip, which he methodically withdrew and presented to Pete.

"*Hier iss schon a Peitsch.*"

"What do you mean, a whip?" the younger man said irritably. Turning, he saw what the old man had in his hand. "Here — where did you get that? Put it back before they see you!"

With gentle disdain, *Kleinsige* shuffled toward the buggy and replaced the borrowed whip.

"Now, you will remain here!" Pete directed, his annoyance having reached its limit. "If you go into the store with me, you'll be sure to see something else you want."

"Huh!" The old man shrugged his shoulders. "So it must be, then . . ."

Muttering to himself, Pete entered the store, leaving his charge alone on the street. After a few moments he returned and resumed his seat beside the old man, who waited with his tiny hands folded upon his lap.

"Now at least we can go home without you getting into trouble," Pete declared as the horses began to move at their own casual pace. "Why didn't I bring a whip? he reproached himself.

Kleinsige then reached beneath the seat. "Well, here is one if you want it," he said, holding in his hand the whip from the buggy that had stood next to them on the street.

Anna's Dream

Anna Hännes was troubled. It was something she could not altogether comprehend, this dream of hers — if that's what it was — that came every night. In the dream she saw a man with a burning taper. Each time he held it before her face, and, when she awoke, she could still feel the flame's warmth upon her cheek. What could such a dream portend, she wondered. For three days now it worked upon her mind. After all, any dream — particularly one of this sort — had its meaning. It might even be a prophecy. . . . But of what?

Prophetic dreams were not unusual in Anna's family. Her brother Jonathan had seen things that later came true, and she, herself, had even dreamed of angels. Yet it seemed always as though one never knew the meaning of such an experience until the event it foretold had already taken place. But Anna felt that there was something about this particular dream that was essential for her to know.

So she reviewed it once again as she went about her morning chores. . . . There was the ominous-looking being in a dark coat.

He approached her bedside and looked directly into her face. His expression was neither sinister nor malevolent — yet somber, admonishing. There was a glimmer of flame at the end of the taper he held so close to her face. She could feel the heat and recoiled from it. Yet the flame remained, refusing to be shut out or turned away. All this she remembered upon awaking. Seeing it again in her mind, she could only wonder. Perhaps she should tell the family about it. But they would only laugh . . . and for now there was work to do.

"Martha" she called to her daughter, who was standing with little Esther by the window, "go upstairs to see if the clothes are dry." Because it was winter, the laundry had to be hung in the upstairs rooms where it would not freeze. So Martha hurried up the steps as she was directed. The boys, meanwhile, had already gone to milk the cows. The daily activities had to be seen to.

Forcing the dream out of her mind, Anna returned to the cradle where baby Katherine had begun to cry. There were thirteen children in all — a sizeable family to care for. Anna rocked the cradle and spoke softly to the baby.

There came a sudden cry from the stairs. At first Anna thought it was only a playful shriek such as the girls gave when they teased one another. Then the words came again — more distinct and terrible: "Mama! The house is on fire!"

Fighting the terror that stabbed through her heart, Anna hurried up the steps where Martha stood, her face pale and frantic. Opening the upper door, Anna was struck by an avalanche of smoke and flying ashes.

"Outside! Quickly!" she ordered the children after she closed the door. "Hurry! The cradle! Take the baby!" Only a few things could be saved. But which? There was so little time. All thought seemed to be paralyzed. Martha struggled with the sewing machine, for which they had saved their money for so long, and managed to pull it onto the porch as Hännes and the boys came running toward the house.

Already the yard was filled with smoke. Flames burst from the roof and seemed to melt against the deep, cold sky. Anna stood outside with the children and watched helplessly, the baby in her arms. At least all of them were safe. Already neighbors were gathering and alarmed voices called out to one another.

"A ladder! Someone get a ladder!"

"No! Too late!"

In silent dismay they watched now as the house wilted and crashed beneath the wind-driven flames. The children wept, but Anna could only stare at the fire. There would be strange beds for them to sleep in that night, and it would be a long time until things would again be as they had been before the fire foretold in Anna's dream.

Die Weisse Frau

"There is talk,' Skurgilie said in his droll voice, "that some have seen a woman in a white dress walking about the country." Taking a handkerchief to blow his rather bulbous nose, he continued: "I for one do not believe it. But there are those who say it is so and that they have seen her."

A jovial little man with a love for humor and gossip, Skurgilie — who had been given the diminutive form of his father's Russian nickname, *Skurra*, or "pelt" — wore the typically full beard that characterized the men of his generation. But unlike many of his contemporaries, he was neither severe nor sanctimonious. His small stature and quizzical eyes gave him a most extraordinary, gnome-like appearance; and no one was more eager than he to tell a good joke or to repeat a tale that caused his listeners to chuckle — as much at the manner of its telling as at the tale itself. His favorite was the story of how a cyclone had once lifted him from the ground and deposited him in a nearby lake. Tonight, however, there was a different kind of story — something mysterious, even sinister.

"It is so, because I have seen her myself," someone announced when Skurgilie had finished. "I was cultivating my corn only last week. I came to the end of the row and lifted the machine out of the ground. Then I noticed something at the other end of the field. It looked like a woman wearing a wedding dress.

"It took me a long time to cross to the far end. By that time she was gone. But what did I find? The marks from bare feet in the dust — big tracks."

This drew gasps of astonishment from everyone in the room. the old men stroked their beards nervously and looked at each other. Lamplight played upon their wrinkled faces.

"Such stories were told in the old country," one of them remarked.

"Maybe it is an *Irrlicht*," someone else suggested, referring to the lights seen along Turkey Creek.

"But one sees those only at night. And the tracks . . .!"

From a corner of the room Skurgilie's young grandson, Willis, listened intently. His father had drowned in Turkey Creek years earlier; and when the boy's mother remarried, the second husband abused Willis so badly that he was taken to live with his grandparents. Having no one near his own age, he was compelled to endure the company of the old people, whose talk generally bored him. Yet tonight the conversation was of a remarkable and tantalizing nature — something to arouse the imagination. He listened with interest.

"Perhaps, too," another speaker observed, "it is someone who has lost her mind. But who can it be?" No one seemed to know.

"If in fact there is a woman at all," put in an incredulous voice. "The imagination does many things to a person."

"What I saw was no imagination!" protested the first speaker.

Having reached an impasse, the conversation wandered to other subjects; and the *Weisse Frau* or White Lady, as they called her was forgotten. Willis, growing bored once again, left the room and ambled out into the warm spring night.

It was not long until he returned — his face flushed with excitement: "Grandfather, the corn crib is on fire!"

With whatever speed they were able to muster up, the elders hastened to the site. The fire was already impossible to stop, the blaze eating through the dry corncobs with ravenous eagerness, lighting up the entire yard. As there was no danger of its catching onto anything else, the spectators stood helplessly watching the destruction of that part of the past year's crop, while the dogs barked frantically.

Willis's voice was tremulous. "I saw her," he gasped. "The woman in white was here!" A search with lanterns revealed nothing among the outbuildings. But in the morning a set of incredibly large footprints appeared on the ground about the burned corn crib.

So the story began and continued throughout the summer as more and more people began to see the elusive woman in a white dress. Gardens were pilfered; bedded livestock was aroused; shed and granaries were found open; and always the same large footprints remained as the characteristic testimony of the visitor.

Skurgilie, like the others, found all of this most disquieting. Although no one had been actually harmed by the apparition, its persistence constituted a major nuisance. But, more than anything else, it was the unknown nature of the entity, itself, that disturbed the countryfolk, their well-ordered lives allowing little room for the para-normal. While the elders saw this intruder as an ungodly threat to the accepted order of things, the younger members of the community, on the other hand, found it an exciting diversion. When individual attempts failed to capture the woman, the young men determined that only an organized effort could accomplish the end.

"It is undoubtedly some moon-struck girl who wanders about without knowing what she is doing," concluded the more prudent ones of the group.

"She is too clever. Whoever it is, she knows what she is after," refuted others.

Still there were some voices who said, "She is a ghost. And how do you catch a ghost?"

Ghost or not, they would be ready for her. At the first sighting, the alarm would be spread so that all could join in the chase.

They had not long to wait. It was early morning a few days later when the White Lady was reported seen in Skurgilie's own cornfield. Soon every telephone in the vicinity was ringing. Neighbors within shouting distance of one another answered the alert. The ghost hunters came on horseback and on foot with dogs and rifles to surround the field. A camera was brought to record the capture for the Freeman newspaper.

"Da rübber! Over there! *Ich han sie schon gesieht!"* So they shouted to one another, riding up and down the hot, dusty rows, chasing something that none of them could actually see. The horses, excited by the shouts of the men and the yelping of the dogs — who found it all a great sport — became confused and nearly collided with each other. In every direction they hunted among the broken cornstalks while Skurgilie looked in dismay at his ruined crop. Willis, who rode with them, suddenly called out. . . . He had found something.

Quickly they gathered at the spot in the center of the field. "What is it? Have they found her?"

Something lay between the rows. "A dog! Someone killed a dog."

Dismounting in a group, they approached to find the pathetic animal, bludgeoned to death, upon the ground. That — and the footprints. The White Lady was nowhere to be seen.

They did not find the *Weisse Frau* that day or ever. Nor was she seen anywhere again. If a ghost, they reasoned, perhaps she was propitiated by the dog's blood; if a mortal, no doubt she was frightened by such a show of force. So they returned home to resume their work and tell their stories . . .

As the frustrated ghost hunters dispersed, Willis laughed to himself. "Such fools!" he muttered, thinking how ridiculous they had looked, the people who always called him "Hickie" after the English gangster Hickman. It was a name he detested as much as he did his grandfather's dogs. Now he had his revenge. Perhaps some day he would tell them that he was, in fact, the woman in the white dress. But for the present it was well to let them talk and wonder. Such an amusement, after all, was best left to itself.

The Day the Gypsies Came

There was a good deal of contention that fall concerning the election. A new senator was to be chosen in a contest between Crawford and Kittredge (or "Digrich", as Uncle Christ called the corpulent candidate). There were special trips on the train to Pierre, colored flags and badges and animated speeches about the Panama Canal and other matters that really meant little to the Mennonites.

In church they debated a matter that was of far greater significance to their world. There was a proposal that the church sell insurance to its members to cover losses from fire and hail. It was a new concept and seemingly one that would be welcomed by any farmer. Yet there was opposition. The entrenched reactionaries saw this idea as a worldly reproach against the will of the Almighty.

"You are taking away God's means of punishing you," lamented old man Sturrai. "If your crop is destroyed, it is His will. You are defying Him with your impertinence."

"*Dummheit* — foolishness! John retorted. "That was what they said when the first lightning rods came out. Where would any of us be with such thinking? It is like a wheel spinning in the mud — going nowhere."

"*Nay, nay! Du bist falsch,*" accused some others; and so the arguments persisted.

Crawford, the Progressive, won the election narrowly; and the Mennonites determined that God could deal in insurance as well as salvation . . .

"I know what your real name is," Freddy teased a little boy who was just beginning his first year of school. "You are called Zonzel."

"No — Mueller!" replied the mystified child, who as yet had not learned his family nickname.

"No, you are Zonzel!" Freddy laughed.

"Mueller!"

"Zonzel!"

"Mueller!"

That was Freddy as they knew him — a prankster who was always forgiven because his pranks made life bearable. So autumn passed into winter and winter into spring . . .

"Summer time — summer time, the best in all the year," they sang on their last day of school, a song composed for them by Dundilie — the little boy with the sack of sugar, who used to lisp. Now he was their teacher. And for John's family it would be a special summer indeed, although they did not know it. . . . It was to be their last in Dakota.

* * *

The Fourth of July was a momentous day to be anticipated many weeks ahead — an "English" holiday they called it ironically, since, after all, all non-Germans were "English." It began with a series of explosions from the Freeman blacksmith shop where a quantity of powder was placed in the forge to produce the effect of a cannon shot. At once, upon hearing the noise, Eddy and Hardwig, as well as Freddy, were out of bed and ready to share in the excitement. "We are going to Julius Ewert's!" they cried jubilantly in anticipation of the promised journey, while John and Joe, never in a hurry, methodically hitched the teams.

"Be patient. It's a long day," the men laughed.

It was a annual gathering at their brother-in-law's farm some miles north of Marion. A red-complexioned, serious man, Ewert was a prosperous farmer, somewhat aloof, especially toward children — yet a cordial host. He met them as they arrived after several hours of tedious travel in the two wagons.

"Here come Uncle John and Uncle Joe!" young Bernard Ewert called out to the others, happy at seeing his cousins. Tante Freni came on the porch and shielded her eyes from the intense summer sun. It was indeed a happy time — another family gathering — a day of laughter and shared joy. Ewert escorted the men into the front room.

"So you are still looking for some land, John," he said in English. "Have you considered trying North Dakota?" Ewert, although German, did not speak the Schweitzer dialect and preferred conversing in the new language.

John told him of the fruitless trip he had made to Chamberlain. "But a few of the fellows are talking pretty strong about Montana," he said.

Outside, the boys found adventure among the trees and along the small creek.

"I have a new fishing pole," Bernard boasted. "I already caught some fish today, too."

They continued their juvenile conversation as they explored the many wonderful places on the farm until Freddy spotted a group of wagons approaching.

"Gypsies! They come every summer," Bernard explained. "Sometimes they even come to the house for food or oats. Pa says they are only beggars."

The others listened, intently eyeing the ominous wagons. "Do you think it is true that they steal little babies? What do they do with them?"

"Maybe they eat them!" Everyone shuddered at the thought.

There were, from the days in Russia, many tales concerning these strange, pagan folk — dire stories telling of child abduction — and humorous accounts of trickery and theft.

"At night we can hear them sing," Bernhard continued. "But you will see. Pretty soon they will come to the house, I bet."

Presently the call came for dinner, and later that afternoon two old, dark-skinned hags approached the house. With them came three children — two barefoot girls in long dresses and a boy with a red bandana. From another time they came, dressed in a manner that resembled a kind of foreign barbarism — the like of which Eddy and the others saw in their geography textbooks. The dark youth examined everything with slow, acute eyes that betrayed little. Left to themselves, the boys might well have befriended him. But the talks they had heard from their elders instilled a mutual fear.

Meanwhile, the *Zigeuner* women began to bargain with Tante Freni for a loaf of bread. Calmly indulgent, she listened to their broken German. It was evident that one loaf between the two was not satisfactory and that each woman desired her own.

Entering the house, Freni returned with a large kitchen knife. "You can easily cut this one in two," she suggested sarcastically, upon which the two women turned away in disgust, taking the one loaf with them.

It was then that the Gypsy boy caught sight of Bernard's new fishing pole; and, before the unfortunate Bernard knew what was happening, the dark youth held the pole tightly, indicating to the others that he wished it for himself.

"No, he cannot have it," Bernhard protested anxiously. "It is mine!" Tears began to well in his eyes.

Ewert, who had watched the events with quiet amusement, approached the young Gypsy. "You can have the pole," he offered, winking at the other men. "But first these little girls must dance for us."

There was some deliberation among the strangers in their own language. The women spoke to their children in emphatic tones. Then the boy began to sing, beating the rhythm upon the fishing pole, which he still held. With considerable animation, the two small girls began to dance, their bare feet pounding upon the packed earth in front of the house. Their gestures, as spirited and wild as the strange song, expressed moods of furious gaiety and even passion. Their audience stared at them with delight and intrigue in the way that the civilized mind always acknowledges its own barbaric origins.

Ewert would not let them stop. "Go on, giggle-gaggle!" he urged them. So they continued to dance, the song rising in pitch and fervor.

"They are tired. It is enough," Freni cautioned her husband, who smiled gleefully.

"Not yet! Go on! Some more!"

At last it became evident that the two girls would soon drop from exhaustion.

"They cannot dance any more. It is cruel," Freni pleaded until Ewert at last relented and told the boy to keep the fishing pole, much to Bernard's consternation.

So passed a day's amusement for people who saw only infrequent glimpses of another life outside their own. So passed the summer — the Dakota days — the things remembered and forgotten. It was the summer of 1909 — when a new world had begun, unknown to anyone save a few gifted with understanding.

And what became of the Gypsy youth, of the fishing pole and of the girls who danced for it? Such questions one might ask only of the imagination. "For each is always bound to his own way, and no one can follow another's course," the elders often said. . . . Yet for a moment the Gypsies had become a part of the Mennonites' lives and had touched them in a way which they could neither define nor forget.

The Gypsy Dancers.

Part V

THE MOVERS

The Railway Depot at Freeman.

Swallow's Nests

So passed the remembrance of those days — of a time that seemed it could not end, alternating cycles of winter and summer, forever the same. So the early years of Eddy's life were begun, completed and abandoned, made of an impermanent substance, like the swallows' nests which hung above the porch. And each spring the swallows came to build new nests with mud from the lake shore, spurning their past work as though it did not exist. Eddy and Hardwig watched them from the doorway, studying the birds' engineering.

"Who taught them to do it?" Hardwig would ask; and Eddy would reply:

"God showed them how. . . . At least He told the first swallows what to do. Then they showed their children."

"But why don't they use the same nests every year?"

"They know they're not supposed to. The old nests might break off from the house and kill the young ones."

"But how can they know it? They're only swallows."

"Still they know."

Also with spring and throughout the summer came wagons along the road — wagons with families, household goods and supplies for farming. These were the "movers," as Henry called them — people bound for Montana and Wyoming. "They are going to take up homesteads," he explained to his brothers. . . . "Just like Grandpa did in the old days." Eddy and Hardwig watched the wagons and waved to them, intrigued, wondering what it would be like to move West.

John, too, had been thinking of the West — particularly of Montana. Later that year, Poltauwitz-Joe — the old wolf hunter's son — and Roger-Jäk — whose house had blown over in the great wind — filed on land near a town called Glendive on the Yellowstone River in Dawson County. They encouraged John to come with them. "It's an opportunity, John," young Poltauwitz urged, twitching his mustache. "There's land for everyone, by George! But you have to act soon. All you need to do is prove up for five years and it's yours."

John listened and thought . . . "So," he told Caroline, "if we go, we leave it all behind — the people we grew up with, the things we always knew. But maybe it is for the best. Who knows? It is what the old people called 'Weltgeist' — the spirit of the world — always changing."

Caroline hesitated before speaking. "Still," she said, "things can go badly for us there. What my father said is true; the cherries always look sweeter in the other man's garden."

John looked away, still thinking. "The weather will soon be

cold," he said at last. "If we go, we must wait until spring. We have a long time yet to decide."

Eddy listened to their conversation, not yet aware of the consequences it bore for his own life. A course of events had begun that would lead them all forever beyond the provincial confines of the Dakota settlement toward the *"Weltgeist"* of a new way. The severance had begun.

John walked out onto the porch, looking beyond the already barren elm trees toward the flat Dakota sky. A fringe of feeble twilight shone from beneath the burden of sporadic clouds along the empty horizon. Eddy stood beside his father, his hand resting upon the head of the old dog. The dog looked up at him with its dimmed eyes that always seemed so very sad to Eddy.

"Is it far to Montana?" he asked John.

"Not too far! A day and a night by train." John poured some tobacco into a cigarette and moistened the edges with his tongue.

"Maybe Uncle Jake will want to move there, too."

"He says it is a good place. But he won't go. He has been in Dakota too long already. He would not know how to live anywhere else." John lit the cigarette. The smell of the smoke was pleasing to Eddy — it was a smell he had come to associate with his father.

In the house the lamps were lit again. Eddy followed John indoors. He could only speculate about the distant place where there were hills and wild animals — perhaps even Indians. If they were really going, he thought, it would be a wonderful thing. But they were supposed to have gone to Chamberlain earlier, he remembered. He and Hardwig had even dug a quantity of wild turnips — "Indian bread" — to trade with the Sioux who lived there for a bow and arrows. They never saw Chamberlain, however, or the bow and arrows. Perhaps this Montana venture would not materialize either . . .

It was February of 1910 when Poltauwitz and Roger took the Milwaukee train for Terry, Montana, accompanied by Poltauwitz's brother-in-law Tieszen. John decided to go with them to see the country for himself.

* * *

Never before had he felt such a fresh exhileration of spirit. "it is as if I were a boy again," he thought, as he examined the hills of Yellowstone Valley from the train window. "Here is something good — a place to invest one's life — an opportunity."

Transferring to the Northern Pacific train, they reached Glendive on the second afternoon. "It's a railroad town," Poltauwitz explained. "They have the biggest roundhouse I ever saw. And that hill to the east is called 'Hungry Joe.' They say a man froze to death up there one winter."

John looked at the stark gray badlands that rose, splotched with snow, above the town. The settlement was divided into two parts by the railroad tracks where bulky steam engines groaned and wheezed in the railyard. The main street ran along the track with all of the shops and saloons facing it from one side. Along the west side of town lay the river bordered with cottonwood trees. That was Glendive.

Directly across from the rail depot a sign read "Hotel Jordan." The four men trudged across the mud-filled ruts with their luggage and, entering the hotel lobby, signed their names in the register book, becoming, as they did so, a part of the town's daily transactions and a part of what was to be remembered as the "homestead era." They had reached the midpoint of their lives and were now embarking upon this great venture with a renewed youthfulness — John, nearly forty, small and petulant — Roger, tall and benign — and Poltauwitz, often impulsive, always agreeable.

"We need to find our locator," Poltauwitz said when they were again on the street. The electric streetlamps began to gleam against the chilly evening.

"What is his name?" John asked.

"Buller — a Mennonite of the Old Order. He wrote to me that he would meet us."

Roger shrugged his shoulders. "Well, he knows we are coming. He can find us tomorrow. Maybe we can kill some time and see what the saloons are like in this town."

Among the Glendive saloons were the Stutz and the Niederhof, operated and patronized by Germans. A third — The Midnight Sun — was run by a Norwegian named Andrew Helland. After sampling the whisky in all three, the newcomers found their way back to the hotel and settled themselves until morning.

The following day arrived — a bit early for John and the others, who were recovering from the past night's exploits. Returning from breakfast, they were approached by a rather short, serious-looking man whom Poltauwitz and Roger recognized at once. After shaking hands, he presented John with a card that read: "Abe Buller, Land Locator."

Buller belonged to a more conservative faction of Mennonites than did John and his comrades and spoke a different dialect of German. Still he was to them a welcome ally in the strange new place.

"This is the man we met on our first trip," Poltauwitz explained. "He showed us some good homesteads."

"I think I know a place you might want," Buller said addressing John with an important air. "It's good land — filed on by a

111

Custer's Lookout in Montana.

man named Slagel. He isn't going to prove up on it — says his wife's health is bad. That's an excuse they give sometimes when the going gets rough."

After this perfunctory introduction, the homesteaders followed Buller to his wagon and began the long trek to the Slagel site. "It's good land," the locator repeated as he guided the team along the street. "No rocks and not too many hills. The only bad thing about this part of the country is that it gets pretty dry in the summer."

"And how long have you been here?" John asked curiously.

"It's going on four years now," Buller replied. "I came with my father's family in six. We filed on adjoining land. . . . No, it's not a bad place — especially when we have an open winter the way this one was.

The wind, in spite of the winter season, was warm, leaving only a few patches of snow upon the hillsides. A "chinook" Buller called it.

"The river will go out in February this year," he remarked as they crossed the bridge leading out of town — a bridge which Roger said must be a half mile long. "Everybody is making bets on it."

They proceeded north past a flat-topped hill that Buller called "Custer's Lookout." John recalled the stories he had heard about Custer — the man who stood off the entire Sioux nation with a pair of revolvers. The land was rugged and sparsely-settled. Many of the hills seemed unable to support any vegetation, save a few rugged clumps of sage and some small scrub cedars. As they continued west and north, however, the terrain became more gentle and the hills less barren.

By late afternoon they reached a farm belonging to another Mennonite, whom Buller introduced as C. J. Schmidt from Indiana — a very proper man of average height with a well-groomed mustache. Schmidt had come with Buller's father in 1906 and was in the process of threshing his past year's harvest. "It wintered in on us last fall," he explained. "But the weather has been good enough now to let us finish."

John, at once impressed with Schmidt's poise and prosperity, examined the grain. The kernels of wheat were the largest he had seen. He felt encouraged.

Andrew Buller, Abe's father, was present to help with the threshing. In contrast to his neighbor, he was short, stocky and wore a full white beard in accordance with Old Mennonite custom. His terse, almost abrupt, sentences were generally prefaced by the word *juscht* — an expletive peculiar to his own people.

"We are very satisfied here," Schmidt continued cheerfully. "This was our second choice, though. We bit into a sour apple, so to speak, when we first came. They put us on some government land out West, and we had no idea what we were getting into. But this is fine country — yes indeed.

Schmidt, speaking English all the while, continued to relate facts about the land and his experiences at homesteading. Inviting the newcomers to spend the night, he showed them a book deal-

113

ing with dryland farming techniques. "It's called the Campbell Method," he said. "The seasons are shorter here, and there is less rainfall. We had to learn a different way of farming when we came."

In the morning young Buller again guided them north along what he called "The Redwater Road" — a trail originally used by early ranchers to drive their cattle to market. The trail skirted an area of high table land for a few miles until it finally crossed a divide that lay toward the northwest. Buller did not take his clients across the divide, however. They had reached the Slagel homestead.

The house — a tall, narrow structure with a loft and a small lean-to beside it — stood perched upon a hill on the southeast corner of the section. Although no fence or furrow could be discerned anywhere, John knew that he had found his farm.

Klaus, the Carpenter

When he agreed to take up the Slagel homestead, John returned with the others to Dakota, where they entertained their families with talks of the hill named "Hungry Joe" and of the bridge that was said to be one half mile long. To people who had seen only the small wooden bridges of Turner County, a suspension bridge of such magnitude seemed incomprehensible.

"Not only that," Poltauwitz added enthusiastically. "But they have a warm wind that blows sometimes in the early spring — they call it a chinook. There can be a foot of snow on the ground, but when that wind comes, the snow disappears in a day."

"Not quite all in a day," his wife, Netha, laughed in protest, well-acquainted with her husband's tendency toward exaggeration.

"That's what they told us, by George!" he insisted. "And look at the wheat they grow there." From a small tobacco sack he poured a sample of Schmidt's grain onto the table for all to see.

Eddy and Hardwig watched and heard all of this with wonder. "If Pa saw it, too, it must be so," they reasoned.

But cousin Freddy, who was also on hand to hear of these marvels, was estatic. "Please let us go to Montana, too," he begged his father tirelessly. Joe Vetter, whose placid temper remained unshaken, merely shook his head. So Freddy had to content himself by exulting over his cousins' good fortune.

"And in the summer you will go there," he told them. "And you will go across that long bridge."

"Yes," Eddy thought, "we are really going there. It is true, after all." An acute sadness suddenly seized his young soul . . . to leave Dakota . . . the lake and the school! How could he be happy anywhere else? Until now the thought of Montana had been like a child's imagined adventure. Now that the reality of it seemed evident, Eddy realized that such a trip meant leaving home forever. He knew that these were feelings he must keep to himself, however. John's mind was made up. They were going to Montana.

* * *

Arrangements were soon made to sell the land in Dakota. John also sold the corn cultivator and other implements that would be of no use in Montana where the season was too short for such crops. The house, too, was put up for sale and purchased by an Englishman named Bailey, who was later to sell it to Jockilie. Everything that John owned and that gave his family its sustenance was being wagered for something as yet only hoped for. The dividends would come in a new place where, with a little good fortune, life would reward them.

In April Caroline took Hardwig and the three small girls to stay with Grandfather Jacob and Marie, while Lydia and Ida were sent to Uncle Christ's house. Eddy, however, remained reluctantly with Joe and Julia, within view of the empty house that had once been his home. He wondered years afterward why he had never gone to visit the house once more. Perhaps fear or remorse prevented him from doing so, for he looked at it only from a distance; and each time he could see the old dog sitting upon the porch, waiting. "Pa should have taken the dog," he would say to himself when he heard it howling late at night.

Meanwhile John and Henry were preparing to leave again for Montana to build their new house, as were Poltauwitz and Roger with their oldest sons, Paul and Gust. On the day they went to the Freeman depot to order boxcars, Henry noticed a muscular, rather rustic-looking man talking with Roger. "Who is that?" he asked.

John laughed. "That is our carpenter. He can't read or write, but he can pound nails for us — if he stays sober . . . Klaus!" he called out to the stranger. "This is my son, Heinrich."

"Well, this looks like a fine young man," declared the carpenter. "He'll make us a good helper."

As the day progressed, Klaus and Henry became good friends. Klaus, who, Henry noted, bore a striking resemblance to the portrait of General Custer in his history book, sported a heavy growth of mustache beneath which protruded a soot-blackened pipe . . .

"*Was sagt es da?*" he drawled to Henry, indicating the names printed upon the boxcars.

"This one says 'Northern Pacific'" Henry explained. "The others say 'Chicago Milwaukee.'"

"Oh, I see," Klaus replied with a sage nod of his head.

Inside the depot Klaus listened with interest as the agent described the boxcars that would be used to take farm machinery and furniture on the trip. "This car has a forty-foot capacity; the others are thirty-foot," the agent explained brusquely.

"Yes, forty-foot capacity is best," Klaus declared, puffing upon his pipe with an important air. "But we need a Northern Pacific car, you see."

"Well, I'll agree to a forty-foot car," Poltauwitz told the others. "We can use the extra space to sleep in." No one seemed to have heard Klaus' remark. But after all, was it not the Northern Pacific Railroad that would take them to Glendive?

"It's a Northern Pacific car we want," he repeated.

At this, the agent, true to the inhospitable reputation of his profession, became irritated. "What the devil does it matter?" he snapped, slapping the lease paper upon the counter. "There's your car!"

Klaus raised his head indignantly to conceal his embarrassment. "*Las uns gehen,*" he said huskily to the rest and left the depot. Yet he remembered the word "capacity" and used it at every opportunity thereafter.

* * *

The cars having thus been arranged for and loaded, Klaus agreed to accompany the three boys on the passenger train, while the other men traveled with the freight. "We'll probably be a day or so late," John said. "So don't let the boys get lost." Once they boarded the train, Henry, Paul and Gust found seats together. Klaus was forced to share a seat with a stranger, whom he eyed nervously. After a bit, however, the stranger smiled, extended his hand and introduced himself. Relieved by this gesture of friendship, Klaus at once began to boast of how he had been commissioned to build houses for a group of homesteaders in Montana.

"So you're a carpenter!" the other man exclaimed in delight. "Well, that is my trade, too. Say — I have a book here that you might find interesting. It has to do with some new techniques." So saying, he handed a bound manual to the illiterate Klaus, who accepted the volume reluctantly and began paging through it with feigned interest.

"Now what do you think of that?" the stranger asked.

Klaus cleared his throat. The three boys, who were sitting immediately behind him, could no longer contain their laughter. "*Seid still da!*" Klaus barked. Then, returning the book, he said, "Well, I see a lot of good points here," upon which the youthful giggles burst into loud hilarity, while Klaus bore his chagrin in silence.

It was a certain kind of pride that gave Klaus this need for importance. He was a man without home or family, unable to read, victimized by an appetite for alcohol. Yet, conscious as he was of these deficiencies, his pride would not allow any concession of inferiority; and it was thus that he often found himself trapped into humiliation. Still the others tolerated him — perhaps even with affection — in spite of his prepossessing manner. He was always affable and fun-loving — the kind of man who is often called a "sport."

When the train reached Glendive, Klaus began to explore the main street with the boys. "We will have to stay in the hotel tonight," he told them. "Tomorrow the freight should come in." Continuing to ask Henry to read the signs above each store, Klaus soon was able to find a saloon. Cautiously the boys followed him into the acrid, smoky room.

It did not take Klaus long to establish a conversation among the collection of cowboys, farmers and railroad men, who found this newcomer a source of amusement.

"A long time ago when I was a boy," he told them. "I learned a stunt. Maybe it's worth a drink or two." Immediately there was an audience of curious, intoxicated men.

"Well, what is it?" an impatient voice demanded.

When he was sure that he had everyone's attention, Klaus looked about him with an attitude of pronounced self-assurance and then, tilting his head backward, opened his mouth in a wide yawn. Suddenly, strange bell-like noises began to emerge from deep within his throat. These continued for several seconds; and when the performance concluded, Klaus, the carpenter, was no longer a stranger in Glendive, Montana.

The Farewell

The air in May tasted of spring. Ducks prattled noisily upon the lake as they moved about their nesting places. Uncle Joe worked at his forge sharpening plow shares, while in the straw at the barn Eddy played with the new-born kittens until he fell asleep. A man named Samuel Clemens died that spring, and a luminous enigma known as Halley's Comet glowed in the evening sky.

"*Katzevater*, wake up!" Eddy suddenly felt someone shaking him by the shoulder. He stirred and looked about. The old cat lay

117

beside him, purring and nursing her kittens. Eddy was used to his nickname — "Cat Father."

"It is suppertime," cousin Freddy was saying. "Tomorrow you have to leave on the train."

Tomorrow — yes, he remembered it now. He would see his mother again — and Hardwig and the girls. Tomorrow they were to start for Montana to join John and the others.

During the past weeks Eddy had spent much time alone, declining to play with Freddy or to indulge in any school games. "I think he misses the folks," he heard Julia say to Joe Vetter one night as he lay quietly, not yet asleep. Yes, he missed them. At first he had not wanted to leave. Yet as the days of waiting increased, he began to look less and less toward the empty house and longed more to see the new place where his father and Henry had gone, until the thought of being reunited with his parents was all that mattered. What he had once known as his home would no longer retain any allure for him, except as a memory.

So when Uncle Joe told him that it was time to leave for the Freeman depot on the following day, Eddy was eager to go. Feeling simultaneous exhilaration and impatience, he sat beside his uncle, jostled by the springs beneath the wagon seat as they rode together past the old house. The movement was sufficiently slow for him to contemplate the narrow building from every perspective in the morning light. In spite of the brightness of the day, the house looked gray and empty, as though it were dead. On the porch the dog waited, lifting his head only slightly when he saw the wagon.

For a moment Eddy wanted to leap from the wagon and to run once more across the pasture, into the kitchen that he knew so well, and up the steps that led to his bedroom. Again he felt the despair and terror of separation from the familiar. But life, he knew, had gone from that house. At last it disappeared behind the newly-leafed trees and into the endless haze of the Dakota sky.

Uncle Joe seemed to sense Eddy's feelings. "There is always something in us that wants to go back," he told his nephew. "We hold onto it, because we are afraid of what is to be. But soon life takes us where we are intended to go. And that is always best, even when we think otherwise." Eddy remained silent, realizing at that moment how deeply he loved his uncle.

Much later — at least so it seemed — as they approached the depot, Eddy saw Caroline waiting for him on the platform with Hardwig, Bertha, Othelia and little Anne. The tiny girl clung to her mother's hand and cried out gleefully when she saw her brother. Grandfather Jacob was there with Marie, both looking old and somber. He saw, too, Uncle Jake and Marja Bas, old Poltauwitz with Netha and his grandchildren, and old Schrag with his grandson, Erhart — the only one of Roger's children still in Dakota. Erhart had remained to help his grandfather with the spring seeding while Katie went ahead with the other children some days earlier. Netha was busily collecting the last pieces of luggage to be loaded onto the baggage car, instructing her children all the while as to the behavior expected of them on the train. Caroline looked on anxiously as Uncle Joe applied the brake to the wagon and pulled the team to a halt.

"Here is the money John left with me for the tickets," she told him when he had dismounted and handed him an envelope with some bills. She followed him then into the depot with Eddy and Anne and listened as Joe negotiated with the agent.

"Any children over ten?" they heard the agent ask. Joe named Ida and Lydia, then turned to his sister-in-law. "How old is Eddy?"

Eddy felt a chill of apprehension race through his body at the sound of his name. He had turned eleven on the eighth of the month. The agent peered suspiciously over the window ledge. "He'll have to pay full fare."

"But only a few days —" Joe protested.

There was more debate until the agent conceded to make a special pass for the boy.

"Show it to the conductor," he instructed Caroline. "Maybe he'll accept it."

When they returned to the platform to resume their waiting, Eddy heard his grandfather calling to him and Hardwig. The old man approached the two boys. In his hand were two tiny boxes. Eddy, feeling an instinctive dread of the family patriarch, looked downward as his grandfather placed one box in each boy's hand. Opening his box, Eddy found a large pocket watch from Kaufman's jewelry store and looked up, amazed to see tears in the old blacksmith's eyes.

"And are you going also to Potana?" Marja Bas asked little Anne and hugged her niece dearly.

"Not Potana!" sister Othelia corrected the aunt. "Montana!"

Uncle Christ was the last to arrive, bringing Lydia and Ida with him. They had barely reached the platform when Erhart called out — "The train is coming!"

Every head turned to gaze down the track at the column of smoke that grew into a powerful machine as it approached the depot. The engine seemed alive, shrieking its whistle and shaking the platform upon which the onlookers waited. Eddy shuttered at the fierceness of the steam and fire and marveled at the jostling motion of the cars.

There was a sequence of hurried farewells and tears. Grandfather Jacob looked solemnly at the engine, recalling another May and another train. Quickly the children were herded up the steps and into the coach.

The train's interior was a confusion of passengers scrambling for seats. Eddy and Hardwig sat with Erhart. Looking from the window they saw — but could not comprehend — the sad and longing eyes of those who watched from the platform. Slowly at last the train pulled away from the station. A series of small kerosene lamps hanging above the aisle swayed back and forth in precarious momentum. Eventually the conductor opened the door, announced by a rushing noise of wheels and air, and began collecting tickets. Eddy watched anxiously as this dreadful official approached.

With a worried look Caroline extended the children's passes to him. The conductor looked first at the tickets, then at Eddy, who felt another surge of terror and knew that his mother was nearly as frightened as he. When the conductor shook his head, Caroline reluctantly reached into her small purse and produced more money — money so precious that some was even hidden in her shoe.

Across from the boys sat an old Polish man, who spoke to the conductor in broken English and ate a lunch of dried fruits. "Do you see his cap?" Erhart whispered to the other boys after the conductor had left. The man had fallen asleep. Erhart quickly reached across the aisle and, snatching the cap from the traveler's head, tossed it across the car. "Now we will see if he finds it," the usually reticent boy chuckled.

Later, when the train stopped briefly, the children were allowed to leave with careful instructions to remain within close range. The Pole awoke and began searching for his cap. Another passenger pointed to it. Grumbling, the man quickly retrieved his property. Erhart bought a sack of marshmallows before returning and ate them sparingly during the remainder of the journey. He offered none of the coveted delicacy to either Hardwig or Eddy.

The trip grew long as the Milwaukee lumbered across the monotonous Dakota flats, stopping frequently at tiny hamlets and farming towns with strange names and faces. Ida and Lydia chatted steadily with the Poltauwitz girls, but their talk remained of little interest to Eddy. Night approached. The talking grew more hushed and drowsy. Eddy continued to listen to the train noises until, before he was aware, sleep overtook him.

He was awakened when the faint light of morning revealed the outline of dark objects against the sky. It was another moment before Eddy determined that they were hills. They were the first he had ever seen and caused a thrill to leap within him. He watched until they became more distinct, and saw at last that they were high, barren cliffs of gray and yellow clay, studded with sage and other strange shrubs. Later that day he saw a broad river valley with green cottonwood and yellow sand bars. That afternoon the train reached Terry.

Eddy was excited as he set foot upon the platform of the Milwaukee depot. Terry was a cowboy's town — the last remnant of a fast-vanishing time. Beyond dust-covered streets lay miles of open plain with sagebrush its only crop. A group of tobacco-chewing cowhands sat idly in front of the hotel and watched impassively as the immigrants debarked.

Without hesitation, Netha asked the depot agent where they were to board the Northern Pacific train for Glendive. The agent pointed to another depot that lay across a weed-covered flat. Quickly the procession crossed the tracks, the women and girls trying with great difficulty to hold their skirts above the cinder-blackened ground while the boys struggled with the luggage. They had not long to wait until the arrival of the second train, which rode more comfortably than did the clumsy Milwaukee. It was dusk when the train arrived in Glendive, and from the window Eddy saw John and Henry.

The Homesteaders

The diminutive frontier town of Glendive seemed awesome to Eddy and the other children, who had never before left the confines of their Mennonite settlement. Yet with John and Henry already there, encouraging them with laughter and embraces, it became at once fascinating and enticing to their young eyes. Above the town Eddy saw the hill that must be "Hungry Joe," catching the last light of day. He saw Roger and Poltauwitz, Gust and Paul, and — of course — Klaus, the man who looked like Custer. The three united families comprised a sizeable congregation at the depot.

Above the clamor, Klaus' laughing voice resounded. "Yes sir! Here they are, safe and sound. Now we can all go and eat."

"That sounds good to me, by George!" Poltauwitz agreed.

So, en masse, they crossed the street to a place called the New Yorker Cafe — which Roger pronounced "New York Safe" — while people on the street gazed at the procession.

"It's a chink restaurant," remarked Klaus, who was sporting a new hat with a dull-gray band.

"That's a cowboy's hat," Eddy overheard Henry telling Caroline. "And that's a real rattlesnake skin hatband."

"*Ach,* such a thing!" their mother observed with disgust.

Inside the restaurant pigtailed waiters scuttled across the floor in their flat-soled shoes. "Ham-n-egg-por'-chop-beef-stew-french-toast-coffee-tea-lemonade!" they recited in rote sequence at each table, for there were no written menus. None of the children, not even the oldest among them, had ever eaten in a public dining place before. What was more, the orders were taken in English, which presented some difficulty for German-speaking people.

When his turn came to order, Gust looked quite frightened. "H-ham?" he finally managed to stammer.

"Ham and what?" the waiter barked.

"H-hmenade!"

The orders were taken at last and the food served at a cost of twenty-five cents for each person.

After they had eaten and again come onto the street, Eddy was immediately awed by the luminous street lamps. "Electric lights," Henry explained, as they walked toward the Jordan Hotel.

It was at this point that Othelia's hat, which she had grown tired of wearing and was swinging carelessly in her small hand, dropped into a basement window along the sidewalk. "Oh, Mama, my hat!" she cried, a sob catching in her voice. The other boys looked on helplessly. But Gust, eager to redeem himself from the affair at the cafe, leaped with his lanky form into the window and retrieved the hat for the gleeful owner.

On the following morning a string of six wagons left Glendive across the "half-mile" bridge. Eddy rode with Henry in a wagon pulled by Billy and Flory, while John came behind with Fanny and Charley — horses that had come from Dakota and bore names that made them more pets than livestock. The bridge planks echoed ominously beneath their ponderous hooves. Eddy chose this moment to open a precious package of Spearmint chewing gum, which John had bought for him in town. The silver paper fluttered upon the air and flew out over the mass of moving water. Eddy's eyes followed it, as it glistened in the sunlight, until it disappeared into the river.

"They are building a new railroad track," Henry told his brother as they passed the section gang on the way toward the new town of Stipek. "They call it the Sidney Branch, because it runs from Glendive to Sidney — that's another town fifty miles from here. And there's a new town just a ways up there called Stipkey."

These names sounded strange and exciting to Eddy — towns he had never known to have existed — much less seen — now to be a part of his life; and for the first time he began to comprehend the magnitude of the world.

Following the railroad track for several miles, the road at last joined another, winding along a shallow stream. "Seven-Mile Creek!" Henry announced.

Eddy was growing impatient. "Aren't we almost there?"

"No, it's a long way yet," Henry laughed. Heavily-leafed

cottonwood trees, gnarled and ancient, shaded the travelers from the sun's intensity. Pulling onto higher ground, they found themselves among grotesque sandhills where no grass grew. The horses, who had been given a chance to rest at the creek, began to strain against the incline. The countryside opened into a wide, grassy plain where heavy clouds appeared upon the horizon and soon began to cover the entire sky. "It's going to rain," John observed.

He had barely spoken when a sudden burst of wind struck the grass and flying drops of moisture fell upon the upturned faces. Poltauwitz's wagon was equipped with a canvas cover, which he quickly pitched and fastened to protect his family. The others, however, were forced to endure the full discomfort of their own open vehicles.

"There is a tarpaper shack a little way from here," John called out to them. "We can make it that far." Their clothing was already soaked when at last they sighted the shack.

Roger tried the door. "It's locked," he cried. "It looks like no one has been here for a while."

"We'll get in!" growled Klaus, forcing the door open with his powerful arms. The interior of the shack, which had only a single window, was dark and forlorn-looking. "At least it's dry," Netha commented grimly.

Once sheltered, the women kindled a fire and set about preparing a make-shift supper, after which the rain subsided and the sun reappeared beneath the clouds, making the prairie bright and glistening, inviting the children to explore outdoors. Henry and Gust began to torment the girls, swinging at them with the skin of a smoked fish that Netha had brought and furnished as part of the supper. They pursued each other, laughing and screaming, upon the shining damp grass across the hillside behind the small house.

Othelia, who had been given a box of something called "Crackerjack" before they left Glendive, was delighted to discover a dazzling string of colored glass beads among the box's contents. Putting them around her neck, she hurried after the other children, eager to appear "grown-up."

So the day's adventures ended, and darkness came to the Montana plains.

When he awoke in the morning, Eddy heard Klaus' sonorous voice dictating a note while Paul sat at the table carefully recording the message. "Tell them we were a group of four families. We got caught in a bad storm. If there's any damage, they should let us know." The note was completed and left upon the table. When the door latch was repaired, the wagons resumed their journey, arriving at Andrew Buller's farm by mid-afternoon. The day was cool and windy; the prairie glistened, green and moist from the rain.

"It's been dry for a long time," Buller said. "This rain will help, but we need a lot more."

As they prepared to spend the last night, Othelia discovered that she had left her treasured glass beads in a drawer at the tar-paper shack. "We will get you some different beads." John consoled her.

Poltauwitz, who spent the night with Abe Buller, left early the next morning ahead of the others. He had taken a homestead some distance from those filed on by John and Roger. But as his house was not yet completed, he would remain with them for a time at the Slagel house. Roger and John followed later, proceeding north now with the loaded wagons and the excited children until at last they reached the crest of a high hill. It was mid-day and had grown hot. The wind moved across an open expanse of unbroken grass. Summer clouds passed above the distant hills, all of which were dwarfed by a high clay butte that stood upon the northwestern horizon and gazed benignly upon the settlers.

Below, all but imperceptible, two tiny buildings rose on the prairie near an almost treeless gulch.

"We are here; this is our home," John declared.

The boys viewed the scene with eager eyes, oblivious to the dismayed looked upon Caroline's face.

"Let's go back," she murmured. "How can we live in such a lonesome place!" This forlorn feeling was to remain with her from that day until the end of her life, as it did with so many other women of that generation, who were the first whites to raise their families in that place. With a slow, deliberate pace, the wagons crept downhill, crushing the young buffalo grass beneath their sturdy wheels. So the day welcomed them, without reproach.

The section upon which the small houses stood had been divided from east to west, Roger taking the south half and John the north. "Even with so many creeks, John, your side is best," Klaus had told him. "There are not so many hills on it." But there was coal exposed in the gulch on the south side. It was a precious fuel in a place that had so little timber, and there, near the coal, Roger had built his house.

"Come and see us after you get settled," he called to the others as they parted.

John's family proceeded to their own house where Poltauwitz was already unpacking his wagon, Netha was inside, preparing the noon meal for the rest of them. Eddy eyed her suspiciously. After all, this was to be his mother's house, he thought with childish indignation. But, whatever she may have felt, Caroline kept her thoughts to herself.

The house — a mere two-room shanty — was constructed of cheap boards with a single doorway and a pair of windows facing south. It stood on a gentle hillside close to the middle of the section. The Slagel house, where Poltauwitz's family would stay, had been moved downhill to a point close by.

Immediately after they had eaten, the boys set out to explore the countryside, walking along bare clay banks that rose on either side of the deep gulch to be known thereafter simply as "the creek," although it held water only in springtime. The grass came to their knees and was filled with a variety of wild birds — meadowlarks, snipes, curlews and ground owls. A layer of matted vegetation covered the ground — an accumulation of many years without domestic grazing — feeling soft and spongy beneath the boys' feet. In some places the yellow earth was exposed in circular or crescent-shaped depressions which, they later determined, were the remnants of buffalo wallows.

At the corners of the section they found four small holes freshly dug in the sod and a single pile of new earth upon which rested a sandstone marker left by the surveyors. Two more such holes and another stone marked the middle line — the first of civilization's attempts to divide and mark the land.

When the young explorers returned to the house, the evening air was alive with a confusion of junebugs and fireflies — so many that it was hard to keep them from the door and windows. It was the end of a remarkable day and the beginning of a new life for all of them — a life characterized by hardship and toil — but also by an intangible freedom and contentment known only to a few isolated generations.

Part VI

WELTGEIST — THE WAY OF THE WORLD

John Breaking Sod.

Proving Up

Throughout that first summer John was breaking sod. He began, walking behind a single-bottom breaker, along the middle line of the section — east of the house. Henry followed with a four-horse hitch on the new riding plow. The exposed flesh of earth lay in long, dark rows where grass had grown so long unmolested. Its roots clung tenaciously, toughened by prolonged resistance to years of drought and hard winters. Still the earth yielded itself, submitting to the sharp steel — embracing it.

As he urged the horses onward across the prairie, John felt a sense of power and of mastery — felt a triumph in the conquest of the grass. He began in the morning, his shadow pointing west; and as the sun progressed, so did the work, until the shadow lay toward the east and the plow was lifted out of the ground. This was his land, he thought — every foot of it measured by the plow's thrust.

For John, as for the other homesteaders, there was no feeling of remorse or compassion for the dying grass, nor any realization of the prolonged significance of the transformation thus effected — or of its magnitude. They came imbued with resolution and purpose, without any deliberation or universal implication. They began their work with the naivete of children, tampering with forces beyond their comprehension, seeking to make the land their own by fencing it, by building houses upon it, by planting crops and groves where no grain or tree had ever grown. And, later, when the dry years came and the dust blew from the arid fields into small drifts among the fences, the crops died; and the men learned a bitterness from which they were never to recover.

There were no stones to clear away, as there had been in Dakota. But there were bones — the bones of hundreds of dead buffalo that had been killed a quarter century before — bones that now littered the prairie — enormous skulls, crowned with brown husks of horns, gazing with empty, dispassionate eyes. Eddy and Hardwig were set the task of collecting these into stacks like kindling wood; and when the bones were sold and gone, there was nothing that remained to tell that such great animals had ever existed in that place.

But the prairie harbored other elements with which the newcomers needed to contend. Even before coming to Montana the boys had heard about rattlesnakes and speculated upon them. "They are not like the garter snakes we knew in Dakota," said Henry, who had often made a game of capturing those innocuous reptiles to terrify the girls. "These are dangerous things, and they make a rattling noise when they are angry." It was truly a subject to stir the imagination.

"They must look like this," Hardwig suggested one evening while they sat at the table where the single lamp burned. the others looked at the picture he had drawn of a serpent with a ball-shaped rattle on its tail.

"Do you suppose they chase after people to bite them?" the girls asked in dismay.

"No, they are probably as afraid of us as we are of them," John reassured them. "But always be careful, especially if you walk through deep grass or brush."

It was not long after, when the boys were leading horses to the well in the creek, that Henry suddenly held out his hand in a warning gesture to Eddy. There was a buzzing noise, unlike anything Eddy had known before.

"Rattlesnake!" Henry cried. "Call Pa!"

Soon the entire family was running toward the place where Henry stood. The children cried excitedly as John plunged his pitchfork into a large badger hole where the snake had vanished. Again Eddy heard the buzzing, and soon John extricated the fork upon which was impaled a sinister, undulating mass of coiled rope.

Hurling the snake upon the ground, John thrust at it repeatedly, beating it until the buzzing ceased. "It's dead for sure!" he announced then.

"*Ach,* no wonder God cursed such a creature!" Caroline shuddered as John carried the fork with the limp carcass triumphantly back to the yard. The rattles were removed for a souvenir.

"Now you saw what a rattlesnake looks like," John laughed, handing them to Hardwig. "Each of these little balls is one year of the snake's life," he explained.

But Eddy could feel only sorrow as he thought of the dead snake that had wanted only to be left alone.

Eddy was on hand some days later when a second, larger snake appeared. Henry had begun plowing on the northwest corner across the creek. It was a large, open flat where, John and the boys determined, there had once been an Indian encampment, attested to by flakes of flint, broken arrow points of irridescent moss agate and a granite maul that Eddy found as he followed Henry along the waves of broken earth. There, in the open furrow, Eddy found a delectable feast of wild turnip roots and wild onions. He had peeled and devoured a number of these when his eye caught a movement in the plow's wake. This time there was no rattling noise, but the snake's repulsive undulations left no doubt as to its identity. Eddy felt a chill of strange, primitive terror; it was a moment before he was able to call to Henry, who killed the rattler with a spade.

Turned out of their hiding places by the plow, however, the snakes soon disappeared, retreating to the badlands along the

130

divide, as did the prairie owls and snipes, when the grass was gone. And men followed even there, cutting the twisted juniper that had grown for centuries where nothing else would and using it for fences. Soon the sections were marked by rows of posts and barbed wire, so that the improvised trails that cut across the land, irrespective of drawn boundaries, could no longer be used. The wounds of civilization had begun to appear.

But for the children, this was a life characterized by a kind of ineffable freedom. In contrast to the tameness of their Dakota days, these times were filled with an excitement of which, before, they could only have dreamed. They wandered among the hills as far as the Clay Butte. They swam in the small pond near the place called "Sandhill Springs," a mile from John's house. There they found still more arrowheads, some of which were still unbroken, and colored agate rocks with scenes of hills and trees, which they took home to decorate the windowsill. And, when evening came, there was the faint smell of smoke upon the air and the reflection of yellow light against the windowpane.

The nights were warm and liquid and dotted with fireflies. When the air was still, one could hear the shrieks of coyotes; and every night the glowing comet hung like a torch in the sky — "the Star of Bethlehem," Caroline marveled.

"It is a wonderful thing," John said, studying it from the porch for hours with an empirical curiosity. Untutored in any school, he still explored the essence of every natural phenomenon, pondering its meaning, wondering. But, when at last he had probed as far as he might and discovered some secret, there was no one with whom to share the revelation.

"Of what use is there to tell anyone?" he thought. "Who would understand? If I told them, they would only look at me."

But there was much to inspire his satisfaction. By the end of that summer he and Klaus had built a sod-roofed cow shed, a root cellar and a granary, which now stood with the dwelling shack and the Slagel house. And Klaus was always there, laughing boisterously whenever he repeated the story of how Roger and John had drawn lots for the house, and how he had winked to John as a signal.

As in Our Father's Time

Although Dakota life was far away, the church — so essential to Mennonite solidarity — could not be forgotten. During that summer the Mennonites came together for Sunday school — sometimes at John's house, sometimes at Roger's or Poltauwitz's; and, afterward, there was always food and laughter and the goodness of an afternoon spent together. In such a way the Sabbath became for them a restoration. They took turns in teaching the Bible lessons, praying in the old language and singing hymns from the *Evangeliums Lieder* — the long, dark-covered book they had used in Dakota. There was also the shared happiness of telling stories, playing games, planning and remembering.

Similarly, the Schmidts and Bullers met for their own services until someone suggested that all of them hold their Sunday meetings at the new Independent Schoolhouse. The formation of a church would be the inevitable outcome. It was a matter to be approached with much deliberation, each adult giving his feelings expression in this miniature democracy.

The nature of their sect had long been predicated upon the concept of congregational autonomy. Decisions in matters of religion were made by popular consensus with Holy Writ the only authority. "It is not altogether as in our fathers' time," they said, recalling the days when the word of the elders was final in every matter. Still some structure had to be applied, and no one knew exactly how to go about this.

"Who is there to help us organize?" they asked each other. "And where shall we have our church?"

As if to comply with their need, it happened that Andrew Buller's son, Fred, had built a small barn on upper Thirteen Mile Creek. The barn was no longer used, and young Buller offered it as a place of worship.

"By George, that will make us a good meeting house!" exclaimed Poltauwitz, whose temperament was generally agreeable. "*Ich unterstütz* — I second the motion."

So the decision was made. The infant congregation had then to take up the matter of a charter. In August of that year, H. A. Bachman, a German-born clergyman and professor of theology, came from Dakota at their request to instruct them in the writing of a church constitution.

The news of Bachman's arrival was received with the sensation of a minor Pentecost. At once the women began to prepare delicacies for a great feast, while the men cleaned the interior of the barn and built make-shift plank benches. The thought that one of God's messengers had come to them aroused among the Mennonites a feeling of renewal — for at last that most necessary element of their worship, a minister, had been supplied. The children, too, as much as anyone else, felt the excitement of the event.

"I wonder if he will look like Kaufman-Sep or one of the others," Eddy mused as he and Hardwig rode beside Henry in the buggy seat on that important Sabbath morning.

"Schmidt says he is a very handsome man," Henry replied. "He is a real German."

For Eddy the trip to the barn chapel took altogether too long. The road trailed like a dusty vine among the rough, red hills that lay along the creek. Meadowlarks sang in the early sunshine; and snipes — like their Dakota cousins — voiced their familiar, frenzied cries. Nearby was a prairie dog town where small, furry sentinels barked a warning from their yellow clay mounds.

Eddy could hear his father and Klaus conversing as they drove some distance ahead with Caroline and the girls in the grain wagon. In similar fashion, Roger and Katie followed with their children.

"Who is that?" Klaus asked John as they passed two lonesome houses standing side-by-side near the creek, where a female figure was laboring with a pair of enamel-coated water buckets.

"She's a spinster. They call her 'Butcherknife Annie.' And the other place belongs to a man named Graham," John informed Klaus. Then, lowering his voice, he added something that the others could not hear — at which Klaus laughed loudly.

The heat had already become intense when the horse-drawn procession approached the stable. Eddy could see the Buller women in their strange little white caps, carrying covered dishes into the single-room building.

Although the doors and windows were left open, the interior still bore the scent of livestock. Perspiring beneath their dress coats, the parishioners took their places upon rough-hewn benches, their feet resting on the packed, earthen floor. After the customary good-natured conversation, Schmidt rose to address the assembly.

"We are pleased," he announced, "to welcome our distinguished brother Bachman, who has come so far to share God's Word with us and to assist our endeavor to form a church."

Bachman was indeed a handsome man — erect and rather young-looking with a dark goatee and intense, compassionate eyes. There was about him an air of calm understanding and dignity. Eddy was intrigued by the minister's dark coat and stiff clerical collar. When he spoke, Bachman's voice was soft and articulate. The formal German would have seemed affected, spoken by anyone else. But for a learned man — a "preacher" — it was considered most proper and acceptable.

The content of the sermon that followed was of little interest to the eleven-year-old boy. His gaze wandered outside to where the meadowlarks continued their intermittent songs. He wondered if they were happy because it was Sunday — because of the new preacher's arrival. Or did they sing for another reason? Did they even know about God?

After the banquet that followed the service, the adult congregation once more assembled — this time to assail the matter of the charter. Soon growing tired of playing outdoors with the other children, Eddy wandered inside to listen to the proceedings. He saw John carefully copying something into a record book while Bachman dictated the words. Although the minister's voice was gentle, it was evident to Eddy that the harmonious good humor that had existed beforehand had now been replaced by feelings of uneasiness — even anxiety.

"But if there must be foot washing, the young people will not want to take communion" he heard Schmidt protest. "They are embarrassed to wash feet in front of older people."

Bachman fingered his beard reflectively. "It is true," he admitted. "Many congregations are dispensing with it — or at least making it optional."

"*Juscht so!*" Buller fumed at once, his face reddening. "And how can you dispense with Holy Scripture? Did not the Master, Himself, say that those who would not humble themselves would have no part in Him?"

Eddy's interest was now thoroughly aroused. Within himself he sided with Buller. After all, he reasoned, it was in the Bible, wasn't it?

Young Christ Buller rose quickly to his feet to support his father's argument, speaking in terse, rapid phrases. "God's Word is the only foundation. There can be no compromise. If we reject His word, we reject Him." Abruptly punctuating his remarks, he dropped back into his seat. The sides were now clearly drawn, and it was obvious that the conservatives would not relent.

Next, Schmidt's wife rose to speak on behalf of her husband's contention for optional foot washing: "I think it is not right to demand such a thing. The Savior was only giving us an example. He did not fix it to be a commandment."

"What do you know of Holy Scripture?" Buller stormed. "Go back and learn your ABC's, woman! You are too proud to wash our feet, are you? I tell you there is not enough water in the ocean itself to wash your sins away."

Flustered and humiliated, poor Mrs. Schmidt resumed her seat and gazed upon the bare clay floor of the stable. The entire congregation fell into a nervous silence. Buller, perhaps realizing the brutality of his words, left the building to seat himself upon the tongue of his wagon, where, muttering to himself, he began to whittle a small stick of wood.

The meeting by this time was reduced to a general uproar. Others began to wander outdoors, speaking and gesturing emphatically to whoever would listen. Bachman made his way toward Mrs. Schmidt.

"I guess now we will have no church," she lamented as he placed his hand upon her shoulder.

"There, now!" he consoled. "These things are inevitable at such a time. It is like turning a stone in a field. First you try to lift one end. If that doesn't work, you try again another way, until at last you can move it. Then the field can be plowed."

John, meanwhile, was pleading with Schmidt. "Someone is going to have to give way. Otherwise everything will be lost. . . . There is no reasoning with that kind of obstinacy."

"So it has to be," Schmidt relented, pulling on the tips of his mustache. "Let them be satisfied."

Later, after Bachman had called them to prayer, the session resumed; and the article pertaining to compulsory foot washing was inserted into the charter.

"All that remains now to be considered is a name," he told them. A pause followed, after which Poltauwitz-Netha spoke:

"I have been thinking on this matter. . . . Our church was born in a stable, just as was the Christ-child. It should be called Bethlehem."

"Quite appropriate!" Bachman replied, smiling. The others nodded agreement, and the church's name became Bethlehem.

Finally came the signatures of all the adult members — those who had received baptism and their first communion. There were, of course, the parent heads of the five established families. But, in addition, were the names of a number of other participants . . . young Gerhardt Boese, married to one of the Buller girls; Fred Schultz, a bachelor from Avon, South Dakota; his cousin, John Boese; Fred Buller, who had donated the barn; and a man named Francis Miller, who had first driven out to his homestead from Glendive on a bicycle.

These, along with a few of the older children who had already taken their catechism, signed the grand document. John Boese became the church's first Sunday school superintendent, and John Schwartz — the blacksmith's son — its first secretary.

The English

As fall approached, John discovered frequent visitors at his new coal mine in the creek bank. They came from all directions, making trails across his land toward the gaping man-made tunnel that opened from the steep clay enbankment. Sometimes the amateur miners drove steam tractors, but usually they came with teams and wagons. The mine was not as large as the one on Roger-Jäk's land, but it probed into the same expansive vein of lignite coal that was the only source of fuel for the area homesteaders. And because the vein was well-exposed at that particular place, it was considered common property for all who needed winter fuel. At first John attempted to discourage the mining by charging each trespasser thirty-five cents per load. But this practice was stopped by a directive from the land office, stipulating that the coal was reserved by the government and could not be sold. So all day long John was forced to listen to the dull powder shots that rumbled from beneath his ground.

"They have no right to be there," Henry protested. "It's our land, isn't it?"

John, equally annoyed, could only shake his head. "There's nothing we can do. If we try to run them off, we will have lifelong enemies."

But Henry, not easily placated, ventured toward the mine to observe the intruders and was met with rifle shots. Quickly he made his way back to toward the house as bullets stung the grass around his feet.

The shots, he later discovered, came from the guns of the mischievous Babb brothers, whose father homesteaded a mile up the creek and who claimed to have dug the first coal from that particular bank before John owned the land. Later, when it became winter, Babb himself walked to John's place to borrow "chawn'" tobacco and, in his own rustic way, extended friendship to the newcomers.

Clem Livingstone, another neighbor, had come as a squatter before the land was opened for homesteaders, living in a log house close to the Clay Butte. With him came his white-bearded father, who was said to have been a veteran of the Confederate Army.

For the first time the Mennonites were compelled to interact with neighbors who were totally unlike them. The Mennonites labeled these people simply, "the English," although in truth most were Irish, Scottish, German or Scandinavian — people who, like the Mennonites, had come to find land and establish farms. But, by contrast, most of these settlers had thoroughly divorced themselves from the language and customs of their ancestors, speaking and behaving now as did the majority of pioneer

Americans.

Among them was Teddy Huffman, an extremely heavy man, who had come from Carolina and settled with his children on the table land northeast of John's farm. It was said that he could hold a swarm of live bees with his bare hands.

In contrast to the large families, were lonely bachelors like Pete McCann — "One-eyed Pete" — who lived alone in a shack to the south. Claiming to be a veteran of the Union infantry, he pursued a solitary and eccentric existence, often tormented by cruel neighborhood children and shunned by everyone else because of his hideously-deformed, sightless eye.

Goliath Smith's homestead touched the northwest corner of John's land. Smith was known for his volatile temper, evidenced by loud curses that he yelled at his team in the field. . . . He could be heard all the way to John's house on still days. Mrs. Smith, however, exhibited a remarkable refinement and entertained the neighborhood young people often at her house, where she performed piano music for them. It was Eddy who, more than the rest, found Mrs. Smith's accomplishments inspiring. In later years, after he lived and studied in Chicago, he was to recall her piano technique as excelling even that of the great Paderewski.

The already-mentioned Butcherknife Annie and her neighbor, Graham, held adjoining homesteads near the Bethlehem barn-church. The story that John had told Klaus — which the children had not heard — was that Graham's romantic advances were not kindly received by Annie and that he had barely escaped castration at her hands. The Mennonites saw them occasionally on Sunday mornings and would wave to them — but never sought friendship.

The Matt Geiger family, because of their German background and their location at the halfway point on the road to Glendive, soon became valued acquaintances of the Mennonites, and brother Henry found a new friend in young Louie Geiger.

There were many other families: Fatzinger; Fuller; Sutton and Boffman; and a collection of single men: Jerry Steffan; Johnny Knox; Charlie Johnson — an ex-cowboy who lived on an old Indian campground below the Clay Butte; young Joe Ziegler, who, John learned later, had built the Slagel house; Freddy Gibbs — a sheep-man who came to visit on foot one winter day and walked home in a snowstorm. There were the two *Ochsemänner* — Swanson and Scarpholt — so nicknamed because both farmed with oxen.

And there were those for whom the desolation of the prairie proved overwhelming. George Klinger remained in his homestead shack only one night. Stopping at John's house on the following morning, he announced that he was returning to South Dakota. "Wind and coyotes!" he lamented. "I've had enough." He left his groceries with Caroline and departed from Montana forever.

A sailor named Ward came with his wife, Retah, to establish a post office near a small hillside spring. Confessing that he could never be happy on dry land, he, too, soon left. The post office, however, to which he had given his wife's name, remained; and the table land upon which it stood ever after bore her name — Retah.

Merle Long, who homesteaded near the Retah post office, was among those who came and remained. His propensity toward practical jokes reached no limit. Passing a group of men fighting a grass fire near the McCone Ranch on Burns Creek, he casually lit his pipe tobacco and then, as he later told with great delight, threw the match upon the unburned side of the fire break. Returning later, he found the entire meadow burned black.

But to John's family, none of these individuals was more memorable — or a greater friend — than Louie Knutson. Young Louie made himself known the day he rode to their house on horseback wearing a pair of chaps and a wide-brimmed cowboy hat. "Hullo! My name's Knutson," he introduced himself with homely formality. "Thought I'd make myself acquainted."

His boots seemed almost to make the floor of the small house tremble, and the children were intrigued by the spurs that were fastened to the man's heels. "A real cowboy! they thought gleefully, longing to ask questions but so thoroughly awestruck that all they could do was stare."

"Yep, these boots saved me from many a snake bite," Louie drawled, proceeding to make himself comfortable in a wooden chair. "They tell of one cowboy, though, who died; and nobody knew for sure what killed him. . . . Well, another feller puts on the dead man's boots and it turns out he up an' dies the same way. Third man does the same thing — same pair o' boots! Well, come to find out — they cut them boots open and there's a live rattler curled up inside just as cozy as can be. Yes-sir!" The listeners shuddered, half believing the outlandish tale. "So they tell me, anyway," the would-be cowboy concluded with a wry grimace.

That was how they came to know Louie. He spent that evening with them, telling stories, and, when he grew tired of the stories, he started singing, of all things, a railroad song — "Come All Ye Rounders" — tapping out the rhythm against his spur, which lay crosswise upon the opposite knee.

"Well," he drawled at last, preparing to leave, "I'll see y' again I reckon. Be good to yourself." True to his word, he returned often to entertain them, announcing himself with a vehement pounding upon the door, once making the little house shake by hitting it with a sledge hammer and roaring with laughter at the consternation he aroused. But he was always welcome because of the good

138

humor and friendship he brought to their isolated lives; and they rewarded him with eggs, jars of cream and homemade preserves.

Although the family soon determined that Louie was not a real cowboy, they did see some genuine examples of those men one day, riding in a group along the Redwater Trail, headed for the annual roundup at the famed HS Ranch. But these were part of a way of life that was already becoming obsolete. Within a short time the homesteaders would claim all of the still unfenced prairie, and the roundups would cease forever.

The Coming of Winter

There was no crop that first year except for a little flax that John managed to sow in the newly-plowed ground and some poppy seed that Caroline planted. The flax did not yield well because it was late and the summer was dry, and, when the poppies came into bloom, Louie Knutson picked them for a bouquet. But now that he had broken sod and prepared his fields for the following spring, John felt encouraged, and approached his new life with revitalized interest and optimism.

Autumn came with its shortened days and chilly nights. Still there was no rain, and the air was filled with smoke. The smoke began first only as a faint, almost pleasant scent upon the still air. But as the days progressed, a veil-like haze grew against the sun and hung about the house like some great, ominous web.

It was on such a day that Roger came walking toward John's house, his shadow moving like a cautious spider through the dark, listless mass. "Is this the end of the world?" he asked, trying to joke. But his eyes betrayed apprehension.

John smiled faintly as the two of them sat together by the small kitchen table. Caroline brought them coffee.

"Your son Willy has nice hair," she said in an attempt to dispel the gloom.

Roger looked up distractedly. "What? . . . Oh, yes — yes! Willy, he has nice hair . . .But have you ever seen such smoke as this, day after day?"

"They say there is a forest fire in Idaho," John said. "Three million acres have been burned. That's what makes the smoke."

The smoke was indeed the result of the Great Idaho Fire of 1910. But the prolonged dry spell caused other fires — prairie fires — one of which came very close to the Mennonite settlement, blackening the countryside from the Missouri River to the Yellowstone. John watched it come that day — a fringe of gray, penetrated by flashes of red, upon the windy divide. At once a procession of wagons and riders was headed in the fire's direction. Among them John discerned Louie Knutson.

"Prairie fire!" he cried, reining his horse to a halt in front of the door where John stood. "That wind's really pushing it!"

Quickly John and Henry hitched the team while the little boys collected woven gunny sacks and shovels.

"How did it start?" Henry asked Louie as they hurried toward the sandhill spring.

"Sheepherder at Fort Peck!" Louie growled. "Damn fool was lightin' his pipe and the grass caught on fire!"

Struggling against heat and wind, they filled wooden barrels and proceeded toward the open hills to meet the flames' advance.

They were greeted by a soot-painted individual who waved at them with a shovel. John recognized him as the old Canadian German whom they called "Alte Urau."

"'Bout time you got here!" he bellowed. "I bin fightin' fires since half past twelve!"

John was tempted to retort, but the fire demanded full attention. The flames hissed like serpents in the grass as the men beat upon them with the wet sacks.

At the same time, Ziegler and Fuller built a headfire in a field of ripe oats. "What the hell's the matter with you?" someone yelled. "That's a man's crop!"

"By God it's gonna burn anyhow!" Fuller snapped.

Returning to the spring, Eddy and Hardwig soon refilled the barrels to take to the men. Louie soaked a large tarp in the water and drew it behind his horse as he galloped along the front edge of the blaze.

Others joined the fight as the fire neared their dwellings until it passed over the hills, leaving smoking lumps of burned animal dung and ant hills in its wake. The country looked hideous, smelling after stale ashes; but the settlers' houses, most of which were protected by plowed fire guards, were saved.

* * *

It was, as always, early morning when Caroline rose. She moved quietly about the small house so as not to disturb John or the sleeping children. The season was getting on toward winter now, and a layer of frost lay upon the ground outside the door. She would have to send one of the boys to get water from the well in the creek. . . . The bucket was nearly empty.

Quickly she had the fire going in the stove and began to grate potatoes to fry with fresh eggs for breakfast. The despair she had felt initially upon coming to this place had somewhat eased. Yet

Caroline dreaded the approaching winter and the loneliness that would inevitably accompany it. It was a loneliness she could confide to no one — not to the children — not even to John. But to herself she would murmur . . . "Oh, Caroline! Where are those good days? The good times with Mama and Papa, with brother Jackob? Where is the joy that you once had?" And she would look at the tea canister with the Chinese lettering — and remembered."

She paused for a moment at the window to examine the new day and discerned a movement upon the horizon as two horses with riders approached the house. "John, someone is coming," she called.

Aroused from their sleep, John and the others quickly dressed. *"Wer kann's sin?"* they asked. Who could be traveling so early? John stepped out onto the porch as a young man, dressed in rather shabby cowboy garb and wearing a pistol, dismounted. He was followed by his companion — a young woman.

"Morning!" the stranger called to John. 'Might we trouble you for breakfast?"

Warily John nodded consent and invited them indoors, where both riders collapsed upon the homemade bench by the stove and immediately fell asleep.

Caroline quickly began frying the potatoes and eggs and cut some homemade bread, noting the strangers with apprehension. "If they should try to rob us . . .!" she whispered in German to John, who sat quietly beside the table, eyeing his shotgun that leaned by the door but making no reply until the food was prepared.

"Did you come from the HS?" he asked after he had reawakened them. There was only a muffled reply, which could be discerned neither as an affirmation nor a denial, as the couple hastened to eat.

Having finished in a short time, the two rose to their feet, upon which the man withdrew a large wallet and threw a pair of paper bills upon the table. Then, without speaking, he left the house.

At once Caroline's suspicions turned to pity. Seizing the money, she attempted to return it. "You have not to pay us," she began in her faltering English. But the woman immediately clasped Caroline's hands in her own, saying in a kindly voice, "No, you keep it." For an instant a gentle look passed between the two. Neither spoke again, and soon the strangers had mounted their horses and ridden out of sight. The family never saw them again or ever learned their names. Where had they come from? Why had they ridden in the night until they were so weary? It was common then for travelers to stop at homes along the road. But John and Caroline could never forget the two riders that had come to them that morning in such a strange and piteous way.

* * *

Winter came earlier than expected or desired. It was a December Sunday when John and Roger took their sleds and teams across the five miles of snow that lay between their farms and Poltauwitz-Joe's. In every direction lay a limitless expanse of white, broken only by an occasional naked shrub or sandstone outcropping. The day was a pleasant one, clear and bright with sunshine. But it passed quickly for the visiting families, and winter darkness settled before anyone was prepared to leave.

"You can easily stay the night with us," Joe offered. "It will be easier traveling in the morning."

This proposition sounded most inviting to the younger members of the party. A night away from home would be a welcome break in the monotony. But John and Roger declined.

"Our fires are banked. By morning everything will be cold," John said, crushing the children's hopes.

"Anyway," Roger added, "the stars are out. It's a clear night."

So the two sleds with their human cargo began the homeward journey across the snow.

Ida and Lydia chatted gaily with Roger-Emma, discussing fresh gossip they heard from the Poltauwitz girls, while the boys called out gleefully to one another from the sleds. To the smallest ones it seemed almost as though they were moving backwards as they lay bundled at the bottom of the open vehicles.

The horses had barely reached the table, however, when a menacing wind began to stir the loose snow. "Can you see the trail?" John called out to Roger. But the wind took away his voice.

A faint, anxious reply came to his ears. "I think we're lost."

Now a silent fear, colder than the December wind, chilled the travelers. "John!" Caroline turned a terrified look toward her husband.

"We will freeze — all of us!" Lydia wept as the wind forced itself through their garments.

Frightened and uncertain, they stopped momentarily and gazed into the dismal veil of flying crystals. Were they to continue, they might well find themselves even further from their destination. Yet to remain could only mean death. Each prayed silently the prayer that is always ready upon the lips of people in despair. If there was a God, it was in His hands, and at such times few people can allow themselves to doubt.

A burst of renewed hope came upon them when Roger at length spotted a lone haystack. "We can wait here for the wind to go down," he said. "At least we will have shelter."

But the wind persisted. After they had waited for what semed an hour's duration, a small conference was called.

"If we stay much longer," John cautioned the others, "we will freeze, regardless. There may yet be a chance if we go on." Roger pondered for a moment and then agreed.

So they continued. Again the horses were urged on against the storm until the ground began to slope beneath them. "We're going downhill," John reassured them. "The wind won't be so strong now."

Suddenly Roger's team, which had been moving ahead of the other, stopped.

"What is it?" John called out.

"I don't know," came the bewildered reply. "They will not go on."

When no amount of coercion would induce the animals to proceed, the two men dismounted and, upon examining the ground ahead, discovered a large gulf. "The horses knew!" Roger announced excitedly. "They saved us from being killed!"

We must be in familiar country then," John observed. "Let them go where they want."

Returning to their seats, the drivers allowed the animals to pull in whatever direction their instincts chose until at last a building loomed ahead through the flying mass of snow. It was Roger-Jäk's barn.

Prosperity

In the spring Eddy went with John to buy seed from Ziegler, the man who had built the Slagel house. Ziegler's homestead lay a few miles across the hills to the southwest — the direction from which, John observed, the rain clouds usually came. They found Ziegler — a short, stocky individual — digging postholes and setting cedar posts for a fence. Nearby, another man was driving a team with a disc across newly-broken sod.

"I understand you have some grain for sale," John announced after he had drawn the team to a halt.

"Yep!" came the curt reply. "It's good seed, too, especially when you put it in fresh breaking."

For a time John and Ziegler talked about Montana, fences and the weather. "The stuff's in the grain'ry over yonder if y' care to have a look at it," Ziegler said then and turned to Eddy. "Run out to my brother there in the field and fetch the key from him. . . . We always keep the thing locked up."

Sensing the importance of his mission, Eddy hurried toward the field and waited until the disc approached. Without stopping to inquire, the driver extended his hand with the key ring toward Eddy, who grasped the shiny object and hurried back.

"This looks like it might be a decent year for crops," Ziegler said as they walked toward the granary. "Lots of folks are wantin' seed."

Eddy watched as the key was inserted into the lock. The door opened easily on its new hinges. Then, with an abrupt exclamation, Ziegler grasped a stick and poked it into the building. After a moment the stick was withdrawn; and Eddy beheld a huge, brightly colored snake coiled around it. Ziegler hurled the hissing caduceus into the grass at a distance. "Bullsnake!" he commented without emotion. "I never kill 'em. . . . Help keep down the mice."

John bought the grain and planted it in the past year's breaking. But the rains were not plentiful, and the hot July wind soon shrivelled the young crop. The following summer, however, was another matter. June was a wet month with gentle winds and cool nights. It looked at last as if it might be a "decent" year.

* * *

The summer of 1912 was one of great events. The crop was especially bountiful that year; it snowed on the Fourth of July; and Uncle Soft brought his family from Kansas. . .

Uncle Soft, huge, imposing and cumbersome — his facile wit always directed toward the telling of some incredible story for the entertainment of anyone who would listen — boasted a personal account of $16,000 upon his arrival in Montana. With this prodigious sum he built a farm three miles south from that of his brother-in-law John. His hospitality was as boundless as his humor, both fostered by a magnanimous heart; and when Independence Day approached, he invited all of his new neighbors as well as his relatives — the *Freundschaft* — to celebrate with a keg of beer and a side of beef.

"I let it age for a few days first," he proclaimed as he sliced it with a huge knife. "It is always best when it smells a little."

Soft — or Zafft, as his name was originally — took pride in showing off his vegetable garden, which he irrigated from an open spring. He planted an orchard, as well, with peach, apple and cherry trees. "*Ach,* so good peaches we had in Kansas," he raved. "But this country is new, John. Here our sons will make even better farms and raise many children." He then proceeded to tell of the Aultman tractor he had ordered for use during threshing and of the engineer named Graber, who would come from Kansas to run the great machine.

Like the others his expectations were limitless. But he would soon see them all perish with the relentless cold and drought that made farming in Montana a hopeless venture for many. And when the depression years dashed his hopes and left them in shreds, he would be left broken-hearted and penniless. This was Soft. Born in Poland of German parents, independent and jovial, he ambled about like an enormous potato sack with his bent frame deformed in a fall from a scaffold years before. The Mennonites laughed with him and adored him, still telling of the time he had led the entire congregation from the Dakota church when the meeting became tedious. Now he was among them again, telling his mirthful tales with a mock seriousness that made him a natural entertainer.

"*Es war einmal ein Mann...*" Thus he customarily began his narratives, as everyone's attention came to focus upon him... "There was once a man who was told by a fortune teller that he was to die upon a certain day."

"Ahh!" gasped the listeners.

"So, he went home then to wait until the day approached; but, when it came, he woke up feeling good as new. 'Well, there is nothing to this, after all,' he thought. So he decided to load up some barley and take it to town to sell..."

By now even the children had left their play and began to listen, while Soft rubbed his nose and continued in his languorous sing-song voice:

"Well, this man starts out and everything seems fine until — hup! The cart hits a stone in the road and turns over. The driver falls onto the ground, and the barley spills all over the road.... Such nice barley, too!" (Again the audience gasped.) "So there he was; and after he had been there a while, here comes a herd of pigs. They see that good barley and start to eat on it. But the man did not move, because he remembered what the fortune teller had said.... Then, at last, he says to the pigs: 'If only I was not dead, then would I ever fix you!!'"

"*Doch nyet!*" Already whimsical from the beer and the warm weather, everyone laughed in delight at the tale's unexpected conclusion.

"*Ach!* How you can lie!" Marhinja Bas reproved her husband, smiling herself at the frivolity.

"*So wird's gesagt!*" So it was told to me," Soft replied, his eyes shining.

It was Roger Jäk who then posed a question for Soft... "So what do you think?" he asked. "Does a man die, then, only when his time comes? Or can he die at any time?" This was an issue that had caused debate as long as anyone could remember. Soft thought deeply for a moment, his faced buried beneath his heavy beard. At last he spoke:

"There is a story that is told," he drawled, "about a traveler who was once walking beside a lake." Curious smiles appeared upon the listeners' faces. "Now it was God's will that someone was to die at that appointed time, and a life was demanded. Suddenly this man heard a voice from nowhere: 'Now is the hour come, and a life must be forfeit.' The traveler, when he heard this, knew

145

that it was his own life that was demanded. So at once he runs to the lake, jumps in and drowns himself!"

"Naa! This is too much!" Marhinja Bas protested again, upon which everyone roared with laughter, and the conversation turned toward other matters.

They were all seated in the open air along the shaded side of the house, where the beer continued to make its rounds, when presently a voice rose above the drone of casual discourse...

"Someone is coming!"

At once every head turned to see...

Approaching the house was a small top buggy, driven by a well-dressed, rather tall man with a neatly-trimmed beard. At once they recognized him as Balzer, an itinerant preacher who had served their congregation the preceding summer. Guilty eyes glanced quickly at the beer glasses.

"*Grüss Gott!*" Balzer addressed them in formal German as he stepped from the buggy. "This seems to be a friendly gathering."

A dismayed sigh caught in Marhinja Bas's throat as she whispered, "Now what will he think of us?"

But Soft, not taken aback, slowly lumbered toward the nearly empty keg and, drawing a glassful of beer, offered it to the minister. "*Du bist auch Deutsch!*" he greeted the newcomer... "You, too, are German."

Balzer, graciously nodding his head, accepted the glass. "Yes," he smiled, "And it has been a long, hot drive." Like Soft, he belonged to that generation of men who knew nothing of ostentation.

The festivities resumed, and the day passed quickly until, at length, dark clouds began to gather in the north.

"They look like snow clouds," John remarked. The others scowled incredulously. It could not be. Yet the air had indeed become uncomfortably cold...

It was then that Klaus, the carpenter, suddenly collapsed in a stupor and had to be carried off to the empty granary.

"Let's go see!" young cousin Herbert giggled when the older men had gone.

"Hold it, kid!" Johnny Soft called to his younger brother in a warning tone. "Let the man sleep."

The younger brother grinned and withdrew.

As the day neared its close the adults continued to talk of the good wheat crop and of the coming harvest that would make them rich. Some of the guests were already preparing to leave when a shout was heard...

"It's snowing!"

At that moment the approaching clouds completely covered the sun, and moist crystals of snow began to fall upon the collection of astonished faces.

146

What the Willows Saw

A massive willow tree grows today along the creek where Pete drowned, its vagrant branches extending over the water that still flows there in the spring and early summer. A pair of decaying limbs that have fallen from the main trunk now lie half submerged in the stream, their decaying bark resembling alligator skin. . . . It is a pleasant spot in June when the afternoon sun warms the steep clay bank where Roger-Jäk once mined his coal. A thick growth of slough grass, buckbrush and wild rosebushes comprises a miniature jungle along the creek bottom. Here buffalo once came to drink, their deeply-worn paths still visible although long overgrown. At a short distance stands a small wooden bridge where a gravelled road leads toward the church; and to the west can still be seen the twin pointed hills, so familiar to those acquainted with the region.

Besides the hills, which Pete would recognize were he to return, there is little that appears as it did on that July day. There was neither bridge nor road then. The church, although planned, had not yet been built; and the willow was merely one of several young saplings clustered along the bank . . .

He was a pleasant youth — very handsome, with dark eyes like his father's. That was how they described Peter Schmidt, C. J. Schmidt's eldest son. Although of a friendly disposition, Pete was a few years older than Henry, which allowed only a polite reserve instead of anything that might be called friendship between the two. It could not have been for any deficiency in his physique that he declined to swim with other young men, for his body was as comely as his face. Yet none of them could think of a time when, even in response to their appeals, he had ever joined them.

Eddy's first verbal contact with Pete occurred early in the second Montana summer when a group of cowboys drove a herd of horses past John's place. Eddy was standing with Henry upon a hill, watching the moving herd, when a rider hailed them. At first they did not recognize him, dressed as he was in chaps, his face shaded by a large hat. Yet, when he called to them a second time, there could be no mistake.

"It's Pete!" Eddy exclaimed as the horse drew up directly in front of them.

The youth's jaspery eyes shone with courteous gentility from beneath the hat. "I'm working at the Cavanough Ranch now . . . five dollars and board. You should join up, Henry."

Henry grinned nervously and picked his nose. "I'm not cut out for that, I guess. I can't quite see myself on a horse."

Pete laughed good-naturedly. "I've got to go. Say hello to your folks."

"He's a good enough fellow, all right," Henry observed as the boy galloped off to rejoin the other riders. "I think he's interested in our Ida."

That was his first visit with them. During the following summer Pete worked for Sam Boese, who farmed a half section of hilly land to the southwest. They saw him often then — like the youth in Gray's "Elegy" — along the creek where he herded Boese's sheep. He came mainly to visit Ida and to bring news, always speaking cordially to John and Caroline, who began to grow fond of him.

Then came the drowning . . .

The July weather was typically hot, and Pete's muscles were sore from the week's labors. He was glad that Sunday had come, giving him a chance to rest. Still that morning there were cows to be milked; and, as usual, they had wandered down to the creek that bordered Roger-Jäk's land. (Roger had since built a new house upon the flat above and no longer lived by the creek.) So Pete rode horseback to fetch them.

A hailstorm during the preceding night had filled the creek; and the water, in spite of its murky color, was enticing. Pete hoped to see Ida after church that day. Surely he would have time to bathe and still finish the milking in time.

He glanced about to be sure he was alone. He listened to the liquid music of the locusts in the crest-headed buffalo grass, blending their song with the water's cold murmur. He heard again the voices of other boys — boys he had known in childhood — calling him to swim with them and laughing because he would not. "Are you afraid?" they mocked him now from his memory.

"No," he replied aloud, "I am not afraid." He looked again at the water. It was so dark he could not see his face in it.

Then, from somewhere deep within him, another voice called. Making sure that the horse was tethered to a post, he proceeded to remove his boots, leaving them and the remainder of his clothing beside the young willows.

The water received his sweat-saturated body, sending a sharp thrill across his skin. It was slightly painful, yet so pleasing. Drawing back, he gasped for air, then plunged headlong into the still, alluring embrace. The water had filled the entrance to Roger's mine, which gaped at him, black and forbidding. He moved toward it until his feet no longer touched bottom.

At that moment he felt an incisive pain as though a knife had been stabbed into his side . . .

Floundering, unable to propel himself, he submerged and rose again in panic. A desperate cry escaped his lips. He looked upward and saw the sky that was so blue and still. The fierce sun glared into his face, and he went under . . .

Beneath the willows the water thrashed and churned

148

momentarily with a sound almost like laughter. Then it became still once again; and the cold, insidious little stream continued on its way toward the far-off river.

* * *

When Pete did not return, Sam Boese's young sons went to the creek and saw the horse grazing alone, still tied to the post. The front of the mine was filled with water, and on the bank lay a man's clothes. It did not take long, after the alarm was given, for the neighbors to gather.

Klaus, as usual, immediately took charge, ordering someone to fetch a rope. "A couple of you boys lower me down and hold on tight," he directed them when the rope arrived. "Hard telling how deep it is, so pull me up when I holler."

He went under and came up at once with a shot. "That stuff's cold as ice," he cried. "I can't see nothin' down there."

"What we need is a hook," Boese proposed; and soon a long-stemmed device was manufactured to probe the water. Again Klaus went to work.

"We found him!" he called out after a short search. "Now all you women turn your heads away. . . . Com'on, boys. I'll need a little help here."

Slowly the hook brought its burden to the surface.

"Careful now! That's good," Klaus's voice boomed.

Soon the sickly-white corpse lay upon the bank, a streak of bright red marking the surface of the skin along the neck where the hook had accidentally penetrated. Eddy looked at the face of the drowned boy who had been alive only a short time before — who had spoken and laughed with them. A shudder of dread mixed with a strange fascination ran through him as he contemplated the old mystery. There was something dreadfully unjust about it all. A young man, who had barely tasted of life, would now never know the fulfillment of whatever dreams or longings he had known. It was not fair at all, Eddy thought. How could it be God's will?

By this time the Schmidt family had arrived, weeping profoundly. "*Was fehlt dem Bu?*" Schmidt cried. "Why did he do such a crazy thing?"

"Our baby — we must take him home," his wife lamented, reaching out to embrace the corpse.

But moving the body presented another problem.

"It has to be recorded," John reminded them.

"Yes — that's so. But who can do that for us?" Boese asked.

"Maybe Reed could do it," Roger suggested. "He's a notary."

Reed, who lived a few miles east, had been known for building the only "legal" or regulation fence in the community — "A fence that a *man* built," he often boasted. Upon his arrival he drew up a paper and asked each adult witness to sign it. Only then could the youth be loaded upon the wagon and taken away.

It was the Sabbath, and the Mennonites had come to break ground for a new church that would be built on the table to the east of Roger's farm. What had been intended as a day of celebration had become an occasion for mourning. . . Pete's body was the first to be laid in what was to become the church cemetery. Above him was later placed a white stone monument that glistened like new snow beneath the ever-returning sun.

Pete's Gravestone.

In the Steps of the Apostles

Since its formation two years earlier, the little church in a stable had been without a regular pastor. A series of various preachers came from time to time to serve the small parish. First among them was Balzer, the itinerant. A dignified man similar to Bachman in demeanor, he had been sent by the Mennonite General Conference and remained with the Montana congregation for part of each summer. In his absence, the worshippers were left mainly to themselves.

It happened one day during this early period that a small buggy came to John's house, and a diminutive, stern-looking man approached the door, introducing himself as the minister of a Lutheran Church at Vida — a small town some distance to the northwest. This introduction was not fully necessary, as something about the propriety and somberness of the man bespoke his profession.

"I have heard," he proceeded, "that the people in this settlement are German, as are those in our parish. Perhaps you would like to join with us for worship."

John at once conducted the visitor to Roger's place where the two Mennonites listened to the clergyman's invitation. "We are of the Mennonite faith," John explained. "We have formed our own church based upon our beliefs. Still we are in need of a minister to bring us God's Word."

At this the little man's jaw stiffened. He looked long and intently at the two Mennonites.

"Perhaps you would want to come and preach to us some Sunday," Roger added.

"*Ach, nein! Das ist verboten,*" the Lutheran declined curtly, rising to his feet and shaking his head to emphasize the refusal.

"So it is always with those Lutherans," John laughed after the minister's abrupt departure. "In Dakota they would even wash off the bench if one of our people had sat in their church."

But another minister — a man named Niemand, who homesteaded in the hills near what was to become the town of Lambert — was more accommodating. Niemand was introduced to the Mennonites through a German family named Pust.

"He is a good preacher," Pust told them, "a Reformer. He will talk to you in your own language."

So John and Roger undertook the fifteen-mile journey through the badlands to visit Niemand.

Finding the small house among the red scoria hills, they were greeted by an attractive, dark-complexioned woman and a small, barking dog.

"Oh, Juno, don't be so rude," she laughingly reprimanded the animal, which she hastily picked from the floor and held to her as though it were a child. "These men won't harm you." Quickly then she turned to her guests . . . "Won't you gentlemen please make yourselves at home? My husband will be in for tea shortly, and we should be happy to have you join us."

Unused to such female refinement, the visitors eyed both the woman and the dog curiously as they entered the house. As his wife had indicated, Niemand soon arrived and shook hands with Roger and John.

"This land is not so good for farming," he laughed. "It seems to be nothing but clay and alkali. A man should raise cattle if he wants to make a living here."

Like his wife he seemed very youthful — small and clean-shaven, with an easy, friendly manner. The tea was soon set, and the four of them sat together while John explained the purpose of the visit.

"Yes," Niemand replied affably. "Brother Pust has told me already of your Christian endeavor. And it is, after all, the love of Christ that is our message. Denominations are secondary always. My wife and I are here to serve our Lord. If we can be of assistance to you, it will be our pleasure."

So it was that Niemand came to minister to the Mennonites.

* * *

Also that summer, a group of Dutch Mennonites from the Silver Lake region in Dakota came to Montana and settled north of the Schweitzers. A restrained contempt felt for each other by both factions had resulted in only limited intercourse for many years and would persist in the form of a generation-long rivalry after the two had merged. The *Plattdeutsch,* as these settlers were called, spoke a dialect of German that was not far removed from Dutch. Hence they acquired the label "Low Dutch" from their Swiss counterparts — a term which the Plattdeutsch detested. Formal High German, used by both groups in church, became the language for any transactions between these two subcultures. Now, by necessity of their mutually small numbers, they would be forced to mingle in one congregation.

The overture was made when a minister named Tieszen paid a visit to John's house. Speaking cordially, Tieszen explained his mission . . .

"The Conference sent me here to form a church. But now I am told that you already have one of your own."

John then produced the book that contained the new charter with the signatures. Tieszen examined it and looked up with a startled laugh.

"Well, then it is done. If the others want to join, all they need to do is sign."

Shortly thereafter a meeting took place at Roger's new house. It did not require much discussion before the newcomers affirmed their intent to join and affixed their names to the charter, making the merger complete. But Low Dutch children eyed the Swiss youngsters with suspicious glances, muttering, "*Plattdeutsch ist besser als Hochdeutsch.*"

As with all human endeavors, large or small, when the survival of a mutually-desirable enterprise is at stake, prejudices remain felt but unspoken. So it was among all but the youngest, who were well-versed in their elders' biases and as yet untrained in social duplicity. The animosities remained to surface later, after the church was on a surer footing.

It was at this time that the enlarged congregation confronted the matter of a new meetinghouse. The location on what was now called Retah Table was chosen for the building, and Klaus, the carpenter — who referred to the Low Dutch contemptuously as *die Gepebel* or "the peasantry" — was to be in charge.

But the Mennonites were poor, and a new church sanctuary required money. Fortunately, a realtor named Phillips donated a ten-acre tract of land for the construction site. C. J. Schmidt, who was well-acquainted with the "English," collected additional contributions from Glendive merchants and corresponded with the Sears-Roebuck mail order firm, which responded with a one hundred-dollar check. It was mid-July, on the afternoon of the discovery of Pete Schmidt's body, that ground was broken for the church.

"If we had done it my way, we could be farther," declared one of the volunteers, as the work began.

"But then we would be too far," John retorted jokingly, referring to a dispute waged over the dimensions of the building.

Hammers clattered noisily upon the hot summer air as if to punctuate the sporadic conversation of the workers. Working upon the structure more or less continually, the parishioners still found time to pursue their necessary farm chores. But harvest was now approaching, and it was essential that the building be completed as soon as possible. So the men took turns, sharing the task as well as the local gossip. They laughed and bantered among themselves, making the project more of a game than a labor. The peaked roof at last emerged upon the crest of the landscape along the old Redwater Trail, which would eventually fall into disuse as an increasing number of barbed wire fences began to segment its course.

Their hearts beat happily, unencumbered by doubt or apprehension, for it was a good year, and the earth gave forth her mighty song of encouragement. Above them they could see the Clay Butte, which seemed to watch their task like some wise sage, austere and ageless — aloof from the transitory schemes of humanity.

"Our Low Dutch friends don't seem to want to help us very much," Poltauwitz jibed, as the group paused long enough for Joe Buller to photograph their work. Indeed, this was no idle observation, for not a single one of the "Silverlakers" was on hand to assist the carpenters.

Although everyone else took a turn at building, Klaus made it clear that the church was his project. *Die Glass Kirche* he called it to the mystification of those who did not know the secret of the many empty whiskey bottles that found convenient disposal between the unfinished walls of the "Glass Church."

The Masterbuilder

A sizable crowd had assembled outside the newly-built church on the morning of the dedication; and, in spite of what would normally have been a time of gladness, a good deal of consternation was in evidence. Reverend Niemand was as yet nowhere to be seen, and the doors of the sanctuary remained closed.

"Why doesn't anyone go in?" whispered a bewildered newcomer to his neighbor.

"The carpenter has the keys," came the disgruntled reply. "And he won't turn them over to anyone but the preacher."

Thus the impatient parishioners debated the matter while Klaus, dressed in a new suit and holding an enormous Bible under his arm, paraded back and forth in front of his building.

Presently Niemand's small carriage entered the churchyard, greeted by a general exclamation of delight and relief. Mrs. Niemand, holding the irascible Juno in her arms, smiled benignly at the crowd that followed her husband toward the church.

"Such a fuss over an animal!" a stern matron scoffed loudly enough for those around her to hear, while Niemand approached the exalted craftsman.

"A fine church you have built for these people," the minister tactfully complimented him. "You have made this day a happy one for them."

Klaus beamed as he reached into his pocket. "I thank you, sir, most sincerely and present you now with these keys in the name of the Father and of the Son and of the Holy Ghost, with my great good pleasure. And for this house of worship, which I have built to the glory of our Lord, I give this new Bible."

So saying, he ceremoniously handed the keys to Niemand; and, when the doors were at last opened, Klaus — the man who would never admit to his illiteracy — placed the huge book upon the sacred desk. For that moment the entire world belonged to him. It was his church — his finest work and achievement; and no one was to question his claim to this grand distinction or to detract from it.

So the church was dedicated with the communion cup and with the hymn *"Was Gott tut, das ist wohlgetan..."* Indeed, what God had done was, as the old hymn said, done well. But Klaus would not allow anyone to forget who had been His foreman.

* * *

It was not long after that John and Roger took Klaus to Glendive to meet the eastbound train. He had been with them for two years, living among them as though he were a family member. But, in spite of the amusement that his often overbearing disposition provided, they began at last to grow weary of his presence. Tolerant of his excessive drinking and of his perpetual hunger for importance, and feeling a kind of pity for his single life, they could not be so brutal as to suggest anything but pleasure at his being there. But, like all drifters, he belonged nowhere and — perhaps sensing this himself — could not long endure a continued stay in any one place.

They paid him his wages — perhaps not a sufficient amount, but all that their means would allow — and spent one last night with him in the way he loved best — at the Niederhof Saloon. But Klaus seemed restless.

"You boys excuse me a while," he told them later that night. "I must have forgot my tobacco at the hotel."

He returned shortly, his hair tousled and his face scratched and bleeding.

"They took it," he wept while the others looked at him in astonishment. "My wallet and all of my money — gone!"

"Someone jumped you?" John asked, helping the man to a chair.

"Right outside — in the alley," groaned the distraught victim. "It happened so quick I couldn't see who they were."

The listeners exchanged incredulous glances, their pity mollified by a mild distrust. But was he capable of going to such lengths to deceive them, they wondered. The story could easily be true; and, if so, they were all but obligated to make some restitution.

"We almost have to take his word for it," Roger concluded after they had talked privately. "Otherwise, we accuse him of lying."

So Klaus was reimbursed and sent on his way...

When, some years later, a visitor came from the settlement

where Klaus had gone to live, John asked the man if he was acquainted with the carpenter.

"Oh, indeed! Everyone knows him there."

John squinted his eyes and asked, with seeming innocence, "Does he still carry that big leather wallet of his? He had it all the time while he was with us."

"Yes, he still has it. There's not another one like it."

"No, there isn't," John laughed.

Savage

Uncle Soft was not the only one of their people who had come that year. John's brothers, Bernhart and Jonath, also moved to Montana as did their childhood comrade, Schenker-Pete. He had managed to smuggle his sons, Bernhart and Carl, onto a boxcar loaded with hay in order to save the cost of two additional fares. When autumn came, the three brothers, together with Roger Jäk and Schenker, formed a caravan of five wagons to haul their wheat to market. It had been a good harvest, worthy even of Soft's new thresher.

"Going to town" generally involved a three-day expedition to either Glendive or Savage — the small railroad settlement to the east. The first day was allowed for traveling, the second for business and the third for the return trip, with evenings reserved for celebration.

It was a momentous day for Eddy when he was told that he could miss school and accompany the men that September. He had heard much about Savage; now he was to see it for himself. Excitement flooded his thoughts for an entire day preceding the trip and allowed him only light sleep that night. Before sunup he was awakened by a series of noises from the kitchen — the clatter of dishes and the grinding of the coffee mill. As he threw on his clothing he heard John's voice:

"So, the boy would rather sleep than go on his trip."

But in a moment Eddy was downstairs, dressed and looking into his father's surprised face.

Still it seemed forever until they were on their way, John taking meticulous notice of every small detail in harnessing his team. The wagon bulged with grain, and every crack in the box had to be stopped with pieces of canvas that John cut and inserted with his pocket knife — not so much as an act of parsimony, but out of a desire to hold on to what was the substance of his life.

"Leave a little for the birds," joked Roger as he waited, observing John's activity from the seat of his own wagon.

"I'll feed the birds!" John snapped and continued his task.

At last the team and wagon were ready, and the grain haulers began their journey. Roger followed behind John as they proceeded up the hill where Jonath, Bernhart and Schenker — the boy who, long ago, had been afraid to go home alone — already waited. With Schenker was his son, Bernhart, who had the same name as Eddy's uncle. There were no exchanges of pleasantries or formalities. Each knew the others' thoughts and habits so thoroughly that verbal greeting became unnecessary.

Later, a sixth wagon joined them.

"Boese! Kommst du mit?" Roger called out to the newcomer. "You also want to sell some wheat."

Boese smiled, happy for the company. "We have a nice day for our trip," he said.

The morning sun had already warmed the ground, and the prairie wind began to chase a few light clouds over the hills. The wagons proceeded across the table and down Burns Creek toward the Bar M Ranch where the teams were allowed to rest and drink. Although autumn was a dry season, the creek remained full and running, its life supplied by many fresh-water springs along its course. There was a ford at a spot on the stream where wagons often had difficulty in crossing the marshy ground.

"We'll need to hitch two teams together," Roger observed as they prepared to relax with coffee that had been brought along in jugs. "That way we'll be sure not to get stuck."

But Schenker and Uncle Bernhart had other matters with which to contend as they warmed their coffee on a small fire.

"It's already too hot," Bernhart complained when he sampled it.

"Well then, mix in some of this from my jug," Schenker laughed. "It's still cold."

This done, each tasted his coffee and, in turn, lifted his head with a grimace.

"Now it's *all* cold!" Bernhart fumed, dashing his jug upon the ground.

The dispute over the coffee was interrupted by the approach of a single-horse top buggy containing two well-dressed men. The horse did not slacken as it neared the ford, the occupants being either inexperienced or in great haste.

"Wait until they hit the water," John told the others. "There'll be some fun."

Plunging into the stream, the buggy tilted to one side and threw the driver from his seat. Instantly the springs recoiled, hurling the other traveler into the opposite direction. The horse, having reached the opposite bank, at once drew to a halt and waited for the two men to pick themselves up, dazed and drenched. Quickly they resumed their trip, pretending not to notice the other travelers for whom they provided such humiliating amusement. By late afternoon the caravan of grain-laden wagons reached its destination.

Savage, Montana, true to its name, was a young and unruly town — a cluster of hastily-constructed buildings with false fronts and plank walks. A collection of railroad workers, their youthful faces made to appear old by dirt, sweat and sunburn, laughed raucously as they walked toward the saloon, their day's labor completed. The teamsters, meanwhile, having left their wagons at the livery barn, entered the roominghouse to arrange for lodging.

"The boy can sleep in the lobby," Eddy heard John tell the clerk. . . . It would be cheaper that way.

Eddy knew enough of the men's habits to anticipate their next venture.

"Come have a drink with us," he heard Uncle Bernhart urge Boese.

Boese — striving to remain true to his Mennonite convictions — hesitated. "No — I better not," he grimaced.

"Well, come with us anyway. We'll buy you a — soft drink."

Eddy followed them into the saloon and saw Bernhart wink to the bartender as he ordered Boese's drink. "Here! You'll like this. It's called benedictine," he explained.

"This is good," Boese laughed, as he sampled the liqueur.

"Well, finish that and we'll buy you another."

Eddy heard a clicking sound that came from a group of noisy cowboys seated about a table at the opposite end of the dimly-lit room. He had seldom seen card games — except for *durak,* which he learned from Caroline — and the earnestness with which these men played fascinated him. Moreover, each had before him a pile of what looked like toy money, which in some cases had accumulated to a considerable amount. The boy drew closer and looked longingly at the poker chips, wishing he would have some of his own to take home.

Among the players sat a singular man, somewhat older than the rest, wearing the largest cowboy hat Eddy had ever seen. He had a friendly face and spoke in a loud but not unpleasant voice. At last the man scraped together his collection of chips and lit a cigar. "I'm calling it quits for tonight, boys," he declared with obvious satisfaction. "Have a round on me."

"Thanks, Bill!" came a matter-of-fact reply. "We'll have a go at it tomorrow."

The man evidently held considerable prestige. Eddy longed to know him.

Rising to his feet, the cowboy went to a small window that reminded Eddy of a bank teller's cage and exchanged the chips for a handful of paper bills. Placing most of the money into a wallet, he laid the remaining currency upon the bar and ordered drinks for the men at the table. Then, turning about, he noticed the half-grown boy.

"Well, what do we have here?" (Eddy felt his heart leap.) "What's your handle, partner?"

Eddy gave his name and, after a series of questions, was able to explain where he lived and why he was in town. Then, gathering his courage, he asked a question of his own . . . "Are you a cowboy?"

"Well, sir," answered Bill as he took a long swallow of whiskey, "you might call me that. At least I rode with the best — old 'Four Eyes' himself — Teddy Roosevelt. . . . Yep, I rode with him to many a roundup. Hi-yah! Hi-yah!" he mimicked, waving his hat so that even the most intoxicated customers turned to stare. "That's how we used to do 'er; an' old Teddy was right in the thick of it . . ."

Abruptly, the cowboy broke off his narrative and took another drink of whisky. A melancholy look swept across his face as he set down the empty glass.

"You know," he said at last, turning toward Eddy with a sad smile, "I once had a boy like you. He was about your age, too." (Eddy stared at him curiously.) "Tell you what I'm going to do . . . I have a small phonograph that used to belong to him. When I get home, I'll send it to you. What was your name, now?"

Overjoyed, Eddy eagerly repeated his name. For a long time he remained near the bar, listening to Bill's stories until the cowboy's companions joined him and Eddy was forgotten. Only as he grew older would he remember the event with profound pity, wondering what had happened to the boy who had been about his age. . .

At last, growing tired of the noise and smoke in the saloon, Eddy returned to the roominghouse and lay down upon the couch, where he fell asleep. Sometime later he was aroused by the sound of excited voices. The front door banged open as John and Uncle Bernhart, followed by the other men, carried Boese into the lobby. Bernhart was tapping Boese's stomach and listening with mock seriousness to the poor man's groans.

"It sounds like appendicitis," he announced drunkenly. "We'll have to operate."

Another groan followed — somewhat louder than those that had preceded it — upon which the landlady appeared to quiet the bedlam.

"We can't help it," Bernhart replied. "We have a sick man here."

"Then get him to his room," the woman commanded with a glare. "It's two in the morning, and you'll wake the whole house."

159

Meanwhile, Schenker was trying to get into his own room where his teenage son, Bernhart — who had gone his own way after their arrival in town — was already asleep with the key. Frightened by the landlady's reproof, Schenker tapped softly upon the door and whispered, "Bernhart! Bernhart!"

Uncle Bernhart, hearing his name being called, came to Schenker's assistance.

"Oh, if it were only Carl," Schenker lamented. "But Bernhart — one can shoot off cannons, and still he won't wake up. Bernhart! Bernhart!"

When at last the youth awoke and let Schenker in, the house became quiet. Eddy had begun to sleep again when he heard a severe pounding at the front entrance.

"Will somebody open this damn door?" an angry voice demanded.

Eddy, frightened by the speaker's tone, did not move; and the pounding continued until another voice came from upstairs:

"What the hell's goin' on down there?"

"Somebody wants inside!" Eddy managed to call out, his voice trembling.

"Let the drunken fool in," ordered the second voice. "He forgot his key."

Quickly Eddy was on his feet and opened the door as the supplicator stumbled inside, cursing and grumbling, and made his way up the stairs.

On the following day the wheat was sold, and John deposited a check for $138.75 in the First State Bank of Savage. The wagons were then loaded with loose lumber, sacks of flour, rolls of barbed wire and a variety of other supplies that included small kegs of pickled herring — a prized delicacy. The return trip in the morning was weary, mostly uphill and against a strong wind that seemed oblivious to everything in its path.

For weeks afterward Eddy waited in vain for his phonograph. But he never again saw or heard from the cowboy named Bill.

Bold Rider

While adults were concerned with matters of adulthood, plying themselves in an endless contest with the land and with each other, there was a generation of boys who found in those days an opportunity for unrestrained happiness. For them it was a time of joy and innocence, of foolishness and growth. The prairie was their domain; and they ruled it with their own form of pure, youthful democracy. Eddy and Hardwig were part of this company of young adventurers that also included the Roger boys, Paul Schenker and Eddy Antelop. (The last-named of these was the son of another Dakota emigrant, Antelop, the auctioneer.)

Although not exempt from the adult tasks of plowing, fencing and haying, they inevitably found time to devise their own adventures, amusing themselves with games known and played universally by boys in every time and in every country. Remarkably incongruous with the anti-military doctrine of their parents' faith were their improvised war games in which they pretended to be soldiers or Indians fighting with stick weapons. And benefiting from what was still something of a frontier existence, they were able to enact their juvenile dramas upon an authentic stage.

They pursued each other across dusty buffalo wallows and along trails that led them among dense growths of bull berry and thorn bushes. They fought their imaginary enemies upon small knolls and clay banks, hid behind sandroacks and decaying buffalo skulls and at times nearly stumbled upon an occasional rattlesnake.

Eddy was often their leader, having absorbed all he could from books on woodcraft by Ernest Thompson Seton and from texts that glamorized the heroes of the American West:

Dead! Is it possible? He, the bold rider;
Custer, our hero, the first in the fight . . . *

He had read the poem often and studied the picture of the gallant general who had faced death with two blazing pistols. . . . It took but little to convince him that he was himself that "bold rider."

For his Indian adventures Eddy made a bow of chokecherry wood, which he decorated with special markings, and arrows with tips cut from barrel hoops. The other boys frequently imitated these patents, even to the point of cutting identical, although superfluous, decorations into their own weapons.

When they grew tired of such sports, they hunted gophers and rabbits, dug "Indian" turnips and ate wild fruit in the form of

* "Custer's Last Charge" by Frederick Whittaker (excerpt).

clustered red "buffalo" berries and chokecherries that grew to be the size of grapes. Some herbage proved less delectable. One day Eddy found a vetch-like plant growing along a cow path. It bore small, bean-like pods, which he picked and ate. Before reaching home he found himself besieged by virulent stomach cramps, causing him to fall to the ground and vomit, thus ending for a time his botanical curiosity.

His hunting impulses were similarly and permanently overcome one winter. For months he had admired the picture of a twenty-two-caliber rifle, the "Stevens Favorite," in a Montgomery Ward catalogue. At last he prevailed upon John to order it for Christmas and spent nearly every day that winter tracking rabbits in the snow — rabbits that were a welcome addition to the dinner table. His marksmanship, however, was not always exact. On one occasion a wounded rabbit managed to elude him, leaving a crimson trail upon the snow. When Eddy at last found the creature, it had lost of good deal of blood and lay struggling in pain and terror. When Eddy raised the rifle to shoot, the rabbit cried out pitifully — a cry that would haunt him for the remainder of his life. Like Thoreau he returned home, put away the Stevens Favorite and never hunted again.

Nor was his life without its mishaps. On two occasions he was nearly killed. The first of these was when he and Hardwig were returning from the pasture with the cows and their small dog, *Funke* (Spark), carelessly ran beneath the feet of one of the cumbersome animals. Eddy sought to retrieve the puppy from the dangerous hooves when, without warning, the startled cow kicked against the boy's head.

Later he was conscious of the sound of voices as in a dream, distant and vague — Caroline weeping and Roger-Jäk saying, "I don't think he will make it."

"Yes," he determined with silent affirmation. "I will make it."

By morning he was awake and learned that he had been unconscious for two days . . .

Another time Eddy was riding the plow east of the house when the horses, frightened suddenly by a bullsnake's harmless movement, stampeded with the machine. He clung to his seat until the plow struck a rock and hurled him to the ground, breaking his collar bone — a bone that would be fractured twice again during his lifetime.

Domestic animals were always a part of his life. There were the dogs with whom he found untiring companionship — *Funke* and Funke's mother, who bore the Russian name *Sutschke*. It was Sutschke who boldly and successfully saved her pup from coyotes during the first winter in Montana. Aroused by her vehement barking, Henry and Eddy found her snarling menacingly at her assailants while the tiny Funke cowered behind his mother.

To Eddy the dogs seemed endowed with almost human personalities. To John, however, the animals merely represented a useless waste of food. For that reason, which he did not bother to explain to Eddy, he abandoned young Funke in Glendive, thinking to rid himself of the hungry mongrel for good. Heartbroken, Eddy had at length begun to reconcile himself to his pet's loss when Funke — much thinner but with undiminished vitality — reappeared in the yard, having found his way back over the road which had taken him away. Not long afterward both dogs mysteriously died. Eddy lamented their loss until Marhinja Bas, touched by the boy's despair, told him that John had admitted — even boasted — of poisoning them. It was the only time that Eddy dared rebuke his father.

His disposition resembled John's in many ways. Like his father he was a reader, thinker, craftsman — always probing with an empirical curiosity and always willfully adamant about what he believed. From Caroline he had inherited an alacrity of wit and activity as well as a boundless reserve of energy — which, however, was not always directed toward practical matters. Sometimes when he grew tired of the dullness of his companions, he retreated to the creek to be by himself with his dreams and secret thoughts, unaware that such clandestine fantasies were typical of other imaginative souls.

* * *

Since his arrival in Montana his education was centered at the Independent School, which lay three miles from his home. At school he found himself among an element that until then had been altogether unknown to him. It consisted of a roguish collection of cursing, backwoods boys who spat tobacco juice and derided each other with the same profane vulgarisms they heard from their own illiterate parents. Here Eddy was at first lost, uneasy and frightened; and his dreams of vicarious bravery quickly wilted.

Yet there came a time when his latent courage was to be shown in a sudden and unexpected way. It happened in the winter when John and Caroline returned to Dakota with Roger and Katie for a short visit. Henry had gone with them to prepare for entrance into the Freeman Academy, leaving Eddy alone with Hardwig and the sisters to tend the stock and watch the house. Early one night during their parents' absence, the children were seated about the table, upon which stood a single kerosene lamp. A sharp rap sounded upon the windowpane.

When they turned to look, five grotesquely-painted faces appeared against the glass.

"Indians!" the girls screamed and turned pale.

Eddy, too, felt the terror. But it was drowned by a sudden surge of fierce anger. Thinking only of the family's safety, he seized the kindling axe and thrust himself through the doorway to confront the intruders.

He met with shouts and appeals for him to stop.

"Eddy — no! It's only us!"

The voices were familiar. He paused, holding the axe in readiness until he discovered — first Gust and Erhart Roger, then the Schenker brothers and finally one of the Holtzwarth boys, staring at him, equally terrified.

"It was only a joke — only a joke!" the astonished boys pleaded, amazed at the consequences of their practical mischief.

They looked at the expressions of panic upon their victims' face and at the boy who had often been their playmate — now holding a weapon which he had brandished with such appalling fury only a short while before. Instead of the laughter they had anticipated, there was shame and dismay.

Erhart turned to speak for them as the others withdrew.

"*Verzeihe uns!*" he muttered in apology.

Eddy could not reply. He felt relief mingled with awe, for he had found within himself a kind of courage that he had not known before.

* * *

As he grew older, Eddy's inclination to learn increased — although not often inspired by school. During the summers he pored over Henry's textbooks, finding history and literature most alluring.

"The farm is no place for you," his teacher told him one day. "You like books, and you write well. You must be sure to go to high school."

The opportunity came some years later when Pete Schmidt's younger brother, Johnny, asked Eddy to come with him to Butte, Montana.

"I'm going to high school there," he boasted. "Come along, and we'll room together."

Although he longed to go, Eddy declined. . . . There was no money. Johnny went alone to Butte and died there of appendicitis while his father watched helplessly, listening to his son's pain lament that he was "too young to die."

Eddy was unable to forget the loss of this friend who had wanted education so badly. For that sublime ambition, felt by so few others of the boys he knew, Eddy had shared with poor Johnny.

But music remained Eddy's chief mistress. Since the time he taught himself to play melodies on Uncle Joe's organ in Dakota, he had felt the touch of something in his soul. He never grew tired of listening to Mrs. Smith perform on her piano. And later, when John built a new house and bought him a piano of his own, Eddy was never at a loss for amusement.

A Proposal and a Wedding

John felt a sense of accomplishment as he examined his new house from the top of the carpenter's scaffold. The two-room dwelling that he had first built was intended only as a temporary home — much too small to house comfortably so large a family as his. So in the summer of 1912 he began digging a basement for the new two-story structure, the exterior of which was now nearing completion.

On the rooftop old Katze Tieszen — not the preacher but a neighbor who bore that name — was laying chimney bricks, while on the north dormer of the four-gabled building Henry assisted John's hired carpenter, Bill Clark, in nailing down the rows of new cedar shingles. John's family harbored a secret dislike for the outspoken Clark, a middle-aged man, whom they called "Pumper" after he and John had argued about the proper way to install the new one-cylinder gas pumping engine. But the man was experienced and worked cheap.

"No rain tonight," Pumper predicted as he straightened his back and glanced at the setting sun. "We should finish easy enough tomorrow."

"It all depends on the direction of the wind," Tieszen replied, placing the last brick and scraping the mortar board clean. "You never know when it can switch."

John, thinking about the work that was yet to be done inside, regarded their conversation with only mild interest. He withdrew a box of Velvet smoking tobacco and began to roll a cigarette. The box, now empty, was quickly deposited with a number of its predecessors beneath the eaves of the roof.

"Wind is something I got used to, living in Chicago," Pumper continued, relating one of his many reminiscences to Tieszen. "I was a boy when Lincoln's casket came through town. . . . Seems the weather in Chicago can't even be relied on at a time like that. One minute the sun shines — the next minute it rains . . . I remember that procession, though. There were two old Negro men driving the hearse. They had snow-white hair. . ."

John, who had heard the story before, did not pretend to listen. Instead, he contemplated the land that was now his, the changes that had been wrought in three years' time and the work that remained. In the distance he could hear the pounding of Soft's new tractor with its two-cylinder engine, signaling the start of another threshing season. In the field Hardwig and Eddy were driving the binder through the last of the ripe wheat, most of which now lay in bundles upon the coarse stubble. Further work on the house would have to wait until winter, after the threshing and the coal mining were done.

John's gaze turned toward the west pasture where there was a small grave — a child born earlier that year and gone after only a few days. They had buried it in a homemade coffin, on the hill close to the middle line.

"Well, such is life," John reflected, drawing deeply upon the cigarette.

The day's work completed, the workers retired with John's family to supper in the house, which had not yet been partitioned into individual rooms. As they were seated around the table in what was to become the new dining room, a knock sounded upon the door.

"Go see who it is," Caroline directed Ida, who immediately rose and went to the door.

On the porch, his face barely discernible in the subdued light, stood the new minister, dressed as though to preach a Sunday sermon. He was a young man, newly-ordained — an eastern Mennonite of Hutterite extraction — their first resident pastor. He gave Ida a paternal smile.

"Well — here is my good catechism pupil," he greeted her in a voice sufficiently loud for the others to hear.

Ida beamed self-consciously and invited the lanky visitor to join them.

"If I may," he said, nodding in the direction of the table, "I would like to speak with your father . . ."

It was not the first time that he had openly lauded Ida. Upon his arrival earlier that year, the minister had organized a class to prepare candidates for baptism. This was the church's first such class — and the minister's as well; and Henry, Lydia and Ida were among those chosen for it.

"There is a certain girl among you," he told his pupils after they had met together for a few weeks, "whom I love especially because she is true to God and always knows her lesson. . . . It is our little sister Ida."

Ida, who had never excelled in school work, was elated by this commendation, although it aroused not a slight envy among the other ladies who heard it.

Afterward, the minister managed to find numerous opportunities for visiting Ida's parents. In the haying season he came to help with the work, and during the course of the day Henry observed him glancing frequently in the direction of the pasture where Ida and Lydia visited upon the grass with Emma Roger. Occasionally the girls' voices chimed with sudden laughter, upon which the infatuated clergyman would pause again to scrutinize them and murmur, "A fine girl — yes, indeed!" nodding his head with approval — but failing to take notice of the work at hand until part of the stack sagged and collapsed about his feet.

"Well, my goodness!" he laughed in embarrassment and, with an almost comic alacrity, set about repairing the hay. At that moment a string of horse-drawn vehicles appeared upon the hill, headed toward the church.

"Oh, glory be!" he cried. "Prayer meeting! I forgot all about it."

Dropping the pitchfork, he hurriedly mounted his horse and proceeded to the church with the most unseemly haste.

"We could teach him some good words one of these days," Henry sneered to the others as they watched the departure.

John shared Henry's disdain. Not only did he resent the minister's affected manner, but the man's general appearance was anything but desirable. He boasted no physical comeliness with his ungainly body and long neck. Moreover, there was always a mawkish smirk on his face that made him seem particularly unpleasant . . .

Now this same individual had come to see John on what appeared at first to be little more than a social call. But it soon became evident that he had a special mission — one very secular in nature.

"Herr Schwartz," he began after he and John had stepped onto the porch. "I have come to request the hand of your daughter, Ida, in marriage."

The words had the effect upon the hearer of a thunderbolt in January . . . "We are reminded of what our Father tells us in *Genesis*," the speaker continued, "that it is not good for man to be alone. I have long admired your daughter's good character and industriousness. It would please me very much to call her my wife."

John paused before replying, trying to conceal the indignation he felt toward the supplicator. In spite of the formality with which the proposal was given, the suitor's manner was that of a man bargaining for livestock. John felt an overwhelming revulsion.

"No, I'm afraid what you're asking is out of the question," he declared with biting finality. "First of all, she is much too young. It is wrong to even consider such a thing at her age. Then, her mother needs her at home. The girl still has much to learn before she becomes a wife.''

Like all people the minister had an ample capacity for self pity. Indignant and frustrated over his failure, he turned at once to go, excusing himself with cool propriety. A refusal was something he had not expected. After all, was he not a minister of the Gospel? Who would not think it a singular honor to be asked to marry a man of his status? Like a wounded coyote, he sulked home and refrained from calling upon John's family for some time thereafter.

* * *

By spring the interior of John's house was completed, smelling of new lumber and varnish. Clear maple floors and dark oaken woodwork shone magnificiently in each room. It was a stately, square Edwardian house. The ceilings were of pressed tin and

John's New House.

ornately decorated. (When Katie saw them she immediately ordered Roger to procure the same for her house.) John had built a secretary with glass doors and a fold-out desk top. This, together with the new piano and a three-tier crystal ceiling lamp, graced the parlor. There was an archway, supported by two square columns, leading into the dining room, which contained a homemade buffet and a round oak table. The upstairs portion of the house consisted of three bedrooms and a small sitting room, each with a dormer window that faced one of the four directions. John had seen to it that all dimensions in the house were meticulously perfect from the concrete foundation to the small metal railing that fenced the chimney.

Beyond the house, he had built a blacksmith shop for his new forge and bellows. A turnstile stood in the gateway that led from the shop to the house. A grove of ash trees, planted during the previous year, lay to the south, and a grove of poplars grew along the east side of the yard. Four lilac bushes, given to Caroline by an itinerant salesman who had spent the night with the family, fronted the house. Because it was still March, none of the trees or shrubbery had as yet any indication of budding; but within a few years they would all grow to full size to present an impressive sight for visitors.

This, then, was the place toward which a small wedding party advanced on the afternoon of March 25, 1914. Although an early chinook had melted all but the most tenacious of the winter drifts, a late snow had once again left the ground white. Still the air was warm. Everywhere there was a sense of newness, and the fresh snow was welcome, because it meant moisture for the spring crop.

It was a good day for a wedding — clear and bright. The snow, warmed by the sun's growing strength, had already begun to thaw as the party approached the house in a large horse-drawn sled accompanied by gay laughter and jocular conversation. A somewhat short and portly groom helped the bride to the ground. The groom was Schultz — the young man from Avon who had been present during the formation of the church. The bride was Ida.

Leaving the sled, the party gathered before the house for a picture while Uncle Soft's son, Johnny, assembled his bulky camera equipment. With Schultz stood his brother, Ed, and his new brother-in-law, Henry. Bertha Poltauwitz and Ida's sister, Lydia, attended the bride. Meanwhile, the minister, who had been compelled to wed the couple, stood grudgingly at a distance — out of the camera's scope — as if to show his contempt for such worldly frivolity.

"I could feel his hand tremble when he blessed us," Ida whispered to Bertha.

What thoughts were going through the minister's mind at this time can easily be guessed. His resentment was directed particularly toward the young man who had succeeded where he had not. Why had John condoned the marriage of his daughter to such an ordinary man, he wondered.

First, John had no predilection toward ministers in general — and particularly toward having one as a son-in-law. But the man's profession and disagreeable manner were not the only factors involved . . . Schultz had his own farm beyond the divide and showed every promise of providing for Ida's needs. She would always be close to home, and there would be none of the uncertainties that are always part of a clergyman's life. . . . So the present arrangement constituted a proper match in John's eyes.

Ida, meanwhile, had determined that there would be no slanderous gossip focused on her marriage. There would be no child born ahead of schedule — an event in which the local gossip mongers would take great delight. In her own way she had been most shrewd, carefully selecting her guests, inviting none of the girls who had made remarks against her virtue.

There were, however, some guests from outside the community. John had invited Ufer, the lumber dealer from Savage, who came to the wedding in his own automobile, and Chilson, a homesteader from Burns Creek with whom John often stayed during his trips to town. . .

After much debate and preparation the picture was at last taken, and the party entered the house where Uncle Bernhart, holding his fiddle, called to the others to "promenade" as he played a series of lively square dances.

"Now play 'Skip to m' Lou,'" Chilson called out to Bernhart, who cheerfully complied with the request before any of the dancers had a chance to catch their breaths. The Chilson girls, much the favorites of the young men, performed all of the dances with great alacrity. The house resounded with the rhythmic clapping of hands as the youthful celebrants pranced about the living room.

Meanwhile, Ida's little sisters, who were busily munching the chewing gum that Schultz had given them, found the guests' winter wraps strewn across their beds upstairs and took great interest in trying each one on.

"Oh, we're the Chilson girls," Othelia announced as she mimicked the young ladies' flirtatious airs.

Suddenly there came a strange and frightening roar from outside. Everyone ran onto the porch to see Ufer showing off his motor car.

"Give us a ride!" the boys were begging him.

"First the bride and the bride's maids," Ufer laughed.

"No, it might explode," the girls giggled.

"Go on! Go on!" the others urged until the three were seated behind the driver in the open vehicle.

This was too much for the poor minister. His face congealed with rage.

"Ehegebrochen!" he muttered as the car splashed away through the melting snow. "Already they have broken their vows."

This accusation of broken faith did not at all alarm the other guests.

"Nothing is broken except his pride," sneered Uncle Bernhart.

When at last everyone had taken his turn to ride in the wonderful automobile, the older women sat about the final ritual of dishbreaking, the symbolic observance of a new beginning. Marhinja Bas had particular difficulty with a cup that she hurled repeatedly against a large rock. At last the cup shattered.

"And I do not lie," she said with emphasis. *"Ich han's fünf Mol probiert."*

"Five times?" Uncle Soft laughed. "Then the marriage will last a long time."

So the wedding day passed. But the Chilson girls were treated to an unpleasant surprise when they went to put on their hats and found a quantity of used chewing gum thoroughly stuck within the linings.

Schools, Politics and Programs

When Johnny Schmidt asked him to go away to Butte, Eddy had not yet completed his eight years of grade school — years that were protracted by long intervals of absence when he was needed to work at home. They were years involving many changes in Eddy's life. Since the day that Ben Poststarr taught him to write his name on a slate, he had attended three schools in all. The Dakota school seemed now to belong to another lifetime — a time of play and sunshine. In Montana the Independent School had seen his transition to adolescence and to another kind of life that was less secure, even frightening at times, but always adventurous. Finally there was the new school built on the northwest corner of John's land and named "Fairview."

The old Independent School, which both English and Mennonites attended, was a considerable traveling distance for many neighborhood children, particularly in winter. By 1915 a sufficient number of families had established themselves to enable the construction of two more schools. But the location of these soon became a matter of angry controversy and intrigue, which began on the day Rhody Strapp paid an unexpected visit to John's house.

Eddy listened as the irascible Scotsman sat cross-legged in the living room, smoking his pipe and squinting his narrow eyes at John.

"Y' see, Schwartz, we know you folks want a school on yer place. An' ol' Clem Livingstone — well, he wants it up north. Now over by us there's the same tussle. But most of us want the Schrag place for our school.

"Now here's what I bin figgerin'," he proposed, pointing with the stem of his pipe. "If'n all a y' wuz t' help us out by votin' our way, well — we'd be apt t' do th' same fer you. . . . Now ain't that just plain common sense?"

John smiled approval at this scheme, and in a short time the plot became a general resolve — those wanting the Schrag site agreeing to support John's faction and the others reciprocating in like manner. When the voting was completed, Livingston counted the ballots twice before hurling them upon the judges' table with the sullen exclamation, "Well, you got it!"

The Fairview School was the last that Eddy — already approaching early manhood — was to attend. Ted Bunley, a robust, boisterous carpenter, who delighted in amusing the children with his ability to hold a chair aloft with his teeth, was in charge of its construction. The building was completed in short order so that Harriet Williams could begin instruction that fall.

Miss Williams was a young woman possessed of both gentility and erudition. Affectionately called "Hattie" — or simply "the teacher" — by both parents and pupils, she was adored by everyone. Eddy found in her a compassionate friend and mentor. He would remember her always, for it was she who encouraged him to read; and, although he was never to follow her counsel to go to high school, he remained devoted to books for the duration of his life.

* * *

School began after harvest and ended with the commencement of "spring's work," when boys were needed to help with plowing and seeding. For the Mennonite children, there followed a few weeks of German grammar school, usually taught by the minister — a practice that would soon cease with the approach of war. Although each child knew his own dialect well, it was deemed necessary by the traditionalists to read and write formal High German — *Bibel Deutsch*.

But the school provided more than education. It was a social gathering place — the cultural nucleus of the community. At no time was this more evident than at the annual performance of what was generally known as "the Christmas program" — a repertoire of trite, hackneyed recitations and slightly off-key singing. Little

Willy Schenker was among the recitants that year. Unable to speak English when he began school, he had been shown a picture of a bird and brusquely declared it to be a *Voegele*. Now at his first program he was able to repeat:

"Dear Santa Claus — not much I ask, for I am very small. All I want for Christmas is a horn and drum and ball."

Henry Roger, unable to sing with any semblance of tonal precision, was assigned the task of accompanying each chorus of "Jingle Bells" with a set of harness bells which he held in his hands. Taking the words of the song literally, he continued to ring the noisy instruments "all the way" throughout the song's duration.

The program, however, was generally lauded as a fine thing by every parent who saw and heard his or her child perform; and each child, in turn, received a special Christmas gift from Hattie. Eddy was pleased upon opening his to discover a new book to add to his small library. The book was an adventure story called *Boy Scouts in the Northwest* with the subtitle *Fighting Forest Fires*. It began a term of late-night reading for him, and throughout his adolescence he longed for the never-to-be realized experience of being a Boy Scout.

In contrast to these happy times, there were moments when conflicts arose — primarily between German and English boys. At one time a fist fight, the cause of which no one remembered when the fight was over, raged on until the presence of the teacher brought an end to the brawl. Then, during the spring thaw, the German boys compelled poor little Bert Smith to swim in the creek, which was full of icy water from the melting snow. When Bert became ill, Smith came to school and threatened to "skin" the culprits if they were ever to touch his son again. So it was that a vengeful enmity developed among the English toward their German-speaking neighbors — an enmity that was soon to erupt in an unforgettable way.

The Patriots

In his Helena office Governor Stewart scanned a letter dated May 25, 1917. It was one of many that he had received from local councils throughout Montana in support of the registration effort. America had been at war for less than two months, and much needed to be done to get the machinery running. These local boys might be inexperienced when it came to politics, the governor knew; but they were as dedicated a bunch as you could find. This particular letter was from a fellow named Thurston in Glendive. It read:

> Dear Sir:
>
> Your letter of May 22 urging our City Council of Defense to give assistance and aid in the registration is received. . . . We have been in communication with our Sheriff. . .
>
> It would appear that the City officers can greatly assist, if every city in the State shall . . . get cases on all the I.W.W. and bum element. . .
>
> Any suggestion as to our practical activity in any direction will be gladly received.
>
> C. A. Thurston*

Two months later Charles Greenfield, Secretary for the Montana Council of Defense, an organization formed for the purpose of promoting the "war effort" at the grassroots level, read the following:

> Dear Sir:
>
> At a meeting of the Chamber of Commerce at Glendive last night the question of organizing a home guard was taken up. We have not as yet been bothered in this community with I.W.W.'s but a large number of men here would like to organize a home guard for any emergency which might arise.
>
> yours truly,
> Frank L. Hughes, Chairman
> Dawson County Council of
> Defense*

Although remotely aware of such organizations as the Council of Defense and the "home guard," the German-speaking Mennonites on Retah Table knew nothing of the consequences which these letters would have upon their lives. Since America's entrance

* Archives, Montana State Historical Society, Helena.

into the "Great War," a feverish anti-German campaign had been promoted by the press and the War Department. "Crush the Prussian" became the slogan heralded by the old *Life* magazine, which carried page after page of ludicrous cartoons depicting the German emperor as a horned demon. German-American newspapers were at first censored, then completely silenced. Wagnerian operas were banned from the New York stage, and sauerkraut became "victory cabbage."

While their neighbors were either enlisting in the army or volunteering for the home guard, the Mennonites, secure behind their doctrine of biblical nonresistance, remained aloof. But the war was closer than they could realize.

* * *

As usual, following church and Sunday dinner, the Sabbath settled itself quietly upon the community. For everyone — save the women, to whom fell the task of preparing endless meals — this was a time of unbroken leisure. Haying, threshing and butchering were set aside as the Mennonites amused themselves with conversation in their parlors or in the shade of their houses. This abstinence from labor issued not so much from a sense of religious devotion as from socially-dictated custom. To have violated it would have resulted in an unforgivable affront against tradition and propriety. For the younger people, however, it was an occasion for seeking entertainment — a thing impossible on working days. Their chief amusement was visiting; and, since automobiles were as yet a novelty reserved for the wealthy and capricious, their only recourse was to travel within the compass of foot or carriage.

"It's a good day to walk to the Smiths' place," Johnny Soft proposed to his cousins on such an afternoon. "Mrs. Smith always has something good to eat."

Johnny, who was Henry's age, spoke in his usually casual and unhurried way. Like Henry and Eddy he enjoyed intellectual pursuits — music, reading and photography. On this particular day he had brought with him a sheet of music that bore the picture of a young couple riding in an up-to-date touring car. Across the top of the page a set of bold letters spelled out the words "The Motor King."

"Mrs. Smith will play it for us. She can play anything at sight," Henry said as the boys proceeded across the pasture. . .

They always called her "Mrs. Smith;" there was no thought of being so brash as to refer to the cultured English lady by a familiar name. The boys saw in her something quite extraordinary, a "worldly" person unlike any other farm woman they knew. "A real lady," they described her, unaware of the jealousy she aroused among the less accomplished majority of women in their community. . .

"Well, what have we here — three boys lost!" Mrs. Smith greeted the youthful visitors at her door, her round face glowing with cordiality. It was a pretty face, although the woman's figure had grown decidedly plump over the past seven years. "I was just telling my husband that I hoped someone would come today."

Inside the house Smith was sitting upon a comfortable rocker and reading from a newspaper. The corners of his mouth hinted at a smile as he rose to shake hands with the boys, studying them acutely with a curious expression.

"Yes, sir," he welcomed them. "Always glad for company."

After generous helpings of tea and cake, the boys prevailed upon their hostess to perform for them. Smiling, she took the music sheet from Johnny and went to the piano.

"That's a cheery little piece," she said when she had played "The Motor King" twice. "Let's see — what shall I play next? I know — there's a new song I got in town just last week called 'There's a Long, Long Trail.' It's very popular with the soldier boys."

Intrigued, they listened as Mrs. Smith played and sang the new song for them.

"Once more," she cried, "And this time I want to hear some male voices."

So the boys joined the singing. This was followed by "Maid of the Mist" and various selections from *The Etude* music magazine. Eddy would never forget the facility with which the woman performed. In coming years he would hear others — artists, masters, Paderewski among them. Yet he would repeatedly affirm that even they did not excel this obscure woman living on a Montana farm.

"There are some fine music conservatories in Chicago," she told Eddy more than once. "Perhaps you could arrange to go to one. The cost isn't really that much."

Eddy gave a grim sigh. "It's a lot when you don't have it," he replied.

Still the idea that she planted remained with him, fed by an insatiable desire to gratify what he had discovered when he played on Aunt Julia's organ in Dakota. Years later, after he returned from Chicago, he would long to show Mrs. Smith the results of her encouragement. But he would never be able to play for her or to hear her again. . .

Smith, who until now had said little, suddenly spoke. "You fellas are gettin' close to military age, ain't y'?" he remarked with a peculiar glint in his eye.

"Guess so!" Johnny answered cautiously.

"Tell me — what branch of the armed forces would you want to be in?"

It seemed a harmless question, asked out of conversational curiosity. Yet the implications were profound. Perhaps, the boys reasoned silently, Smith was unaware that Mennonites opposed military service. Yet none of them was willing to reveal this and subject himself to the Englishman's contempt. It was commonly known that Reverend Franz, the fiery young preacher who had recently succeeded to the pulpit, had taken all the Mennonite boys of conscription age to town and registered them as noncombatants — all except Carl Schenker, who vowed that he would go to prison before wearing a military uniform, a pledge that he would soon fulfill.

"Oh, I guess I'd go wherever they put me," Henry said at last, nervously picking at his nose.

Smith glanced significantly at his wife. "Well, now I'm gettin' past the fightin' age. But what I'd like to do — mind you, if I was t' go — would be to drive one o' them tanks. I hear they're quite the machine.

"Y' know that Kaiser Bill must be one low-down cuss," he went on. "Now take the way he marched through Belgium, cuttin' off kids' arms an' legs. An' what them Germans done to the poor, helpless womenfolk. . . . Why, it's enuff t' make any decent man fightin' mad."

An awkward silence followed after which the boys politely excused themselves.

"What did you make of all that?" Johnny asked Henry after they had left the house.

"Oh, he's just curious, I guess," Henry shrugged. "Wants to see what we think about the war. After all, we are German."

There was, indeed, a substantial pro-German feeling among even the nonresistant Mennonites. Goering, Schrag and even Uncle Soft had openly declared their German allegiance in emphatic terms. Moreover, some of the non-Mennonite German men had already returned to fight for their ancestral homeland.

"Wilson wants to rule the world," Soft proclaimed when the United States entered the war. "But we will win out yet and show those Yankee bluebellies."

John echoed this contempt for the president, whom they had all along suspected of being pro-British. "What does he know of European matters?" he fumed when he read the newspapers that lauded Wilson's speech to the Congress. "We left the Old Country to get away from all that."

Locally the Mennonite community continued as always with its church services in the old language. But every Sunday that

177

summer brought a set of English visitors to the church, visitors that included the Smiths.

"They have come to spy on us," the Mennonites concluded; and Franz, upon seeing Mrs. Smith among his congregation, promptly instructed the church to kneel for prayer — a thing that was not often done during Sunday worship but that required humiliating effort for the heavy-set woman.

"For once I made her get on her knees," Franz boasted to John that afternoon.

Shortly afterward a local member of the home guard observed the Holtzwarth boys playing war games with stick weapons in their pasture. A large family of modest means, the Holtzwarths, whose father was virtually blind, were known for their abundant humor and for a propensity toward practical jokes. Although their games were innocuous, the climate of the times endowed them with the most sinister implications.

"They're gettin' ready to fight! Somethin's gotta be done!" the patriots cried.

On the following week the county sheriff paid a visit to Franz.

* * *

Franz was not secretive of his indignation over the sheriff's visit.

"He glared at me like a tiger," the minister told John in describing the incident. "But I looked back at him like a lion."

Small in stature and always meticulously well-groomed, Franz was a man possessed of a most assertive and willful personality. He was well-read, had a strong speaking voice and fancied himself something of a scholar. Unfortunately he was inclined toward a measure of prepossessing egotism, which was to a great extent responsible for what was about to transpire.

"He told me that because of the war our service should no longer be in German," he stormed, "and that we should quit our grammar school. . . . Who is he to dictate to us? A mere county sheriff!"

What Franz did not know was that his rebuff toward the sheriff was a nearly fatal error. Shortly afterward, a local election took place at the Independent School. John was not there to witness the events, but Franz told later how a car containing masked figures came into the yard shortly after he and his wife had arrived to vote. The strangers seized him and fastened a noose about his neck. His wife was hurled to the ground when she attempted to interfere. Swiftly securing their captive in the back seat of the car, the abductors sped south for some miles until they came to a poplar tree on Deer Creek.

What happened there has since been subject to dispute. Franz affirmed that he was taken to the tree, where the rope was fastened to a limb. During the initial struggle he had been able to maneuver his hands inside the noose so that it would not tighten about his neck. The masked men argued for a time before undoing the rope and returning their frightened hostage to the car.

Some maintained that the entire episode was merely a macabre joke played to terrify the man into compliance and that no lynching was ever planned. In any event, the hanging was not performed; and Franz was taken to the county jail in Glendive. . .

The courthouse was filled with spectators that night for the hearing that followed. Present were the district judge, the sheriff, the abductors — all members of the Council of Defense and the "witnesses" from the Retah Table home guard, called to provide evidence of the minister's disloyalty — among them Mr. and Mrs. Smith. When the participants were assembled, the judge called the session to order and proceeded to interrogate the accused.

Did he consider himself a loyal American?

Was he discouraging his congregation from supporting the war effort?

Obviously shaken and much subdued, Franz responded, declaring that he was a loyal citizen and that these allegations were totally false.

What was his justification for using the German language in defiance of national anti-German policies?

"The old people," Franz replied, "have trouble understanding English. German is what they have always used in their church."

Throughout the interrogation the judge, his legal eyes discerning every nuance in the man's expression, continued to scrutinize this so-called spy. When he had finished with Franz, he turned his attention to the witnesses. . .

Upon what basis had they made these assertions against the minister?

They looked at one another like reprobate children. Caught in the zeal of propaganda-induced patriotism, they had convinced themselves, as well as the entire county, of the existence of a conspiracy. Now the conspiracy was revealed a myth. The war's conclusion would see all of them sell their farms and leave the community, never to be heard of again. The charges against Franz, unsubstantiated, were dropped; and the minister was released on probation.

On the Sunday following his release, he addressed his congregation for the first time ever in English.

"Starting today," he announced, "we must do things differently than they have ever been done. Our church will no longer be the same."

179

The language sounded strange and out of place; but the declaration proved to be prophetic, for although the German language would eventually be restored for a time, the change to English ways had begun. The old language was dying and with it a traditional way.

Meanwhile the county authorities confiscated all German-language hymnals and Bibles. (These were returned after the war, smelling of formaldehyde.) A war bond rally was held at the church, conducted by a Glendive attorney named Hildebrand.

"In the history of our great nation," he began, speaking as though he were running for office, "we have been faced with three great crises. And each time we have been given great men to lead us in these crises. . . . In 1776 there was George Washington; in 1861 there was Abraham Lincoln; and in our present crisis we have our third great leader — Woodrow Wilson!

The people listened with intimidated awe to this "English" politician extolling the virtue of the hated Wilson. But they bought the bonds and became loyal citizens. The Mennonite women baked their bread with oatmeal and knitted socks for the soldiers (although Uncle Soft continued to use his own wheat flour and preached for the German cause until the end of the war). The boys of the community went for military service — some even consenting to carrying rifles. . .

On the day in 1918 when Henry put on his uniform and prepared to leave for Camp Lewis, Washington, a woman came riding horseback to the house. It was Mrs. Smith, who presented the young soldier with a copy of *The New Testament* in English.

Some Lessons in Brotherhood

The "crisis" that the Great War thrust upon the Mennonites served temporarily to diminish the older, internal rivalry between the church's two linguistic factions. Following the war this truce between *Schweitzers* and *Plattdeutsch* ended, and local conflicts resumed. Not once, however, was the deeply-entrenched competition directly referred to either from the pulpit or at congregational meetings. This was in part to preserve the myth of a unanimous fraternity among the believers and in part to avoid what might have become a complete severance. Nevertheless, it was generally known that the "Low Dutch" sought tirelessly to wrest control of the church from the Swiss — an objective which they eventually achieved.

The conflicts — for the most part personal and petty in nature — became at last so numerous that a general meeting of the congregation was called; each parishioner was prevailed upon to forgive his neighbor any and all past enmities. In spite of some balking, all of the members rose to their feet in silent affirmation of this general amnesty. But the road to brotherhood is subject to numerous detours, and the mountains of prejudice are not quickly eroded. Low Dutch children continued to mock their Swiss antagonists with the hated taunt: *"Plattdeutsch ist besser als Hochdeutsch,"* an affirmation which was always made, ironically, in High German. Their indignation aroused, the Swiss youngsters plotted revenge.

The occasion presented itself one day when some of the Low Dutch children passed the Swiss settlement in a horse-drawn buggy near the place where Othelia and Anna were playing with Clara and Elsie Roger.

"Let's block the road and see what they'll do," Othelia proposed with malicious glee.

The other girls submitted to this plan with equal delight, helping to form a human chain by locking their arms firmly together across the roadway. The vehicle continued its pace, seemingly oblivious to the obstacle before it. Still the human blockade refused to yield.

The situation now constituted an unmistakable challenge; to relent on either side would be a matter of disgrace. Only one outcome was possible. . . . The wagon passed through the barrier and directly over poor Clara, who was forced to fall to the ground to avoid being struck. The challenge had been met, and the hoped-for revenge had decidedly backfired.

Confrontations among adults in the community, if not less vindictive, were at least less blatant. They commenced when the man nicknamed *Menschefresser* appeared in church and was recognized immediately by Uncle Bernhart as the individual who had once been so presumptuous as to interrupt the fishing at Silver Lake.

"Huh! *Dort iss unser Fischwarden,"* he whispered to John, recalling the long-ago incident.

Thus the old resentments were perpetuated, reaching a climax with the formation of what would come to be remembered as the "shit committee."

It should not be thought that the use of what some, even among the present generation, might consider an obscenity could in any way have depreciated the significance or seriousness of this ad hoc body. Although never officially designated as such, the "shit committee" was so called for two reasons: first, it had no other name; second, its function was to investigate the indicated subject.

The circumstances that led to the formation of this illustrious committee occurred one night after evening church services when old man Schonfeld, one of the more wealthy of the Low Dutch parishioners, went to his newly-purchased automobile and reached for the crank. Immediately upon grasping the handle he felt a substance the nature of which, even in the darkness, was unmistakable. Schonfeld's reaction was no doubt anticipated by the anonymous conspirators who had perpetrated so pernicious a deed. . . . He was furious.

The question of whom to blame for the outrage came before the church elders. After some deliberation, Uncle Bernhart proposed what would seem to have been a most reasonable explanation. Schonfeld, he suggested, had unwittingly struck some pedestrian in the rear with the car. This, however, did not satisfy the plaintiff; and upon his insistence the "shit committee" — although not as yet designated as such — was formed.

Its members were, not coincidentally, all Low Dutch. The chairman proceeded to interrogate as many of the Swiss boys as he felt capable of such mischief. One suspect was Eddy Antelop. Incensed at the implication of guilt for a crime of which he was genuinely innocent, Eddy later greeted the chairman at the church with the cordial, "So how's the shit committee?"

Thus the committee received its name. The chairman immediately demanded an apology from the boy under the threat of excommunication (*Meidung* in old Mennonite terminology).

"Well, that's what it is, isn't it?" argued the defense.

So the matter was laid to rest; and the committee, unsuccessful in its endeavor, closed the case, becoming a memorable footnote in the church's history. But the feelings would persist for an entire generation afterward until family and linguistic differences were obscured and forgotten by grandchildren who neither remembered nor cared.

Two Indians

Except for a pair of hawks that glided above the hills and the whirring clatter of summer locusts in the grass, the day was still. The midday sun burned upon the Clay Butte's wrinkled face as it looked across a serene landscape. A sudden whirlwind tore at the crisp strands of needlegrass and at the twisted juniper bush that clung to the side of the ancient promontory. Beneath the juniper, gazing from among a cluster of exposed roots, a horned skull lay exposed to the sun.

Secluded as it was among the badlands, it had escaped the bone collectors and remained now, flecked with patches of dry moss, to see a changed world. The plains it had once known and grazed upon with its kindred were now wheat fields bound by an enormous spider's web of barbed wire fences. Together with the buffalo skull and the two circling hawks, the Butte, itself unchanged, continued its vigil.

Across the hills to the south, along the lines of fence, ran a dirt road from which rose a cloud of dust. A car was approaching the Mennonite settlement. The driver was a small, bearded man, a minister. With him were two aging Indians. Well-dressed and dignified in their new suits and big reservation hats, they seemed oblivious to the summer heat as they looked impassively upon the changing countryside. . .

They had seen much in their time — these two men called Standing Elk and Yellow Fox. They were chiefs, men of honor among the *Oemisis* — the people whom history would remember as the Northern Cheyenne. Standing Elk, appropriately named, was tall and erect in spite of his years. An orator in his own language, he spoke only a little of the white man's talk while Yellow Fox, short and heavy, in contrast, could make himself understood in the alien tongue.

Not long ago they had been compelled to fight the white soldiers who came against them. Now it was a white man who had befriended them and with whom they were travelling along this dusty summer road over hills that were still familiar in spite of many changes. These changes made both men feel somehow much older. Their very presence constituted an anachronism, for they belonged to another time — to a world that had vanished.

They remembered that world and the subsequent changes in spite of the rapidity with which the events had happened. There was a time of buffalo-hide teepees — always in a circle on the un-broken prairie — of great hunts and of the Sun Dance that renewed the earth and men's lives — of fights with the Crows and the ripen-ing chokecherries. Then there were no more buffalo. Instead there was pursuit, flight — and death at the hands of the soldiers when Morning Star's camp was burned on the Powder River. The soldiers had done that to avenge the killing of Long Hair — the man called Custer. The people were then sent to Oklahoma. Some escaped north. Others were killed. That was a nightmare they could not forget.

At last now it seemed that things might be getting better. They had a good place at Lame Deer agency — good water and grass for the ponies — and they had this white missionary named Petter, who had brought them a new religion which was really the old religion spoken in a different way. They called him "Cheyenne Talker" because he spoke their language, and some had even hoped that he might be the prophet whose advent had been promised by the "ghost dancers." If he was, in fact, no prophet, he was still a good man; and on this day he was taking them to visit the white man's church.

183

The car was coming to the crest of a high ridge from which one could see in every direction the great circle of the earth. Yellow Fox saw something in the north and motioned to Standing Elk, who looked for a long moment and smiled. There on the horizon, seeming almost a part of the clouds, shone the bright yellow Clay Butte, unaltered. Yes, they remembered that place — where the old people used to catch eagles. It was always a good place to talk to God.

The Clay Butte

The Clay Butte.

Part VII

THE LOST AND THE LONELY

„Einmal hatte ich a Frau."

The Widower.

Leavetaking

It snowed the night before Eddy was to report at the induction center for his physical examination. The harvest had been late that fall, and some of the wheat still stood in snow-covered shocks, waiting to be threshed. But John said that the snow would not hurt the crop. Besides, there was still coal to be mined. He hitched the team to the sled and drove Eddy across the ten miles of white country to Bloomfield where Eddy would meet the Nelson boys.

When the sled reached the crest of the Bloomfield Hill, the snow had changed to mud. John and Eddy left the sled where it stood and rode horseback into the Village where the Nelsons waited in their Oakland car.

"Had a hell of a time gettin' over here," the older brother remarked. "Mud up to the axle in places."

Eddy knew the brothers well and liked them. Like many of their generation, inspired by Zane Grey's novels, they fancied themselves cowboys. Eddy thought himself too mature to show them the sadness he felt at leaving his father.

"So long, Pa," he said in English. "You'll still have Hardwig to help you."

He knew he wasn't going to be inducted immediately. The results of the examination would still have to be processed. There would be a few days' waiting period. Also, there was talk that the war was nearly over. Still he felt as though he were leaving home for the first time — even if it was to be only for a day.

John smiled and raised his hand as the car pulled away.

Besides Eddy and the Nelson boys, the car had two other occupants — the little Jewish storekeeper from Bloomfield and another small man, who spoke with a strong Scandinavian accent. They talked among themselves about the snow, the harvest and the war. The little Jew was sullen.

"You boys harvest your grain and thresh it, and that's all you have to worry until spring," he lamented. "You could leave. But who will take care of my store if I have to go away?"

"I wouldn't fret too much," the older Nelson consoled him. "We're gettin' mighty close to the end of it, they tell me."

Eddy felt sorry for the Jew.

The car continued to plow through mud that clung like wet mortar to the fenders.

"By God, I think we got a flat," the older brother announced suddenly as he struggled with the steering wheel.

He stopped the car and got out, followed by the others. Eddy and the small Scandinavian helped the brothers change the tire while the little Jew stood at a distance, grumbling to himself.

"I wonder — is he a pro-Yerman?" the Scandinavian whispered

to the others.

"Hell, no!" Nelson scoffed. "He's just kind of a queer duck."

The tire was fixed, and the young men resumed their journey along Deer Creek. They passed the tree where the minister had nearly been hanged. Of those in the car, Eddy alone knew its significance but made no point of revealing it to the others. He was not, he told himself, ashamed of being either a Mennonite or a German; and he knew that his ethnic identity was no secret to his present companions. Still, he was now no longer among his own people and was well-acquainted with the second-generation immigrant mentality that prided itself in being "American."

He recalled his baptism — a thing he had submitted to as a matter of course with all of the other Mennonite youths of his age. Did it make him any different from the boys who had never been baptized — from those who knew the church only as a place for weddings or funerals? No, he reasoned. He was no better than they. He thought, too, of how his father had taken him to Glendive to be registered — of how the clerk had spoken so kindly to him, until she learned that he was a noncombatant. To such people being German meant being a traitor, being Mennonite — a coward.

"You fellas remember your flu masks?" Nelson asked as he drove them across the bridge that led into town, for the epidemic was at its height. But in a moment the masks were forgotten.

"What do you s'pose is goin' on?" the younger brother wondered aloud when they heard the music of a marching band and the blaring noise of automobile horns. . .

They found themselves riding amid a procession of cars, wagons and bicycles. A throng of ecstatic spectators had gathered along the street. Flags hung from stores and office windows. Nelson drove past the courthouse.

"Well, boys, looks like we made the trip for nothin', he smiled as they read the makeshift banner that hung from the balcony. "They've signed the armistice."

* * *

So Eddy returned home and continued for the next five years to farm with John and Hardwig. Few of them were good years. Crops were often poor, and people had little money. It was prohibition; and some, even among the Mennonites, resorted to bootlegging their home-distilled liquor to provide money for their taxes.

The boys of Eddy's age had long ago given up their childhood games for escapades that proved more alluring. They knew very well which of their neighbors cooked whisky or made the best "home-brew" beer, and often an illicit brewer would return to his cellar or barn to discover that his stock had been noticeably depleted. But the youthful thieves did not always escape with impunity. . . . Although they were seldom apprehended, they often paid for their deed with a ferocious hangover. They learned also to crave the brown, moist snuff that came in small, round cans and that was generally referred to simply as "a chew." Such was their induction into manhood.

But Eddy had not lost his desire for learning. He continued to read — not only the "dime novel" western stories that were popular — but textbooks on history and literature. He discovered Poe, Emerson, Shakespeare and Thackeray and kept lists of words he wanted to learn. Although he could seldom afford new books, he was able to purchase used volumes at auctions and to borrow from others who shared his devotion. He saved the music magazines that Mrs. Smith had given him, studying them until they were all but memorized; and at night, after the family had gone to bed, he practiced his technique on the piano and learned the works of Beethoven and Chopin.

Then came a year when there was no crop at all. The grain remained hopelessly stunted in the field so that there was nothing to harvest. It was then that Eddy determined to go to his mother's sister and her husband, Uncle Reich, who lived in North Dakota where the crops had been good. It was, he knew, a chance to earn money; and John, who knew that Reich was well-to-do, would not object. He spent the remainder of the summer there and worked on into the fall, learning to pick corn, to pitch rye bundles until his back ached and to milk cows unti his hands were numb. He soon discovered that for his mother's people there was only one activity — work; and work he did even in his sleep.

He was happy to return home and to show the family his new wealth, for it gave him an almost noble status among them. So when John approached him and asked, almost timidly, for money to pay the taxes, Eddy was exultant. Still there remained a singular ambition which he had kept to himself since his adolescence. Now he was twenty three years old and determined that his goal could be delayed no longer. . .

When he returned from the army, Henry had married and gone to study art at the Chicago Institute. There he and his wife shared a Parkside flat with another couple with whom Eddy was acquainted.

" We have a grand time," Henry wrote. "Each of us has a job, and there are all sorts of entertainment. Eddy, you would have no end of things to do. Last night we heard Paderewski. . ."

So it was that in the fall of 1923 Eddy found himself waiting at the Glendive depot where, thirteen years before, he had come as a child. In his pocket he held a ticket for Chicago and the watch his grandfather had given him when he was eleven years old. For a moment he longed again for his recent boyhood — longed for the grandparents whom he could never see again, for both of them had died — longed once more to steal watermelons with the Holtzwarth boys.

He would return to Montana some day, he thought. But the life he had once known would be, from that day, lost to him forever.

The Uncle

The prairie wind stung his eyes and drew tears from them the day he drove to town to buy Esther's coffin. He muttered to himself as he wiped them away with his sleeve. It was nothing — merely another winter; and he had lived through many, both here and in the Old Country. Although the pain in his back and legs seemed to have gotten worse during the past few years, he complained to no one. "*Das iss mir nichts!*" he scoffed when his children told him to remain indoors during such weather. He could still work harder than any of them. . . . He could still tie knots in barbed wire with his bare hands. All his life he had worked through every season and through years that had been both good and bad.

The good years returned to him now as he guided his team and sled over the snow-encrusted roadway — years when he and his family dug fat potatoes from their Kansas field and picked peaches from their own trees — the Montana years when he and Graber threshed together with their new separator that spewed straw and chaff like an erupting volcano while the Aultman tractor's cylinders hammered upon the autumn air. Yes — good years, he thought. He had seen his sons grow and marry and had bought land for them.

"Fine good, sturdy women," he had told them. "They make the best workers."

But Herbert had married a small woman instead. She had given Herbert two children; and now — only one day apart — both she and Esther, the old man's beloved daughter, were dead of the flu.

"Dead!" he thought as he sat hunched upon the cold seat.

"Dead — dead!" echoed the heavy sled runners as they dragged upon the packed, frozen snow.

He had at last reached the river. Here the wind did not blow as hard as it did upon the hills. Yet the tears still came to his eyes. Again he wiped them with the sleeve of his sheepskin. A few reluctant snowflakes began to fall from the cold sky to mingle with the flying ash from many chimneys as he crossed the bridge into town. The town smelled of wood and coal smoke.

He drew the team up along the street. Painfully climbing to the ground, he put on his flu mask and made his way to the Lowe brothers' furniture store.

"I want a box for my daughter," he announced to the clerk in a voice that was labored but unfaltering.

With well-rehearsed commiseration the clerk showed his customer a seven-hundred-dollar model.

"We have a fine one here," he said, opening the lid so the old man could inspect the lining. "White plush!"

"Yes, that one will be good," the old man sighed, his great, callus-toughened hands touching the soft material, and opened his checkbook.

The white plush box was loaded on the sled, and the old man began his return trip. Esther had her coffin. Herbert, he concluded, would have to see about the other one himself.

That afternoon, their bodies wrapped against the winter cold, Esther's cousins picked through the frozen sod in the churchyard until they had made two open graves. They spoke only at intervals, struggling to keep their breath against the persistent wind, which seemed somehow to mock the whole affair of death and human suffering.

Because of the flu the double funeral was held outdoors, pallbearers and mourners standing in shivering silence with their masked faces. The old man, his eyes drawn and weary, stood with his wife in stoic contemplation of the ancient mystery. The wind grasped the words of the final hymn and cast them away without consolation.

From then on it seemed as though the whimsical light that had always gladdened his many friends ceased to shine in the old man's eyes. He still went to town, always by himself, and continued to cook whisky in his cellar to the embarrassment of his family. But the jovial story-teller had become a saddened, withdrawn man. The people had lost their prophet of wit.

At home there was no consolation for him. His wife and son nagged him mercilessly.

"You are making a fool of yourself," Herbert rebuked him, "going to town and trading whisky. Think of your grandchildren. You must help to care for them now that their mother is gone."

But the old patriarch was not a man to endure contumely for long.

"My children I have raised," he argued. "And how do they treat me — their father? Myself I can care for, as I have done always; and if I am so bad a person that my own family is disgraced by me — well, then I shall leave."

True to his word, he left, moving onto a section of hilly land west of John's farm, where he lived by himself in a small shack, cooking his whisky and pursuing his own affairs in perfect contentment. But such outrage was beyond his childrens' endurance, and their mother was hysterical with shame. Herbert, convinced that the old man had indeed lost his mind, determined to act.

"We're going to get Pa home, and if he won't come we'll tie him and take him with us whether he likes it or not," he told John one day, stopping at the house with Graber and Graber's two sons, one of whom held a stout hemp rope.

"It might be good if you came along, too," Graber proposed to John. "He'll listen to you maybe."

John stared with intense disgust at the almost droll spectacle and spoke harshly to the would-be abductors:

"See here — I'm not going to tie a man up like that against his will. He's older than all of us and knows well enough what he's doing. If he wants to be left alone, it's his affair."

Although Herbert's mouth tightened sullenly, Graber nodded agreement.

"Yes, I suppose you're right. Maybe we should only talk to him."

"There's been enough talk!" Herbert snapped. But John cast a peremptory glare at his nephew, who did not venture to say more.

"Take the matter to the *Vorstand*," John proposed then. "If they can settle it for you, well enough. If not — leave the man in peace."

So the thing was brought before the church elders. The reprobate uncle came willingly enough in his single-horse buggy and sat listening with impassive silence to the arguments put forth by his children and to Graber's admonition that he return home. Finally the old man rose to speak.

"So much fuss over a little schnaps," he said in his slow, deliberate manner. "Always it seems that what I do is not right. But there has always been food for my children to eat and money for my wife to buy what she needed. When my son's wife died, I was told to care for his children. I did not argue. But it seems now that I am just a crazy old man who doesn't know anything.

"Now I cook a little whisky once in a while so I can have some money. Times are hard. . . . So they criticize me because I trade a gallon or two of it for a little meat from the butcher. But the meat was good enough for them to eat, too. And if I did not sell my whisky, where should we have gotten our meat then?"

"*Nicht wahr!*" Herbert exploded, seeing that the sympathies of the elders clearly fell toward the old man. "It is all not so!"

"*Nun!*" the uncle replied with a strange laugh. "Then there is nothing to it after all."

"Then you will go home to your family?" Graber asked.

But the uncle was already on his feet. Seeing nothing more to discuss, he ambled out of the church, as he had done in Dakota so long ago.

"Then there is nothing to it, if it is all untrue. Graber will rule the church and Wilson the world," he quipped with some of the old light in his eyes.

They followed him to his buggy, imploring him to listen. But nothing could persuade him. The matter, as far as he was concerned, was settled. Returning to his small house, he remained there until Herbert was able to remarry. Only then did the old man come home to stay. As for the grandchildren, Herbert's new wife had no idea that they were intended to become her charges. When their grandparents brought the children to their promised new home, the supposed-to-be stepmother protested loudly and tearfully.

While the family quarrelled over the childrens' future, the smaller of the two girls ran about the house, crying excitedly, "Where will I sleep? Where will I sleep?"

"At home!" retorted the grandmother in disgust, leading them both back to the wagon.

The Ernest Affair

The boys slept as late as possible on the morning of the first day's threshing until at last the peremptory call came from below:

"Sun's up! Time y' git yer horses fed breakfast'll be ready."

The young men laughed at the sing-song chant as they buckled their overalls, repeating it among themselves until the words became a refrain:

"Time-y'git-yerorsesfed-breakfast'll-bexeady."

Breakfast was noisy business at the main house, with prodigious quantities of scrambled eggs, fried ham, coffee and Russian cheese pancakes topped with sour cream — accompanied by the clatter of dishes and the din of lively voices. After they had eaten, the crew members harnessed their teams and moved out onto the field where the engineer blew a whistle on the threshing machine to announce commencement of the day's work.

The bundle wagons formed a line that extended from the field to the monster, steam-operated thresher, which blew straw into one enormous pile as it consumed one after another of the stacked grain shocks fed into it with pitchforks. Each wagoner then returned to load more bundles while a second group waited in turn to have their wagons filled with hard, red spring wheat, which the horses then bore to be unloaded at the granary. Then the empty wagons returned to the thresher to resume their respective places in the line.

Into the midst of this involved operation came little Ernest, moving his wagon into position wherever it suited him, much to the annoyance of the other crew members.

"Ernest, wait your turn!" shouted an irate wagoner. "You're gettin' us all outa time."

Ernest, who always seemed to be late for work, lifted his head indignantly, replying in his thick Swiss accent:

"I'm kinda shlow gettin' shtarted — but vhen I go, I go!"

This brought laughter from everyone, and the work proceeded until the noon bell announced dinner.

Dinnertime — which in a rural locale always meant noon — provided the threshers with a chance for rest and an opportunity to help themselves to the copious variety of food prepared by the women, who were thanked with an occasional, flirtatious jibe. There was much laughter and loud conversation.

"Hey, Ernest," someone called out loudly to the little fellow who had been so bold that morning as to upset the work routine and who was now engaged thoroughly in gorging himself, "tell us about the war."

This was said with a knowing wink to the others, who smiled in anticipation of the droll account.

"*Ach,*" scoffed the voluble little foreigner. "I come to America to file on a homeshtead. Den dey tell me I haf to go fight; so to France I go. Dere I am in dose trenches — and vhat happens? Dey find out I'm not a citishen after all, so here I come pack again."

There was a roar of laughter, followed by another question:

"Ernest, how's Lizzie? I hear you're planning to marry that old woman?"

Ernest's frequent visits to the recently-widowed Lizzie were an embarrassment to the widow's entire family; so much so that her son-in-law had threatened to beat Ernest should he ever encounter the undesired visitor at the house.

"Vell, maype — maype not!" Ernest shrugged, helping himself to a boiled potato.

Secretly, Ernest — who had never been married — was hoping to prime the widow for a proposal. It did not matter to him that younger women avoided him or merely laughed when he spoke to them. An older, more experienced bride would do just as well, he reasoned. So when Sunday arrived at the widow's farm, so did Ernest — with a Bible and a bottle of whisky. If he could not persuade her with scripture, perhaps a drink or two would put her into a more amenable frame of mind, he reasoned.

Looking about cautiously to make sure that the antagonistic son-in-law was nowhere to be seen, Ernest officiously rapped upon the screen door.

The son-in-law was not there, but the widow's youngest son was and immediately slammed and locked the door in the suitor's face.

Unabashed, Ernest began pounding furiously, calling out to the widow to open the door. His appeals had no effect, and at length his frustration reached its climax. He sat down upon the steps and wept loudly, indulging in the most mournful wailing imaginable. But his lamentations served only to draw the attention of a covey of strolling barnyard hens and an underfed cat. So the rejected admirer returned to his farm to contemplate his defeat.

Entering the small house that he shared with no other human being, Ernest situated himself upon his single wooden chair and opened his bottle. Taking a substantial draught, he smacked his lips and grimaced.

The table at which he sat was heaped with yellow newspapers and past issues of *The Saturday Evening Post*. A single cup and plate — the latter encrusted with the remnants of that morning's breakfast — remained where he had left them, with a knife and fork tossed carelessly to one side. The table was covered with grease and fly specks.

As he drank, a tortured look emerged upon his face. There was anger and bitterness. There was pain.

"Dey all laff at me," he complained to the flies that crawled along the windowpane. "But I show dem. Dat poy who treats me like dog — maype later I go giff him plack eye."

Satisfied with this proposed revenge, he finished the bottle's contents and stumbled to his bed, where he fell into a sorrowful slumber. . .

But Ernest had no opportunity for retaliation against the widow's son, who went to town on the following day to sign a complaint. Soon after, the county sheriff came and took Ernest away. His land was put up for sale to the avaricious neighbors who had so often made the pitiful man the butt of their idle humor and who now bid against each other for what had been his.

After a term in the state hospital, he returned to Switzerland, never to be heard from again. But for years after, whenever the threshers gathered, the story of Ernest was bound to be told; and someone would be sure to repeat his well-remembered affirmation:

"I'm kinda shlow gettin' started — but vhen I go, I go!"

The Calling of Harvey

Upon returning home from prison, where he spent the duration of the war for refusing to wear a uniform, Harvey determined by means known only to those so fortunate as to encounter such a mandate, that he was "called" by God to preach the gospel. ("Goshpel" he called it with profound veneration.) But, because even such divinely-ordained careers require money, the calling was delayed for some time until Harvey's mother was able to secure the necessary funds, setting aside what she could from the farm income for her son to attend Smith Bible Conservatory in Chicago. Through perseverance, thrift and prayer the money was earned, and Harvey became a student at the famed Conservatory.

Eddy was already living in Chicago and learned of Harvey's presence in the city from a visiting friend, who happened to be Harvey's cousin. Although a few years younger, Eddy had known Harvey since boyhood and agreed to go with the cousin to call upon him.

Harvey was not in good humor.

"I came to learn to preach the Word," he moaned. "Now they want me to study college English." So saying he produced a book on basic composition, showing his guests a section on sentence diagraming.

Eddy smiled as he paged through the book and recognized lessons he had been taught in the seventh grade.

"Keep your chin up," he consoled Harvey. "You'll get it in time."

Harvey responded with a sour grimace.

Later, as they walked toward the "L" platform, Eddy and the cousin discussed Harvey's situation.

"Poor Harvey," Eddy laughed. "We learned that stuff in grade school. He wants to be a preacher without knowing his ABC's."

But neither Eddy nor Harvey's own cousin could know the depth of Harvey's determination. He completed his courses and left the Conservatory a fully-licensed evangelist with an endorsement in sacred music.

When he returned home, Harvey was placed in charge of the church choir. He set up auditions and sent invitations to those whom he selected. Long nights of arduous rehearsals followed in preparation for Harvey's first Sunday concert; and, indeed, nothing could surpass the spectacle of that performance.

Harvey stood upon a small podium in the little church and led his singers with an alacrity that astounded everyone. As the choir sang, "Send the light . . . the precious gospel light," there was sufficient dramatic force in Harvey's gestures to accommodate a performance of the Berlioz *Requiem*. A similar program was in store for the church upon the following week and every week thereafter.

But Harvey was not content in his capacity. No one, not even the minister, had asked him to preach a single sermon. On top of this some of the congregation had the audacity to imply that the choir's singing was not as good as it had been before Harvey had taken over as conductor. In short, Harvey simply was not appreciated.

Yet, taking to heart the biblical affirmation that a prophet is without honor in his own country, the aspiring evangelist determined to travel west.

"God's spirit is moving in that part of the country," he encouraged himself. "There is a new field that needs to be worked."

So he left with his mother's blessing. But within a few months Harvey returned home and spoke no more of the "new field."

Although some impious souls now ventured to suggest that God may have made an error in judgment where Harvey was concerned, this was by no means the end of his endeavors. . . . He had a divine mission. He must not fail. Convinced that he had not been given a chance to prove his capability, he soon announced his intent to conduct Sunday services at the local schoolhouse.

This might have succeeded, had his meetings taken place during evening hours instead of coinciding with regular morning worship at the church. A few loyal or curious parishioners did come to hear Harvey. But these, even reinforced by some of his own relatives, were not enough to sustain a congregation. The meetings at the schoolhouse collapsed soon after their inauguration.

Disillusioned and bitter, Harvey retired to his mother's farm. During the day he remained indoors, engrossed in contemplation. At night he complained of insomnia and took long excursions upon the lonely, moon-lit section roads. He had given the world his best, but the best had not come back to him. He had sought to elevate humanity, and humanity had rejected him. All that remained now were his mother and his God. They, at least, did not scorn him. Somehow, he reasoned, God's purpose would yet be made manifest in his life. He had but to study and to wait.

At length Harvey's brother, weary of doing the farm work by himself, approached their widowed mother.

"What's wrong with Harvey? Can't he do chores sometimes?" the brother complained.

The old woman's eyes flared defiantly as she defended the son in whom her confidence had never wavered.

"*Ach, nein!*" her shrill voice cried. "You should know that he has not time for such things. After all, he must study his Bible. . . . There are so many lost souls that must be saved."

Rediscovery

Gemmer stood that morning at the window of his studio in the Kimball Building and gazed at the traffic below. His form, blurred by the brilliance of the sunlight, seemed more like the subject of an impressionist's painting than a living man. Although no longer young, he was still handsome — poised and slender.

"So what do you intend to do when you return to the farm?" he asked Eddy in a voice that was almost scoffing. "What do you have there? A cow, no doubt. . . . Now what inspiration is a cow? Tell me that!"

These questions were put to Eddy in a way that made it clear no answer was expected. Rather, they constituted part of a lecture to the young student, who sat at the piano nearby.

"You have already said it isn't a question of money," the instructor continued, still addressing his remarks to Eddy without turning from the window. "I have even offered to work with you for nothing. . . . And I should hope that you are not afraid of opportunity. Not that you're going to be featured on a concert bill anywhere for a while. But you can certainly hold your own until something comes along. . . . There's still an immediate demand for pianists in the downtown theaters — in spite of talking pictures. And all it takes is someone with a discerning ear to hear you and to know you've got talent. . ."

He turned from the window and faced the young musician, who for two years had been his pupil. There was compassion in his eyes as he spoke:

"Eddy — I'm preaching at you, I know. But I won't let someone like you go without protest. No, because I know that you've got the touch. You had it when you came to me. . . . And you're ready now, damn it. Tell me — are you still doubtful?"

Eddy, who had listened until now without comment, smiled awkwardly. This time the question required an answer.

"No," he hesitated. "I guess I've got a pretty good chance, all right. It's just . . ."

He paused, unable to come up with anything that sounded convincing. He could not tell those scrutinizing eyes — so much like those on a bust of Caesar — what longings he felt — to see the Clay Butte once again, to smell the smoke from his father's cigarettes and to taste his mother's cooking. Somehow the city had not been able to eradicate those elements still so fundamental to his being. . . . Finally, there was the letter from John, which he had shown to Gemmer, telling again of no money for the taxes.

"They need me at home right now," he managed, almost apologetically.

Gemmer shook his head. "No, that's not it at all," he replied in a voice that reminded Eddy of his father's. "Your problem is homesickness. You've discovered that life is hard and that you have to keep putting your best foot forward just to keep above water. You think that by returning home you'll find life simple and idyllic. . . . So the only solution may be for you to go home for a while and discover that things there are no longer as you knew them. You will soon find yourself dissatisfied and more than anxious to return to the city — because you belong here."

He approached Eddy and placed a hand on his shoulder.

"Who knows — maybe a vacation will be good for you," he said in a gentler tone. "Now — if this is to be our last session for a while, let me hear the Chopin *scherzo* once again."

So Eddy played Chopin, whom he had learned to love as dearly as his own soul. The theme of the *scherzo* accompanied him as he left the studio for the last time and followed him along the street. . . . He did not have to go to work until afternoon and determined to spend the remainder of the morning in the Loop, wandering up Michigan Avenue and across the park to the lake shore. Still the music followed in his thoughts and would not leave him.

How grand it was, he thought as he viewed the city of which he had recently become a part and which he was about to forsake. It would have terrified him to have seen it as a child. Now he had to remind himself of its magnificence, for it had become almost ordinary to him; and the thought that he might never see it again made him sad. He recalled Gemmer's remonstrances, which he knew were true. Still he could not bring himself, as others did, to worship such things as opportunity and talent.

Such people annoyed him. What was talent but a potential that each person had within himself, that could emerge through interest and hard work? If a farmer could be a musician, couldn't the reverse as well be true? A man was still a man, no matter what he did in life.

He also distrusted people who settled themselves upon a creed — whether religious or secular — as their entire basis for living. He had listened for a time to the socialists and applauded their call for revolution. He had debated evolution and discussed theosophy with Henry. With Gemmer he had explored aesthetics. But those who propounded these doctrines were after all, he reasoned, still human beings; and, no matter how adamant they were in their beliefs, still none of them had the whole answer.

The answer — if there was one — lay, not in complexity, but in simplicity — not in words, but in honesty. Such were the things important in life, and those who sought importance without them were deluded.

* * *

That afternoon Eddy left his job at the Gardner Wire Company and walked with his friend, Herman, to the elevated platform to wait for the train. It was Friday, and both men had their paychecks. But Eddy was in no hurry to return to Parkside, where he still roomed in the same flat that Henry and Laura shared with a young osteopath and his wife. The sorrow he had begun to feel that morning returned to him now as he realized that the good times he had shared with them were about to end.

"What will you do, Eddy, now that you got paid?" Herman asked as they walked together.

Although they saw each other only at work, Eddy had learned to think of this kindly, unassuming Jew as a good friend — one he would be sorry to leave.

"I'm going home," Eddy replied in an abrupt voice.

He had not meant to be curt with Herman, who was often the butt of jokes at work; but there was so much on Eddy's mind. . . . How could John have let the taxes go unpaid? Surely the crops had not been that bad. . .

Herman glanced curiously at Eddy.

"On Parkside? The whole weekend?"

"No — not Parkside — Montana!"

"Back to Montana!" Herman's voice revealed his disappointment. "Well — I guess that's where you belong, after all, eh?"

They had reached the ticket booth, where each put down his fare, and mounted the steps that led to the platform.

"You know," Herman resumed, "I never thought you was cut out for the city. Me — it's different. This place is all I know. But I'd give anything to have a farm like you do."

The platform was crowded, and Eddy had to raise his voice to be heard.

"You'll have to come visit me. Bloomfield, Montana — that's all the address you need."

"You know, that's just what I'll do," Herman grinned. "Someday you'll look up the road, and there old Herman will come walking. Just wait!"

"I'll be looking for you." Eddy laughed to conceal his sorrow.

Already they could see the westbound train approaching. Herman would have to wait, for he lived in the opposite direction.

"So long, old friend," he said, shaking Eddy's hand. "I hope you have a good trip — I was going to ask you to go with me to a Harold Lloyd picture show tonight, but I guess you'll be busy packing."

"Yes, I have to leave early," Eddy managed to say before the doors opened and he was pushed into the train.

From the window Eddy was able to catch a final glimpse of Herman and wave to him. But Herman did not see; and, when the train pulled away, he was lost from Eddy's sight.

200

Return

From the train window Eddy could see Hardwig and Othelia waiting for him. . . . At least they had gotten his telegram, he told himself with relief. He noticed that, even in two years' time, Glendive was changed. There were more people now and more automobiles. He had to look closely to see a horse or wagon anywhere. Only a few, older men still wore their beards and handlebar mustaches.

After the laughter and handclasps were over, his brother and sister led him from the depot and across the same street they had seen for the first time in 1910 — now no longer a mud-saturated wagon road. They had only walked a short distance when Hardwig stopped beside a new Chevrolet automobile, opened the door and put Eddy's suitcase into the back seat. Othelia began to laugh at Eddy's dumfounded stare.

"You can get in," she told him.

"Now we can take Pa and Ma to Dakota," Hardwig said as he took his place behind the steering wheel.

Eddy was dismayed. If there was no money for taxes, the car was a foolish extravagance, to say the least.

As they drove the familiar road from town, Eddy began to question the others. The crops, Hardwig told him, had been good; and there was wheat in the granary. But John had grown increasingly indifferent toward any business connected with the farm. When he spoke at all, it was only in monosyllables. He was often irritable and complained of illness, but the doctor could find nothing wrong.

"Then there was Richert's bull," Othelia said. "Our little bull kept getting out of the fence and fought with Richert's — and his was a registered bull. Then, one day, our bull came home with blood on the horns. So Richert came to Pa and wanted him to pay for the registered bull. Pa offered him ours instead — but no! 'Mine was a better bull,' Richert insisted. 'Well,' Pa said, 'it seems that mine was better if he killed yours. . . .' So now Richert says he's going to sue us."

"We didn't think about the taxes," Hardwig explained. "Then one day the sheriff came and told us he was going to serve papers."

"And Pa got letters from the courthouse," Othelia added. "They were in the bookcase. He never opened them."

Eddy shook his head. But, when they reached the house, he saw his father and knew at once that what Hardwig and Othelia had said was true. John spoke politely — almost formally — to him, asking about Henry and the weather in Chicago. Then he withdrew to his chair and seemed engrossed in his own thoughts until mealtime. He ate little at supper and spoke less — except to complain that the food was not cooked properly; and, after he had eaten, he left without comment for bed.

Caroline seemed not to notice his behavior, but Eddy had not seen her smile once during the evening. With Eddy back among them the children at home now numbered five, for Lydia had gone to South Dakota to be married. Caroline looked at her two sons and addressed them in a voice that was both beseeching and imperative:

"My boys, if there is to be bread, it is now up to you."

On the following morning Eddy and Hardwig hired trucks and a small elevator and arranged for the wheat to be hauled to town. The taxes were paid, and there was enough money left to buy paint for the house. Later that year Hardwig took John and Caroline to Dakota as promised, and upon their return John seemed somewhat cheered. He spoke of past events, laughed at the antics of old acquaintances and even resumed his work at the forge long enough to devise a new type of gate hook, which his neighbors later adopted.

Then his former distraction reappeared; and the familiar gloom — the cause of which no one could determine — reclaimed his spirit.

Pete's Last Bivouac

No one knew for sure if One-eyed Pete was a real Civil War veteran. True, he spoke of having been with the Union infantry on Cemetery Ridge. But because he had no family and few friends — and because his neighbors considered him to be a "queer duck," his claim was seen as suspect. He sought no one's company; and his companionship was, likewise, desired by few. So whatever was said regarding Pete consisted primarily of rumor and supposition.

All that his neighbors knew for sure about this pathetic, lonely man was that he lived by himself in a tarpaper shack along the road to Bloomfield, that he drove a one-horse buggy — even after everyone else owned cars — and that he drank a lot of whisky. Some said that he kept a loaded, double-barrel shotgun — its hammers always cocked — hanging over the door inside his house. But, since no one could actually attest to having been in the house, this matter, too, was questioned.

Whether or not his deformed eye was a product of Gettysburg, of an accident, or of birth was also unknown. But it was his most remarkable characteristic and, therefore, the source of his nickname.

Eddy had known Pete and seen him often enough since coming to Montana, although he could not recall a time when either he or John had spoken to the solitary bachelor. Like everyone else who had seen Pete, Eddy was struck by the grotesque, twisted eye that seemed to be looking back into the man's brain. But Pete was accepted as a fixture in the community, and his buggy was often seen on the road going to or from town.

So it did not seem unusual to Eddy and Hardwig when they saw Pete's vehicle in Bloomfield not long after Eddy's return from Chicago. He and Hardwig were on their way to Glendive in the new Chevrolet and had stopped in the village for gasoline when they noticed a crowd of school children capering about a lone buggy.

"That's One-eyed Pete," Hardwig laughed. "Those kids always give him hell."

Indeed this was no exaggeration, for the children seemed almost demonic in their taunting of both horse and driver. Pete, standing in his tiny buggy, struck at the imps with his whip, which caused them to shriek in mock terror and then to giggle.

"Little bastards!" the furious driver cursed them. "I'll break your bones — the lot of ye!"

The spectacle revolted Eddy. He could not forget the pitiful scene — even after spending half the day in town; and that night, when the two brothers drove through Bloomfield again on their way home, Eddy cringed at the sight of the place.

"We should stop in and visit old Pete," he told Hardwig. "We go right past his place anyway."

"He might use his shotgun on us," Hardwig joked at this unusual suggestion.

They had gone another seven miles when Hardwig spotted an object in the moonlight. Only as they drew up beside it could they determine that it was Pete's buggy. It stood facing north upon the roadway a short distance from the shack where he lived. The horse also stood waiting, still harnessed between the traces. Hardwig stopped the car.

As the two approached, the horse turned its head and snorted at them. They found Pete lying in the seat, his face turned upward with both of his eyes open, staring at the moon.

"He must have passed out," Hardwig suggested.

Eddy shook the man and called his name.

"I'm afraid he's dead," he told his brother. . .

Eddy waited with Pete's body while Hardwig went to Fuller's house to call the sheriff. When Hardwig returned with Fuller, the three of them remained to await the sheriff's arrival. The moon rose higher and cast its rays full upon the dead man's face. The light reflected from his one good eye. The men's talk subsided into an uneasy silence during which they could hear the horse's soft breathing.

"Must have had a heart attack," Fuller proposed when Eddy told him what they had seen earlier that day. "Them kids prob'ly got the old boy pretty worked up."

When the sheriff came, Fuller lit a lantern and led the way to Pete's house a few yards beyond the road.

"Take it easy," he cautioned when the sheriff attempted to force the locked door. "That man kept a loaded shotgun in his house. Careful you don't set it off."

The sheriff looked at him incredulously.

With a little effort the lock was broken, and the four men entered the tiny dwelling.

"What'd I tell ya?" Fuller laughed as he raised the lantern over the doorway to reveal an ancient, double-barrel shotgun with both hammers cocked. . .

They took Pete to Glendive and, after an unsuccessful search for his relatives, buried him the in the county cemetery. But Eddy would never forget the haunting, vindictive expression he had seen on the face of the one-eyed veteran, who had lain there that night, staring helplessly at the moon.

Heaven's Flowers*

There was no greater source of pride for Gantschook than to be known as the people's auctioneer or "crier," an avocation practiced by his ancestors for many generations. No one — either in Dakota or in the Montana settlement — would have thought of hiring anyone but him for the task of selling everything from furniture to livestock. Descended, as he maintained, from a noble line, Gantschook bore himself with the air of a minor count. He loved to tell jokes and to recite droll proverbs, his pointed teeth gleaming amid a mass of graying whiskers, whenever he conducted a sale; and he was most disdainful of those who suggested that his bold and uncouth jokes at auctions violated all propriety. After all, who, he asked himself, knew the tricks of auctioneering better than he? Those who disparaged him were, he determined, merely envious.

He was among the loyal Germans in the community, and it was to his great delight when, following the war, he was called to conduct sales at the farms of those English patriots who had sought to inform upon their Mennonite neighbors. But, as time passed, Gantschook found that he had a competitor in the person of a local man named Vogel, who lately was managing to score a number of sales for himself. Not to be outdone, Gantschook determined

* All names in this chapter, except for those with which the reader is already familiar, have been fictionalized.

204

to show this upstart how a truly expert auctioneer performed.

Now the Mennonite people knew Gantschook and tolerated his sometimes outrageous humor. But with the English it was a different story. It happened that at one sale the crier held up a milk bucket to the bidders and announced:

"Here is a nice milk pail for anybody with a fresh cow."

In the crowd stood Mrs. Bailey, who was in an advanced stage of pregnancy. Seeing her there with her husband, the auctioneer added:

"Or maybe Mr. Bailey wants to buy it for his wife. She will soon be fresh."

Mr. Bailey promptly showed his amusement by punching the unfortunate comedian in the nose.

No one could have been more surprised at this turn of events than Gantschook.

"*Nun, was iss?* he cried out, his humiliation complete when Vogel was asked to finish the sale.

Returning home to nurse his wounded pride, Gantschook soon learned that his auctioneering talents were no longer in demand. Vogel's cordiality and good manners had won for him the distinction of replacing Gantschook as the neighborhood auctioneer. Gantschook felt betrayed. His own people had rejected him, and he longed for a chance to publicly condemn them.

His opportunity for revenge came when the women's mission society sponsored a church sale, choosing Vogel to be their auctioneer. During the course of the activity a severe wind arose, forcing the crowd to move indoors — into the sanctuary of the church. Hearing later of this, Gantschook knew he had the substance for reprisal. Soon after, the church assembled for a debate to determine if the moral status of the world was improving or deteriorating. Gantschook rose to his feet. Wiping his beard in his handkerchief, he began to speak:

"No-sir-eeah! The world is gettin' worser an' worser! Now we have seen everything when there is buying and selling in the very House of God."

His voice became increasingly shrill as he vented his wrath. . .

"When our dear Lord drove the moneychangers out from the temple, He said that it was a den of thieves. Then He used only a small piece of rope. But today He would take a blacksnake whip to such people as we have in our church. They would all be chased out — and the preacher too!'

At this he threw a virulent glare at the minister, who had sanctioned the impious sale. His revenge complete, Gantschook again wiped his face and brow with the handkerchief and resumed his seat.

The young people who had heard this could barely contain their mirth until they were outside the building. There they fell upon the ground, abandoning themselves to wild hysterics.

"A blacksnake whip!" they repeated, tossing about in fits of laughter.

Among this group of less than compassionate youths was Eddy, then only a boy in his teens. He, like the others, had always known Gantschook, who lived along a branch of the creek that passed through John's land. But a time came when Eddy would learn to pity the singular old man.

It occurred in the early days of the depression when Gant-schook's wife became ill. Eddy was working in the field and saw the familiar figure of Gantschook walking along the creek that would always bear his name. His children gone, he was left alone now with the ailing woman.

"I must go to town for pills," he told Eddy. "Her bottle is already empty, and the doctor said she should have them every day. But I have no car."

"We can go with mine," Eddy offered, unable to refuse the helpless petitioner; and the two of them set out.

The trip, even by car, took more than an hour over the coarse gravel. The old man spoke of his family and of his childhood in Russia. . .

"It is true — we come from a noble family," he insisted. "Our name belonged to a count. But no one wants to believe it."

Mainly, however, he talked of his wife. . .

"She is the most wonderful woman in the world — always so good to me. Even now she does not complain. But she knows. . . . She knows."

He became quiet then for a time. Eddy tried awkwardly to console him.

"Don't give up yet. She can still pull through," he said.

"It is as God wills it," the old man replied; but he shook his head. . .

And for the first time Eddy sensed a simple dignity in the man who, for so many years, had seemed merely eccentric.

After they reached Glendive and refilled the prescription, Gant-schook seemed somewhat relieved.

"Come, I will buy you supper," he proposed to Eddy as they left the drugstore.

They entered the Grill Cafe, where Gantschook placed his order. . .

"A beef sandwich — a hot one!"

Having eaten and paid the bill, which amounted to sixty cents, the two of them began the return trip. Again Gantschook spoke of his wife.

"I am already getting too old," he lamented. "And if she must die, I shall be alone."

It was nearly evening when they reached his house that stood amid a cluster of trees.

When Eddy saw the sick woman, it was evident to him that she was indeed dying. Gantschook produced the small druggist's bottle and gave it to his wife. Then he noticed a bouquet of lilacs in a glass of water near the bed.

"Such nice blossoms," he said, making a pitiable effort to be cheerful.

"The girls picked them for me," the woman smiled weakly, yet with obvious pleasure.

"They came to visit me when you were gone."

At this the old man gave way to his long-confined tears.

"In heaven you will have nicer flowers," he cried, burying his face in the familiar handkerchief.

On the following day the woman was dead.

The flowers still stood by the empty bed, as did the newly-opened vial of medicine, when Eddy came into the house.

"She didn't need the pills after all," sighed the bereaved husband. "We made the trip for nothing."

Before Eddy had a chance to reply, a car drove into the yard; and a well-dressed man came to the door.

"I've come about this bill you owe on your tractor," the caller said, presenting an invoice to Gantschook.

The old man looked uncomprehendingly at the paper.

"Well, do you have the money?" the agent demanded.

It was then that Eddy came to the door.

"The man's wife just died," he said softly. "Your bill can wait until another time."

At once the agent's manner changed.

"Oh — I'm glad you told me," he apologized. "Yes, I can come back later."

As he waited with Gantschook until the family arrived, Eddy looked again at the lilacs that still bore their original freshness, as though they had never been cut. He did not know if there were flowers waiting for the old woman in heaven. Nor did he know if the claim to nobility was accurate. But he knew that no sorrow could eradicate the splendor of those blossoms.

Caroline

During the first year in Montana a peddler came to the house. Caroline determined through her own means of deduction that he must be a Jew. Recalling warnings given by her parents long ago, she harbored a profound distrust for Jews. This man in particular, with his tiny, scheming eyes, seemed to personify all the duplicity and avarice that she associated with that race. Moreover — as was often her plight — Caroline had very little money to spend on frivolities. Much deliberation preceded even the smallest purchase.

"*Kein Geld* — no money!" she protested after a brief but perceptive scrutiny of the man's goods.

The peddler, however, knew well the art of salesmanship. Determined to sell something, he produced a sample of calico for Caroline to inspect.

"This you can surely afford," he assured her. "Think of the dresses you can make for your daughters."

So saying, he winked playfully at the small girls.

Caroline examined the material carefully.

"It will fade," she announced.

"Impossible," the salesman scoffed. "I do not deal in poor merchandise."

Caroline hastened indoors and took a basin of warm water. She rubbed the cloth with considerable vigor until the cotton became a bleached pink, then held it out triumphantly before the salesman.

"You see!" she announced.

Promptly seizing the cloth and hurling it into his wagon, the tradesman leaped up onto the seat.

"This is the treatment a man receives!" he snarled. "*Kein Geld! Kein Geld!*"

Spitting into the air, he drove off to a farewell chorus of jeers from the children.

This was not Caroline's only battle with the members of the merchant class. Sometime later she and Roger-Katie attempted to sell some homemade butter to Albrecht, the Amish storekeeper in what was to become Bloomfield. The ten-mile trip in the hot sun had given the product an almost liquid consistency; and, when Albrecht lifted the cover from one of the jars and looked at the contents, he sneered, pronouncing it "baby's shit." The outraged women departed with an indignant "Goodbye forever!"

Forced by the confines of the society into which she had married and limited by her lack of education, Caroline endured a life that consisted of unending labor. She accepted it as the norm of her existence.

"Rest now! Sit down and let us do the work," her daughters

sometimes insisted.

But Caroline was incapable of remaining still when there was work to be done. There existed in her an indefatigable urgency — a need to pursue some task. Perhaps it was due to the established habits of a lifetime. Yet there was something else — a need to conceal with a fury of activity the profound longing that she kept within her. Just what it was that constituted this longing she did not quite know. But there were times when, unnoticed by anyone, she would weep to herself. Then, on Sundays when the weather was warm, she wandered into the hills to search for agate and other small stones. She would return with a handful of such treasures tied in a cloth and deposit them in a pile beside a post in the yard, leaving them to the grass. . .

In the pasture beyond the house lay two infant children to whom she had given birth and from whom life was taken before they had become personalities. She alone knew them. They were a part of her. And for the eight surviving children she had the task of providing bread. At times the fare was little more than fried potatoes and scrambled eggs — milk, if the cows were fresh — but always there was something for the children to eat. When they became ill, she was there with tea and toast in her aging hands. Even in the flu years she refused to become sick, knowing that she had to remain strong to care for the others.

She was compelled to keep her anxieties to herself, for there was no one in whom she could confide. . . . John remained lost in his own frustrated purgatory of unfulfillment and provided little company for her.

When she thought of her parents, it was with sorrow, for she did not even have a photograph of them and had never been able to visit their graves. Before his own death, brother Jackob had sent her a picture of himself with his family. . . . She saw that he had gotten fat. The tea cannister he had given her remained in use, scratched and dented but with the blue and gold Chinese lettering still evident. It was her only memento.

Of the women whose acquaintance she shared, there were none whom she could consider friends. Once she committed the error of confiding to one of them the location of some wild plums.

"I would have shared them with her," she despaired when she learned that the woman had betrayed her trust. "But she goes ahead of me and takes them all for herself."

There was, too, the remorse that had grown over the years since her marriage to John — since those happy times at the Unruh farm. She remembered the suitor whom she had rejected in order to marry John. Would John, she wondered, have done the same for her? Was there, perhaps, someone long ago whom he would have preferred to her? She did not know. John became angry when she spoke of such things.

He had struck her once. Yes — with the buggy whip — when he had had too much whisky and she had tried to take the reins. Eddy was there beside her and tried to shield her from the blow. He had wept for her. He was her Eddy. He was like her people — not like John's. Of all her children, he belonged most to her. . .

It took but little perception to tell her the contempt with which most of the Mennonites regarded her — a Lutheran and illiterate. She learned early to hate anything that was written or printed on paper.

"Books!" she would scoff. . . . "They are only foolishness."

The one exception for her was the Bible, which she could partly read; and for her the only Bible was that printed in the German language.

"So they will talk German in heaven," she reasoned, no matter what anyone said.

Likewise, when her own children revealed to her that the world was in fact a sphere, she remained incredulous.

"But I can see it for myself," she argued. "and where I look it is flat."

So she continued to rely upon her perceptivity, which, as it is with many who are unlettered, became a highly-developed tool and gave her an awareness of things unknowable to others.

"I saw old man Schultz last night," she revealed to John one morning, referring to the father of Ida's husband. "He was standing in this very room at the foot of our bed."

John scoffed at the dream — until he heard that Schultz died that very night. . .

On occasion she was able to tease John and the children, fabricating stories for their amusement. But it was the agony of loneliness that bore upon her as she grew older. Life, which for her had never been a proposition requiring debate, became a matter of seeming hopelessness. The longing that she had always felt and ignored then became implacable. She wanted suddenly to flee — as if from some unknown terror. But there was no one to take her and nowhere to go. So she reconciled herself to despair and to loneliness until age robbed her at last of her senses.

John and Uncle Jake

Harvest was finished. Wheat shocks stood once again upon John's land, awaiting the threshers. It was a good year — the first in nearly a decade. As he sat on the porch, John looked at the fields; but his thoughts beheld other times. He saw a long-ago village where a cottage stood surrounded by spring flowers. He saw also a man working with a team of oxen, plowing a new field in a new country. John thought often of his father now. It was difficult to comprehend that the blacksmith had been dead for more than twenty years.

John's gaze crept over the stubble fields that lay, warm and bright, beneath the afternoon sun. Beyond the fields stood Roger's barn. John rarely visited his old friend now. It seemed there was little they could think of to say to each other. As for Caroline, John was weary of her ceaseless imploring to sell the farm. Daily she wandered about the yard and the house, which now seemed so empty to both of them.

"It was not so bad," she grieved, "until the youngest left."

They were all gone now — except for Hardwig and Eddy, who did the farming together. Henry was still in Chicago, and the girls were married. Few remained of those neighbors who had once homesteaded with John. C. J. Schmidt lost his farm and moved to Oregon. Soft and Marhinja returned to Kansas, old and defeated. Schenker was dead. Many of the English, too, were gone — including Louis Knutson and the Smiths. Finally Bernhart — John's own brother — sold out and, sick and dying, returned to Dakota. John began to write a letter to him, but Bernhart had died before it was finished. . .

John looked up the road and saw a cloud of white dust upon the horizon. A car was approaching. He knew it was Jake, who had written that he would come after finishing the corn picking in Dakota. John watched the car's advance as if in a dream. After what seemed a long time, the ancient vehicle drew to a stop beside the lilac bushes in front of the house.

"The trip took a little longer this time," John's older brother smiled gently as he opened the door. "But I did not hurry . . . I put a few things in a sack — some gas in the car — then I started out. My one good eye is already getting a little dim. It was not easy to drive."

Caroline came then with two kitchen chairs, which she placed in the shade by the house for the two aging brothers, and retired to the kitchen while they visited. John inquired the circumstances of Bernhart's death.

"He was sick for a long time; he was ready to go," Jake said. . . . There was weariness in his voice.

"And who will be the next one?" John murmured.

"Only God knows. And I trust He will take us when He is ready. Until then He can do without us — but we can never do without Him."

"Like Papa, you have faith," John smiled sardonically. "But I cannot bring myself to think on such things. Always there is a fear in the back of my mind — especially at night when I try to sleep. It makes me shudder inside; and I wonder why it was that I did all these things — why I married and had a family, why I came to Montana. It seems that none of it is mine any more . . . I still fix the fences, and sometimes I sharpen the plow bottoms at my forge. But the boys do all the rest now. It is up to them."

Jake thought for a long time before speaking.

"You know, little brother," he said at last, "the part in the *Schrift* that we have heard even before we could understand — how when you are young you can run anywhere you please; but when you are old they will take you even where you do not want to go. . . . For us that time is almost here. The words are true — in a way that even the preachers cannot see. . . . So all there is left for us is faith.

"Do you remember Poststarr? He came to see Bernhart before our brother died. As he got up to leave, he told him this: "When you come to heaven, greet my wife for me. Tell her I am well.' That is the faith of the apostles."

"Faith!" John retorted scornfully. "Again you sound like Papa when he gave me his Bible — the one from the Old Country. But still I am afraid . . ."

And again he thought of the dog — the devil dog, which he could barely remember, except for the terror it aroused in his small boy's heart of that ancient and fearful enemy. . .

"The old people had faith," he continued, "so they were not afraid. In their honest way they understood, and their belief saved them. But I cannot believe as they did. I have too many regrets — things that I had forgotten until now; and nothing that anyone says can change those wrongs we have done. . . . These things come to me when I lie awake at night, and I cannot chase them away. So I try to remember some good thing I have done. But somehow the good thoughts do not come — only the bad."

"Because the good is already to your credit," Jake replied. "It is the wrongs that you need to contemplate."

Jake nodded. "For a long time, I did not go to church. What the preachers say I know better than they do; and they, too, must question it sometimes to themselves. . . . Then last week I decided I would go there again to show them I had not forgotten. So I walked by myself. But it was not the church I once knew. The newcomers have it all their way now. The people I knew are almost all of them gone, and the young ones have yet to learn what I know."

Jake understood. "There is one young man back home," he said, "who gives revival meetings every night. He must think the louder he preaches the more souls he will win. . . . He asked me if I heard him preach. So I said that I didn't have to leave my bed to hear him . . . *'Ich han Sie schon im Bett gehört,'* I told him."

Both men laughed then — not as children who love laughter for its own sake — but as old men laugh with a trace of sadness upon their lips.

Then Jake spoke again. "Let me see Papa's Bible one more time, John. One eye is gone a long time already, and the other is not good anymore. This might be the last time I can see it."

The two of them entered the house then, where John opened the glass doors of the secretary he had built and produced the old volume. Jake looked at it for a long time before opening the stitch-mended covers.

"The printing is still big like I remember it," he said after turning a few pages. "I can still read it."

"You are the oldest," John said. "It is rightfully yours."

"But you have sons," Jake reminded him. "It is theirs to claim. The times, they have already changed so much. But this must not be lost."

As he spoke, Eddy and Hardwig came into the house to greet their uncle. Jake laughed and embraced them.

"What is this — two grown men already! And Henry in Chicago now. Maybe I will not see him again."

They sat together in the parlor until it was dark. Caroline prepared supper for them, and still Jäk Vetter talked, telling stories of Russia and singing peasant songs in that strange, old language. . . . At last he rose to his feet.

"This has been a good day for me," he announced as he left for bed.

But his stay with them was short; in a few days he was ready to return to Dakota. John and the two nephews followed him to his car on the day of departure.

"Now it will be your turn to come to see me," he said as he shook hands with the young men. Then he turned to John . . .

"Und du — lieber Bruder!" he exclaimed and kissed John's lips — something that John couldn't remember his brother ever having done before.

Jake smiled then, somewhat embarrassed, and wiped his eye.

"This is perhaps the last time," he added before he got into the seat.

As the car slowly moved eastward up the road, John stood alone watching it.

"Yes, brother," he said aloud to himself. "This may be the last time."

But he knew that it was not really important that he might never see Jake again. What was important was that they had seen each other now . . . that they had known each other as boys and worked together as men. When all else was forgotten, it was the joy of their kinship that would always endure. It, alone, mattered . . .

That night John slept well. In his sleep he was talking to Bernhart, whose buggy stood without a horse on the hilltop above his farm. John did not know why it was there. But he knew that he had found the solution.

"We can coast it down the road," he heard himself saying, and both men laughed.

And it seemed in John's dream as though they were boys again and that there was neither sorrow nor death in the world.

AFTERWORD

In the Far Country is the result of a seven-year effort. It is a collective biographical narrative of three generations of my father's family with additional episodes taken from the lives of other Mennonites with whom the family was associated. In 1973 I asked my father to recount the many stories he knew from his own early life — and from the lives of his parents — that constituted the oral tradition, not only of the Schwartz family, but of an interrelated group of Mennonite people. In the process of collecting these stories, I soon determined that in them lay the essence of a biographical novel. The ensuing task included transcribing the stories as they were told to me, researching the related historical data that was available and writing a preliminary draft — followed by three major revision of the text. The manuscript was completed in January of 1980 and revised again in 1983.

The events in this narrative cover a time span of some sixty years. During that time the Mennonites — with the exception of some groups of Old Order Amish — were subjected to a massive cultural metamorphosis. Some time between the two world wars they ceased in many ways to be a culturally distinct unit. In part this book has been a history of this cultural change, personified in the lives of its major characters. It is, therefore, necessary to provide some explanation of the factors which came to bear upon these people prior to — and following — their migration to America.

There are many varieties of people who fall under the general term "Mennonite." For a thorough study of their origins, the reader is advised to consult Smith's *The Story of the Mennonites*, published by the General Conference Mennonite Church in Newton, Kansas. The particular group of Swiss Mennonites who are referred to here as "Schweitzers" originally belonged to a faction of Swiss Anabaptists known as the Evangelical Baptist Brethren. Their beginnings were in Bern Canton, Switzerland, during the time of the Reformation. Their most significant religious doctrines included baptism upon confession of faith (i.e. adult baptism), abstention from the taking of any formal oath and opposition to militarism or any form of violence. Their lifestyle was characterized by simplicity in manner of dress, a general avoidance of "worldly" amusements and — in some cases — communal living.

During the seventeenth century they were forced out of their native country as the result of intense political and religious persecution. One faction fled to Montbeliard, France; another found refuge in the Rhine Palatinate. Kaufman in *Unser Volk und Seine Geschichte* lists the name "Schwarz" (Schwartz) as belonging to a Swiss individual who lived for a time in Bavaria.

In the 1780's a group of the Swiss Brethren, then living in the Palatinate, migrated to Galicia, a Polish province acquired by Austria in the first partition of Poland in 1772. They were attracted to this region by the promises of free land, religious freedom and exemption from military service, which Emperor Joseph II offered to German farmers to induce them to settle in his new province, then in a rather neglected state. When differences arose between the newly settled Swiss Mennonites and others who had settled with them, some of the Swiss, in the early 1800's, moved on to the Russian province of Volhynia, also formerly Polish. In Russia at that time, since the early years of Catherine the Great, German farmers, especially Mennonites, enjoyed many attractive special privileges.

Volhynia, annexed by Russia in the second and third partitions of Poland (1793 and 1795), then had large areas of forested and marshy land waiting for good farmers to develop them. Beginning in 1807, the Swiss Mennonites founded several villages in the Dubno area of the province: Eduardsdorf (Oderad), Sahorez, Futter, Waldheim, Horodisch, Kotosufka. In the early 1870's, the Russian government began to withdraw the special privileges so highly valued by the Mennonites. It is at this point in their history that we first meet the people described in this narrative, then living in Eduardsdorf in Volhynia.

Perhaps the greatest misconception regarding the Mennonites is that of their being an austere, humorless people. True enough, a strict religious discipline was observed in their daily lives, and severe social sanctions fell upon those who violated this discipline. Nonetheless, Mennonite life was replete with its own humor, and traditional Mennonite stories of a humorous nature abound. The reader might also be struck by the social drinking that is depicted within this book. While some groups of Mennonites observed strict abstinence from intoxicants, the Swiss were known to imbibe on special occasions such as weddings. Smoking was also practiced by some individuals, and the description of church elders spitting tobacco juice upon the floor during Sunday worship is not exaggerated.

In considering those factors which made the Schweitzers a distinct cultural unit, one could go on to cite such things as manner of dress, forms of worship and traditional ethics pertaining to daily work and family life. These things are best evaluated by sociologists and to comment further upon them is not within the scope of this present work. The matter of language, however, is paramount in characterizing any group of people. It is necessary, therefore, to make some observations on the Schweitzer dialect.

Centuries of isolation and intermarriage resulted in the Swiss

Mennonites' preserving a dialect of German which was their own — *Schweitzerdeutsch.* It is an unwritten dialect and, due to increasing influences from the "outside," is currently in danger of extinction. Linguistic differences between Swiss and Dutch Mennonites were a factor in the sustained rivalry between these two groups, a rivalry that has diminished in recent years. Also, during their sojourn in Russia, a number of Ukrainian loan words were added to the Mennonite vocabularly — and certain Ukrainian dishes became part of their diet.

The problem of translating Mennonite thought and humor into English was formidable. Because it was essential that the bilingual nature of the characters be preserved, I determined to punctuate the text with commonly-used Schweitzer expressions. In most instances the meanings of these phrases should be evident within their English context. In other cases I have attempted to render a translation that still preserves the original idiom.

Perhaps as a result of the world wars — or simply the inevitable process of acculturation — a stigma became attached to the speaking of the German language in America during the past generation. Increasing contacts and marriages with non-German-speaking people, along with such factors as the automobile, secular education and the mass media, have contributed to the language's decline in recent years. The tragedy in this is that when a people cease to speak their own tongue and begin to adopt the customs of another culture, they often cease to think, react and function in their traditional ways. The result has been that the descendants of the first eleven Swiss families who came from Volhynia in 1874 have lost many of those distinctive elements that characterized their great-grandparents, and thus it is that the book's conclusion marks not only the end of one man's life — but the end of a way of life.

But the spirit contained within this work is not one of pessimism. Its theme is, on the contrary, a testimony to the endurance of a people and to their faith, in spite of the social and political changes imposed upon them. The book's purpose is neither to ridicule nor to lament but to render a tribute to those qualities that sustained the Mennonite pioneers in the far country called America.

Warren E. Schwartz
Richey, Montana
Summer, 1983